LOVE AND OTHER RARE BIRDS

Praise for Angie Williams

Last Resort

"The buildup to romance for Katie and Rhys is slow burn but it's like one continuous foreplay, and when they finally hit the sheets, it's very sexy. They also have incredible banter that is fun to read and made their romance even more plausible."
—*Les Rêveur*

Mending Fences

"This is not a story driven by angst but more of a sweet (but incredibly sexy) story of finding your way home…For her first novel, I think Angie Williams knocked this one out of the park. I will be following what she does next very closely!"
—*Les Rêveur*

"*Mending Fences* by Angie Williams is a heartwarming second chance romance that highlights the importance of following your heart and being true to yourself no matter how daunting it may seem."—*The Lesbian Review*

By the Author

Mending Fences

Last Resort

Just as You Are
(novella in Opposites Attract: Butch/Femme Romances)

Love and Other Rare Birds

LOVE AND OTHER RARE BIRDS

by

Angie Williams

2022

LOVE AND OTHER RARE BIRDS
© 2022 By Angie Williams. All Rights Reserved.

ISBN 13: 978-1-63679-108-1

This Trade Paperback Original Is Published By
Bold Strokes Books, Inc.
P.O. Box 249
Valley Falls, NY 12185

First Edition: August 2022

Credits
Editor: Cindy Cresap
Production Design: Stacia Seaman
Cover Design by Tammy Seidick

Acknowledgments

Thank you, BSB family, for the support, for the laughs, and for always having my back.

A special thank you to Cindy Cresap and Meghan O'Brien for your patience and guidance.

Aurora Rey, Leigh Hays, and Rach Byrne, you guys are the best cheerleaders ever. Thanks for listening to me and all the encouragement you give.

Thanks to my parents for always believing in me.

I couldn't do anything without the love and support of my little family. Meghan and Ryan, you are the reason for everything, and I love you to Pluto and back.

Meghan, we've had a hell of a life together thus far, and now we can add living through a pandemic without murdering each other to that list. Against all odds, I think it's somehow made us stronger and brought us closer. That's pretty amazeballs. You're the first thing I think of every morning and the last thought on my mind before I fall asleep. You're my everything, and I can't believe what a lucky duck I am to have you by my side. You also have a nice ass and are an awesome kisser.

For Meghan, always and everything

CHAPTER ONE

Dr. Jamie Martin stepped into the aviary and drew in a deep breath. The familiar lilt of seabirds accompanied by the gentle cadence of water cascading down rocks at the foot of a waterfall helped ground her to prepare for the chaotic day ahead. It was the calm before the storm, and she appreciated every moment. She loved her job at the Pacific Wildlife Center and Aquarium, or PWCA, but the seemingly nonstop influx of visitors sometimes wore her down.

When she'd dreamt of becoming an ornithologist as a girl, she had always imagined rugged fieldwork, discovering some exotic bird species previously only rumored to exist. She never pictured herself locked in a building all day, explaining the difference between a sandhill crane and a great blue heron. Not that she didn't enjoy talking to people about her passion, but she longed for the adventures. Armed with a backpack and binoculars, her younger self would roam the wooded acres surrounding her home, scribbling her observations and sketches in a leather-bound logbook her dad gave her for Christmas when she was eight.

She missed the father-daughter adventures they'd had before his focus turned toward politics and away from science. He'd had a popular television show before deciding to run for office, and Jamie would often join him when they filmed during her summers away from school. The exotic locations and one-on-one time with her hero made for a fantastic childhood. Once he became wrapped up in campaign dinners and glad-handing, his political career took precedence over his duties as a father. One minute she was the center of his universe and the next an afterthought from his past. That feeling of rejection was jarring for a young girl just finding her way in the world. When she needed him most, he wasn't there.

At first, the strain of that loss had driven Jamie to become someone worthy of his love. She knew in her heart that if she could do something extraordinary, be someone incredible, she would once again be a part of his orbit. She'd wasted years of her life in a futile attempt to make him notice her, but as she grew older, that drive to gain his respect turned into the drive to find success in her career, not for him, but for herself. She no longer wanted to be considered Senator Phillip Martin's daughter; she wanted to be seen as a successful person in her own right. A strong, capable, intelligent person who found her own way in the world.

Unfortunately, her father had cast an enormous shadow. No matter how hard she worked, she couldn't seem to step out of it, and Jamie was eager to feel the sun on her face. She had found success, working her way up to assistant curator of ornithology at the PWCA. It was a great accomplishment, especially for someone in their mid-thirties.

The position garnered her the respect she wanted, but she couldn't help but feel a bit like a fraud. The title brought professional validation but wasn't as fulfilling as she had hoped. She knew the curator would be retiring in the next year or two, and Jamie was determined to prove she was ready for the job. It was merely the next step on her quest to become director of the Pacific Wildlife Center and Aquarium and earn a seat on the board.

If she could reach that level she would have the power to actually make a real difference for the seabirds she had dedicated her life to. Having someone in a position like that who could advocate for the funding that would enhance their research was invaluable.

To achieve that, she needed fieldwork. Accomplishing significant and meaningful research in the field was the only way they would ever take her seriously. With the competitiveness of receiving grant approval, she was doubtful they'd even consider her for one until she could log more time at the PWCA.

"Hey, Doc, did you notice a limp on one of the black-necked stilts?" Jamie's intern, Craig, asked as he entered the aviary. "I thought I saw one limping when I was locking up last night."

"I didn't, but thanks for letting me know. I'll keep an eye out. How did things go yesterday?" she asked, not looking up from the logbook where she entered notes from her morning rounds. Jamie had taken the previous day off to give a lecture at the local community college. The time away left her feeling out of touch with what was happening with her birds.

"It went well. Do you know a Dr. Patricia Carlson? She filled in for you."

Jamie and Patty Carlson had known each other in college. After an almost two-year friendship, they dated for precisely thirteen days before Patty broke her heart once she had given an innocent young Jamie a thorough lesson in the lesbian birds and bees.

"We were in school together." Her memories of Patty were simultaneously fond and painful. "I didn't know she was living around here."

"I guess she just moved back," Craig said. "She asked about you. She said she heard something about a northern curlew sighting in Alaska and thought you would be interested."

Jamie looked up from her logs, a flush of excitement warming her cheeks. "Are you sure she said a northern curlew? The last confirmed sighting was in the sixties. They're technically on the critically endangered list but thought to be extinct. Did she say where she got this information?"

"All I know is Dr. Carlson said someone mentioned something about a sighting to her," Craig said. "She said you could call her if you wanted to know more. I left her number in your office."

Jamie's mind was moving a hundred miles an hour. If Patty was right and she could confirm the bird wasn't extinct, it would not only be a massive boost to her career but might lead to more opportunities in the field. Of course, she'd have to speak to Patty to get the information. She wished she'd just left it with Craig. Talking to Patty was the last thing Jamie wanted to do.

"Thanks, Craig." Jamie closed the logbook and locked it in the hidden cabinet with her supplies. "I'll be in my office if you need me for anything."

"Later, Doc," Craig said as he unlocked the main doors to the aviary to allow the waiting visitors to enter.

As Jamie walked the halls to her office, she practiced likely scenarios in her head of her conversation with Patty. The last time they'd spoken, Jamie was crying and asked her why she was leaving.

Patty's excuse was that she had simply fallen for someone else. Jamie's heart ached for the naivety of her younger self. With any luck, the call with Patty would be short, professional, and free of drama.

Over the years, Jamie had dated women on and off, but none of them understood how important her career was to her or respected the time it would take to accomplish her goals. She preferred a more casual evening with a woman where they could find pleasure with each other, without the dedication a real commitment required. It was what worked for her and she'd never met anyone who could convince her otherwise.

The only one she had ever allowed close enough to break her heart was Patty Carlson. She supposed it was because she was her first, but whatever the reason, she'd never expected to speak to her again.

When she arrived in her office, she picked up the paper Craig had left with Patty's number and dialed it before she chickened out. The northern curlew lead was too significant to allow her stupid, old hurt feelings to keep her from learning more.

"Dr. Patricia Carlson's office. How may I help you?" a woman with a pleasant voice asked on the second ring.

"Hello, this is Dr. Jamie Martin. Dr. Carlson asked me to contact her. Is she available?" Jamie nervously picked at the edge of a notebook on her desk as she spoke.

"Let me see if she's available, Dr. Martin. One moment, please." The overly exuberant hold music was obnoxious and only increased Jamie's anxiety as she waited.

"Hey, Jamie, I'm so glad you called." Patty's elegant voice was a familiar link to Jamie's past. "I couldn't believe it when they told me you were assistant curator at the PWCA. Your dad must be incredibly proud."

Not in the mood to waste time on pleasantries, Jamie got right to the point. "Thanks, Patty. Craig said you heard a report of a northern curlew sighting?"

"I did," Patty said. "I was wondering if maybe we could get together for dinner, and I'll show you what I have."

Jamie couldn't help but roll her eyes. "I've seen what you have, Patty. Maybe you could email the information to me?" The last thing she wanted to do was see her in person.

Patty sighed on the other end of the line as they sat in silence. "I suppose I deserve that. I won't force you to meet me, but I had hoped we could see each other. How about just coffee? I'm not trying to make you uncomfortable, Jamie, but I would love to apologize for my behavior in person. I treated you horribly, and the least I can do is buy you a cup of coffee and a donut. I won't insist, and if you're that against it, I'll courier the information I have for you, but I beg you to give me a chance to say how sorry I am in person."

Suddenly, her irritation seemed much more childish than she had any right to be. The sincerity in Patty's voice weakened her resolve, and Jamie relented. "Okay, I'll meet you for coffee and a donut. Are you available this morning? I have an hour between ten and eleven if that works for you."

"That's perfect. Our usual spot?" Patty asked, referring to the twenty-four-hour donut shop they frequented when they were in school together. Memories of midnight trips there for a sugary snack after hours of studying together came rushing into Jamie's mind.

"That works."

"See you then," Patty said.

"Bye, Patty." Jamie hung up and stared at the phone. She wasn't happy about this situation but knew if the information on the curlew was accurate, it would be worth the effort.

Three hours later, Jamie walked into the donut shop, where she found a stunning older version of the beautiful girl she once knew. "Hey, Patty." Jamie slid into the booth across the table from her.

"Hey, Jamie, it's so good to see you."

Jamie could tell Patty was just as anxious as she was, which helped settle her nerves. "Do you have the information on the curlew?" Jamie asked, getting right to the point.

"I do." Patty pointed toward a bag sitting next to her in the booth. "Do you mind if we chat a little? I'd love to learn more about what you've been up to since we last saw each other."

Jamie glanced at her phone to check the time. "Sure, I have a few minutes."

"How's your dad?"

"My dad? He's fine. He's up for reelection next year, so he's swamped. Why?" Too many ambitious people used her to get to her father for her to trust anyone who immediately asked about him.

"No reason." Patty shrugged. "Just curious."

There was a time when Jamie wouldn't have thought about

questioning Patty's motives, but that was long ago. She didn't know this adult version of Patty and couldn't be certain about what her intentions might be. Jamie's father had power in many circles that most ambitious people found hard to resist. It was difficult enough when he was only a famous biologist who hosted his own syndicated television show. Everyone was curious about the girl who would sometimes accompany him on his adventures. When he got into politics and became a senator, Jamie's life became more about his career than her own.

The tension between them was uncomfortable, and Jamie itched to get what she'd come for and leave. "Do you have the information?"

Patty regarded Jamie, then pulled out an envelope from her bag and slid it across the table. "Here's everything my colleague sent, including the contact information for the Alaskan Wildlife Refuge where the reported sighting happened. When they emailed me, you were the first person who came to mind. I was hesitant to reach out, but when I was asked to sub for you at the PWCA three days later, I knew it was too good to be a coincidence. I've thought about looking you up several times over the years but was afraid you wouldn't welcome the contact, rightly, I see."

Jamie sighed. She stuck the envelope in her bag and folded her hands on the table. Maybe she was being too critical of Patty. They were adults. Innocently asking about how Jamie's family was didn't mean she had ulterior motives. They both looked up as the server approached and took their order. When she walked away, they sat awkwardly for a moment before Patty finally spoke.

"Jamie, I was so sorry to hear about your mother's passing. I was out of the country when it happened, and by the time I learned of it, it had been several months. I wasn't sure if it was still appropriate to send flowers after such a long time."

"Thank you." Jamie's mother had died of a stroke the year before. She had been a world-renowned entomologist, and her sudden death was something Jamie still struggled to accept. The bell over the door jingled, alerting them new customers had arrived. Jamie watched the waitress rush to take their order before disappearing through a door behind the counter.

"I'm sorry for dragging you here against your will, Jamie. No matter how I acted the day we broke up, I wasn't proud of how I treated you. I was young and stupid, and there's no excuse for my behavior."

The apology seemed sincere. Jamie felt her posture relax, and some of the anger she'd held for so long melted away. She watched Patty rub her thumb against the palm of her other hand, a nervous habit she remembered from their time together so many years ago.

Patty nodded a thank you to the server when she returned with their donuts and coffee. Jamie watched Patty add cream to her mug and take a sip.

"Apology accepted."

"Do you think there's any way we could try to be friends again? I've missed you." Patty placed a delicate hand on Jamie's where it rested next to the plate with her untouched donut.

Jamie stared at her hand, not wanting to assume anything but feeling like Patty might hope for more than a friendship. She ran through several responses in her mind and how she thought each one would play out. In the end, she settled on her typical reaction when someone showed interest in her romantically. It wasn't a lie, after all.

"We'll have to see, Patty. I'm so busy with work that I have little time for anything else these days."

Patty nodded. "I guess I deserve that."

Jamie glanced at her watch and sighed. "I hate to say this, but I have a meeting. Thank you so much for thinking of me when you got this curlew information."

They stood and gathered their things to go. "I know they have fascinated you for years. Hopefully, it's a good lead." Patty pulled a business card from her purse and wrote a telephone number on the back. "Here's my personal contact information. In case you change your mind."

Jamie took the card and slipped it into her jeans pocket. She doubted she'd ever actually contact her, but it would be rude not to take her card at least.

"Good luck, Jamie. Please let me know if the curlew sighting turns out to be legitimate."

"I will." Jamie waved as she walked out the door and into the midmorning sun.

Later that evening, Jamie made her way home and collapsed on the couch, exhausted. When she'd returned to work after her talk with Patty, they had pulled her into one meeting after another until she was sick of the sound of her own voice. With a sigh, she forced herself to change into pajamas and put her dinner in the microwave. While she waited, she pulled the envelope containing the information on the curlew sighting from her bag. Her thoughts that day were never far from what it would tell her, but this was the first opportunity she had to open it and find out.

The first page was a letter from Patty explaining where she heard about the sighting and the contact information for someone Jamie could speak to if she was interested. The second page was a written report from the park ranger who had taken the witness statement.

Ranger Rowan Fleming had gotten a call from a hiker who was an amateur bird enthusiast. He reported seeing a northern curlew in a rocky area near the Kannik River in the Alaskan Wildlife Refuge. The ranger noted the coordinates of the sighting and a few details of the terrain. Jamie had a difficult time believing it could have been a northern curlew, even though the description of the bird and the area seemed reasonable.

Though now thought to be extinct because of habitat loss and unrestricted hunting in the late 1800s, they were once common. With the most recent confirmed sighting being in the 1960s, they were now on the critically endangered list, on the verge of being officially considered extinct.

Jamie's father had always loved birds growing up on the Midwest prairies and had seen a northern curlew on a camping trip with his father. The situation wasn't as dire for the northern curlew then as it was now, but the sighting was rare enough to be a special moment between father and son. By the time Jamie came along in the late eighties, sightings were things of legend, and the chance to repeat that experience with her was only a dream. Every summer when Jamie was young, she and her father would make a pilgrimage to areas in their migratory path, hoping to see one.

Each trip with her father was a bust as far as the curlew, but the experiences they had shaped who Jamie was today. She'd wanted to be an ornithologist for as long as she could remember, and even the remote chance this sighting was legitimate sent a chill of excitement down her spine.

With the papers from the envelope spread out across her desk, Jamie turned on her laptop and pulled up a map of Alaska. After searching, she found the coordinates stated in the report and pulled her food from the microwave while her topographical program built an image of the area. The terrain seemed like a suitable place where they would be nesting. She checked the date, and June was a bit early in the season for one to have migrated that far north, but not impossible.

She felt the excitement build. What if this was real? Jamie picked up her phone and dialed her dad's cell number.

"Hi, Pigeon, how's life?" Her father's deep voice on the other end of the line made her smile.

"Hey, Pops, it's good. Sorry I haven't called you in a while. Work has kept me so busy I hardly have time for anything else. How are you doing?" After her mother had passed away, she and her father had found it even more challenging to communicate with each other than they had before.

"As well as can be expected, I suppose. I'll be at the house for a few weeks this summer. I'd love to see you while I'm there." As a United States Senator, her father spent most of his time in Washington, DC. Jamie did her best to visit him when he was in town, but she knew she should make more of an effort.

"I promise to visit soon. I was wondering if I could get your advice on something. Do you have a minute to chat?"

"I've got all the time you need, Pigeon. What's up?"

Jamie pulled out the report from the ranger and read it to her father. She could hear him typing on his keyboard before asking her to repeat the coordinates stated in the report. "That's north, but just within their known migratory pattern. When was it reported?"

She relayed the date to him from report. "I know that's a little early for one to be that far north, but it's not abnormal enough for me to discredit the sighting."

"No, I agree," he said, excitement growing in his voice. "What if it's true, Jamie? Could you imagine seeing one after all this time? What a thing to have your name next to a confirmed sighting. That would be a great boost to your career."

"I agree. Do you think I should go up there and check it out? It's not much information to go on, but I almost feel like I have to at least try." Jamie knew the tricky part would be to convince her workplace to fund a trip like that for a relatively inexperienced ornithologist.

"I hadn't planned to mention this until I had more details, but do you remember Calvin Adams?"

Jamie knew the name sounded familiar, but it took her a moment to recall who he was. "Didn't he work for the network when you had your show? Tall, skinny guy with blond hair, right?"

Her dad chuckled. "That's the one. He was one of my assistants. Now he's a producer and looking for a new show to create. He contacted me a couple of weeks ago to see if I thought you'd be interested."

"In a show? As in a show of my own?" Jamie had always dreamed of someday having a program like her father's. She'd accompanied him on his travels several times when she was a kid, and they'd included her in many episodes over the years. Watching her father excitedly explain to the camera about the fantastic world of animals filled her with pride. She'd wanted nothing more than to grow up to be just like him.

That version of her father was before he'd become a politician, of course. Once he turned his sights toward Washington, everything changed. The fun-loving, adventurous man she'd always looked up to became somewhat of a stranger to her. The hardest part had been the fact that as a conservative politician, he'd bowed to his colleagues frequently and supported bills that went against everything he'd taught her to believe. It was difficult for Jamie to reconcile the man who'd raised her with the person he'd become. He was her father, and she'd always crave his approval and acceptance, but she couldn't help but feel disappointed in the man he was on some level.

"Your own show, Pigeon. I'm not sure precisely what he's looking for, but I suspect it would be a similar format to what mine was. What do you think about that?"

Jamie could feel her cheeks straining to accommodate her smile. "I think that would be amazing."

"If this curlew thing turns out to be true, it might be something that could get everyone's attention and help pave the way for whatever show you want."

"So, you think I should do it? You think it will be worth the effort even if it's a fool's errand?"

"I think you have to do it. I wish I could go with you. What an adventure it will be. I'd advise you to take an extra camera or two and document everything you can. Besides the field cameras you'll need. If you find something, that footage might be useful to them."

Jamie had learned the basics of camera placement and what shots to get when working on her father's show. She'd have to buy new equipment to take with her, but she thought her father was probably right. If nothing else, it might help convince the PWCA to support her trip if she promised to have something on film to bring back to them.

"That's a great idea. Maybe we can spend time at the beach house together when I'm home to catch up?"

Her dad sighed. "That sounds great, sweetheart. We'll have to see how my reelection campaign is going at that point. A couple new candidates might give me a challenge. Don't you worry, though. Your old dad has some fight still left in him."

Jamie could never admit to her dad that she didn't agree with him on most of his political views. She'd decided long ago it was easier to let him believe she felt the same way rather than cause a rift between them. "Thanks for the advice, Dad. Wish me luck convincing the PWCA to fund this trip."

"I can't imagine they wouldn't see how this discovery could be mutually beneficial for both of you. I wouldn't worry about the PWCA. I know some people I can contact if they give you trouble."

"Dad, no, please don't do that. I can handle the PWCA. I appreciate the offer, but I don't want them to feel bullied into doing this."

"I would never make them feel that way. I only meant I could make a couple of calls for you. Grease some wheels, so to speak."

"Thank you, but no."

"Well, you won't need my help, anyway. The PWCA will see the advantage of sending you on this trip. I know it."

"Thanks, Dad."

She wished she had as much confidence in herself as he did, but the encouragement helped give her the boost she needed. "Okay, have a good night. I have a lot of paperwork to get through before presenting this to the board. Good luck with your campaign."

"Thanks, sweetheart, good night." As her father hung up the phone, Jamie felt a mixture of excitement and fear grip her heart. There was no guarantee she'd be successful, but she was sure she'd at least have one hell of a story to tell afterward.

CHAPTER TWO

Shuttling a scientist around wasn't something park ranger Rowan Fleming enjoyed. The thousands of acres in the Alaskan Wildlife Refuge she called home were a popular destination for researchers of all sorts. Still, they had never expected her to babysit one before. Her responsibility was to the park and to preserve all the creatures that lived within. She didn't know who the person they had asked her to look after was, but she resented them pulling her away from her job. When she'd gotten the call the day before from her supervisor asking her to pick up an ornithologist in the village of Ugruk, fly her out to where the curlew sighting had been, and act as her guide and caretaker for three months, Rowan was sure she was part of an elaborate practical joke.

Sure, they had asked her to fly people to remote locations before, many times. That wasn't the part that frustrated her. That this ornithologist's time was so much more valuable than hers was what drove Rowan crazy. Who did they think they were? What important person did they know was a much better question. Rowan knew when she'd written the report on the sighting that it would be a fantastic find if it were to be confirmed, but this wasn't her job. When she'd asked why, her supervisor had told her it came from the top, whatever that meant.

Rowan checked off each item on the list as she loaded the gear they would need for their trip. With limited space on the plane, she had to be careful only to pack the essentials. Thankfully, she wouldn't have too much trouble trapping or fishing for their food, although they would have plenty of competition for their resources this time of year.

And then there was the idea of living in a tiny, remote hunting cabin for three months with someone she'd never met. Part of the reason Rowan had chosen the career and location she had was that she wasn't a big fan of people. She appreciated her friends, but she valued her personal space, like many Alaskans. Sleeping for weeks in the tight quarters with a stranger was her definition of hell.

Dr. Martin was expecting her at noon, and if she left soon, she would make it right on time. As she walked toward her house to get the bear boxes containing their food, her radio crackled to life. "You there, Rowan? Over."

"This is Rowan. Go ahead, Greg. Over." Greg Thompson was the emergency coordinator for the park, and her best friend. She knew a call from Greg at this time of day would mean her trip to Ugruk to pick up Dr. Martin wasn't happening today.

"There are a couple of rafters who got into some trouble on the Kannick, and they need immediate help. Are you available? One has a head injury, and you're my closest option. Over," Greg said.

"No problem. I need to pull this equipment out of my plane, and I'll be on my way. Could you send word to Ugruk to tell Dr. Jamie Martin that I can't meet them until tomorrow? Over." Rowan began dragging her equipment back toward her storage shed to make room in her plane for passengers and their equipment.

"Roger. Sounds good, Rowan. I'll send word. Thanks for taking the call. It sounds like they're pretty banged up. They'll be glad to see you. I'll send you the coordinates. Over."

"Right-o. I'm on my way." Rowan climbed into her plane and started the engine. "I'll update you when the passengers are on board. Over."

"Roger. Good luck. Over."

Rowan turned the plane and taxied down the small airstrip on her property. As she gained elevation, she mentally ran through potential scenarios she might find when she reached the men and the actions she would need to take to ensure they had the best chance of returning home safely. Everything about flying in Alaska was dangerous, so Rowan had learned to be cautious and ready for any situation.

Her father had been a Navy pilot in the Middle East, flying FA-18 Hornets off an aircraft carrier. He would tell her stories about his missions on the few occasions he was home when she was a kid. She knew he couldn't share details for security reasons, but what he did share fostered a love of planes she never grew out of.

Two hours into her flight, Rowan spotted the men on a narrow beach where Greg said they'd be. One waved his hands to flag her down while the other sat wrapped in a blanket near a small campfire. She dipped her wing to acknowledge she saw them then circled the plane around to find the best place to land. The men jogged away from the beach to get out of her way. Though there were only a few yards between the river and the trees, she thought the beach would be just wide enough, but there was no way she could land in the short distance unless she could slow the plane down sufficiently before reaching the sand. Coming back around to line herself up, she decided she would have to slip her wheels into the river to create enough drag to decrease her speed. She had used this technique before, but the degree of difficulty and opportunities for complete disaster always made it her least favorite option.

Holding her breath, she slowed as much as she could before dipping her wheels into the frigid water below. She felt the plane jerk as the river tried its best to flip her over. She held the controls in a death grip as sweat trickled down her forehead and into her eyes. Come on, girl, she silently encouraged herself as she approached the beach. Thump. The plane jerked as its wheels contacted the beach, and Rowan held on tight as the sand fought her for control. When she finally came to a stop only inches from the tree line, she released a relieved breath and pulled off her headset as the excited hoots from the rafters made her smile.

"That was fucking awesome, dude." The taller man jogged around to her side of the plane. "I can't believe you just did that."

Rowan unbuckled herself and grabbed her first aid kit as she climbed out of the pilot's seat. "Hey, guys." She smiled as she shook their hands. "Which one of you bumped his head?"

"That would be my little brother, Sean. We finally got the bleeding to stop, but I'm concerned he may have knocked something loose in there." The older man gently punched the arm of a slightly younger but almost identical version of himself.

Sean winced as he reached up and gingerly touched the bandage on his head. "Shut up, asshole. I would have been fine if Jackson had listened to a damn thing I said. We came around a bend, and he steered us right into a low-hanging branch. I tried to avoid it but didn't get out of the way in time, and it threw me into the rapids. I hit my head on a rock and passed out before being swept down the river."

"I pulled off the river as soon as I could and waded out into the current to find him. By some miracle, his body floated right past me so I could grab him and drag him up onto the shore without being pulled out myself. It all happened so fast. I still can't believe how lucky we are." Jackson pulled his brother into a hug. "Mom would have murdered me if I killed her baby boy a couple of weeks after he graduated from high school."

Rowan smiled at the brothers as she pointed toward the burning fire on the beach. "Let's sit down so we can stay warm while I get your head wrapped up in case the bleeding starts again. We're going to need to get you to the hospital as soon as possible in case there's more going on than what we can see. We're also going to need to mind our time. If we wait too long, it will be difficult to take off in the dim light and we'll have to wait until morning." The brothers nodded as they walked toward the fire. "Jackson, while I'm checking Sean, can you stow what gear from your raft you want to take with us in the plane and pull the rest as far from the beach as you can? When storms come through, this river can get quite high, so try to get it above that ridge up there if possible. I'll help you drag the raft up and tie it off as soon as I'm done with Sean."

"Roger that." Jackson hurried toward their raft.

"Is your brother military?" Rowan asked as she and Sean sat next to the fire.

"Marine." Sean winced when Rowan pulled the bandage away from a massive gash in the back of his head. "He's been deployed in Afghanistan for the last several months. When we were kids, we always talked about rafting up here, and when his leave lined up with my graduation, we went for it. It sucks that I ruined our trip."

Rowan could see genuine regret in the boy's eyes as he picked up a stick and tossed it into the flames. "Not your fault, man. Things happen, and you're just lucky your brother kept his wits about him and could pull you out. This kind of thing happens all the time, and more times than not, the other person panics and ends up costing both people their lives. I'm sure the last thing on his mind is that your trip is over.

He's just happy to still have a little brother." Rowan smiled at him as she opened her first aid kit and pulled out a small penlight to check his eyes.

When the medical evaluation was complete and his head bandaged again, she helped Jackson pull the boat off the beach and get it secured. After stowing her gear back into the plane, she surveyed her surroundings for the best direction to take off. The trees on the north side of the beach were lower, which meant she would need to take off toward them. Unfortunately, this meant the plane would have to be dragged over to the other side of the beach.

Enlisting Jackson's help, they got the plane in position, and the three of them loaded up as she crossed her fingers and took off. The plane weaved as the wheels dragged through the sand until she could get enough lift to rise above it. They all held their breath as the treetops brushed the bottom of the plane, but they made it over the top and headed toward town. Turning to check that her passengers were okay, Rowan smiled to see them leaning against each other, fast asleep. With a sigh of relief, she finally allowed herself to relax as the sun dropped below the horizon.

CHAPTER THREE

Jamie stepped off the single-engine plane and stretched her aching muscles. After traveling for more than a day, she was happy to extend her legs to their full length. Pins and needles assaulted her feet as the blood returned to her extremities. Eager to meet with her guide and officially begin her research, she found a luggage cart for her bags and pushed it toward a small building just off the gravel strip they called a runway. She had grown up watching television shows set in small Alaskan towns, but nothing could prepare her for the incredible beauty or the true feeling of isolation she felt.

The small village of Ugruk sat at the foot of an impressive mountain range. Imposing rocky cliffs rose high above, ending in snow-covered peaks tucked beneath a blanket of fog. Jamie was glad she'd thought to pack extra memory cards for her camera. She knew she would leave Alaska with thousands of photos to sort through when she got home.

The email she received from the park service had said her guide would meet her at the airport. They would spend their first evening camping near a river, and the following day they would hike to a cabin near the area where the sighting occurred. She'd done her best to look at maps and try to familiarize herself with the terrain, but it was difficult when she didn't know exactly where they were going or where they'd be staying. Whatever was going to happen, Jamie was ready to get started, so she would have as much time as possible to look for signs the curlew had been there. Finding a nest would be spectacular, but probably too much to hope for.

It had been less than two weeks since she'd spoken to her father and somehow found the strength to approach her boss, requesting they send her to the middle of nowhere, Alaska, to search for a bird that was more than likely extinct. She was confident they would get a laugh at her expense and they had initially turned her down, but to her surprise, she got word the following day that the board had reconsidered and agreed to fund her trip.

Her contact had promised to send the ranger who took the report to meet her in Ugruk. He would guide her to where the bird sighting happened. She knew nothing of him other than that his name was Rowan Fleming. The idea of spending several weeks alone with a man she'd never met, in the middle of nowhere, made her nervous. At least the martial arts classes she'd taken several years before, and the canister of bear repellent she planned to always have strapped to her side, gave her confidence.

After sitting in the tiny building they used as a terminal for over an hour, Jamie gathered her bags and slowly made her way out the front doors to see if someone was waiting for her outside. Several people were milling about, but none of them seemed like they were looking for someone. She checked the time on her watch once more and sighed. The last thing she needed was a guide she didn't trust. She checked her phone for messages, but none were there. Another glance at the email confirmed she had the date and time correct. Jamie checked her watch one last time. Now she was officially pissed. Two hours late was ridiculous. She pulled her phone from her pocket to figure out who she needed to complain to when she noticed a woman walking toward her.

"Are you Martin?"

"Yes, I'm Dr. Martin," Jamie answered as she pocketed her phone and reached for her bags.

"I'm the terminal agent, Janet. Greg at the AWR asked me to let you know Rowan was called out on an emergency and won't be able to meet you until tomorrow at noon."

Jamie felt her temper quickly escalating toward its boiling point. She'd already spent two hours waiting for the guide to arrive, only to find out her trip was postponed for a day. She didn't have a day to spare. Every single hour she spent here was an hour wasted not doing her research. "You're kidding me?" Jamie tried to keep the frustration from her voice. It wasn't poor Janet's fault, but it was becoming increasingly difficult to keep her cool. "I'm only here for a limited amount of time. Don't you have someone else who can handle the emergency or possibly another pilot and guide who can take me?"

Realizing she sounded like a petulant child, she took a deep breath and closed her eyes. She was tired and hungry, and there wasn't anything that could be done for her tonight. She'd complain to someone tomorrow. Jamie rubbed her eyes and looked around, taking in her surroundings. "Can you tell me where to find a place to stay?"

Janet silently pointed toward a building across the street with a hand-painted sign that read "Ugruk Saloon" in large letters and "Rooms for rent" in small lettering below that.

"You've got to be kidding me," she grumbled to herself. "There should have been supplies sent a week ago. Do you know if they've arrived?" They sent boxes days before that contained the cameras and other recording equipment she'd need. It was essential for her research, so Ranger Fleming wouldn't be her only delay if it hadn't arrived.

"It's locked up in the storage room."

Jamie looked down at the bags she'd brought with her and decided she really would only need one of them for the night. "Can I store some of these with the boxes? I'd rather not have to carry them around with me."

"We only have room for three of them. You know this is a ridiculous amount of stuff, right?"

"I'm going to be here for months. Most of this is the equipment I'll need for my research." She was driving Jamie crazy. It was none of her business how much stuff she had. "Then, can you take what you can store so that I can get a room?"

Janet nodded and waited while Jamie grabbed the bags she would take with her to the hotel and stacked the rest back onto the cart. So far, this day had been horrible, and she was ready to relax and get a warm meal.

An hour later, a freshly showered Jamie descended the wooden staircase from her room down to what appeared to be an actual saloon on the first floor. She pushed her way through the press of townspeople, to a table in the back corner and caught the attention of a waitress as she hurried by with a tray of shot glasses.

"I'll be right back with a menu, sweetie."

"Thanks." Jamie pulled out her phone to email her dad, letting him know she landed safely and that there would be a delay. She hadn't thought about the fact she likely wouldn't have cell service once they were out in the field, but with only two bars in town, she saw the writing on the wall.

"Can I get you something to drink?" the waitress asked when she returned with the menu.

"Do you have a wine list?"

"We have red or white."

The look she was given told Jamie she should steer clear of the wine. "How about a beer? A stout with fish and chips?"

"You got it."

Jamie watched her quickly put in her order before rushing to another table. The bar was busy for such a small town, but Jamie couldn't remember when she'd felt so alone. The adrenaline rush motivating her since the trip was approved seemed to dissipate with the delay. Her entire schedule would need to be adjusted to accommodate the time lost. Thus far, she wasn't impressed with Ranger Fleming, and she hoped once she could talk to him, he'd have more respect for how vital her research was. She wasn't some eager grad student trying to impress their professor. Her work was serious research that could change the fate of a bird species.

By the time Jamie finished her food and a couple of beers, the bar crowd had thinned. She assumed Monday nights in sleepy little Alaskan towns ended early, even though the sun wouldn't set for at least another few hours. Jamie wondered what it would be like to live in such a small town. Monterey wasn't exactly large, but this village gave her the feeling she was on the very edge of civilization.

"Whatcha thinking about?"

Jamie looked up into hazel eyes she hadn't noticed the last time they'd spoken. In the crowd's chaos, she somehow missed how beautiful her waitress was. "Nothing important."

The waitress reached out to touch the furrow in Jamie's brow. The move was forward but not unwelcome. "I highly doubt that. You look like you're thinking about important things. Can I get you another beer?"

"No, thank you. I think I've had enough for tonight. Besides, sitting in an almost empty bar in the middle of nowhere drinking a beer alone isn't exactly a good look." Jamie didn't miss the flirtatious look the waitress gave her. She wasn't opposed to a casual night with the attractive stranger, but it probably wasn't the best idea when she'd have to get up early the next day.

"What about sitting in an almost empty bar in the middle of nowhere drinking a beer with a friend?"

"Are we friends?" Jamie asked.

"We could be friends. I'm Caroline," she said, holding her hand out to shake.

Jamie took her outstretched arm and noticed what appeared to be the feathers of a bird tattoo peeking out from beneath her sleeve. "May I see your tattoo?" Caroline pulled her sleeve back so Jamie could get a better look. The red and black tattoo was of an enormous bird similar to a bald eagle with a giant beak and exaggerated wingspan. It was a common theme in the art of the indigenous people of the Pacific Northwest, but Jamie had never seen such a beautiful interpretation of it before. "Thunderbird, right?"

Caroline smiled and ran a finger across the design. "That's right. This one was modeled after a totem in the village where I was born. My grandparents still live there. It gives me strength and reminds me I come from a long line of courageous women."

Jamie gently turned Caroline's arm back and forth to take in every intricate design detail. "It's exquisite."

"Thank you. I think you're rather exquisite yourself."

It had been some time since Jamie had been with someone who flirted with her this directly. She could admittedly be a flirt herself, but Caroline's direct approach was intriguing. Spending time with her would undoubtedly take her mind off the disappointment of being stuck in Ugruk for an extra night.

"How about that beer you promised me?" Jamie asked.

Caroline stood and checked the time on her watch. "It's time for me to clock out. Let me do that, and I'll be right back with our drinks."

Jamie nodded and watched her saunter away with a swing of her hips. She was sure it was for her benefit, and she would not complain about her efforts. Caroline wasn't Jamie's typical type of more masculine lesbian, but she certainly wasn't immune to the attraction of a feminine woman.

When Caroline returned, she set down their drinks and slid into the booth next to Jamie. There were only a few people left in the bar, and none of them seemed to notice or care that two women were sitting so close to each other.

"Is it difficult to be a lesbian up here?" Jamie asked.

"What do you mean?"

Jamie sipped her beer and glanced around the room. The younger people in the crowd had cleared out, and the remaining few patrons looked like regulars who had spent most of their lives in this bar. "I just wondered how difficult it was for a young, beautiful lesbian like yourself in such a remote and conservative part of the world."

"It's not as bad as you might think." Caroline shrugged, then took another sip of her beer. "Most of the people who live up here year-round are conservative, but Alaskans do their own thing and don't pay attention to what everyone else is doing. It's probably different in bigger cities, but people don't have time for that out here. Few stay over the winter, and the summer is a constant flood of tourists, seasonal workers, scientists, explorers, and anyone else who thinks they have the balls to make it out here."

"I certainly don't have balls, but I hope I have what it takes to be out here through the summer. If I ever get used to the almost constant daylight." Jamie had done her best to convince herself she'd be fine, but now that she was here, she couldn't help but question whether she had possibly bitten off more than she could chew.

"Remind me to give you an eye mask to block the sun at night. It will be your best friend. You here for research?" Caroline asked.

"Yes, birds." Jamie was a little sheepish to admit she would spend the summer trying to prove that a bird most had written off as extinct was still alive and well. It was easier to stick with the basics. She was pretty sure Caroline was interested in something other than what she was studying, anyway.

"Neat. Lots of them around here." Caroline scooted close enough to slip an arm over the back of the seat behind Jamie. "What else interests you? Besides birds." A slender finger tucked Jamie's hair behind her ear and traced the edge of her jaw.

"I don't know." Jamie took another big drink of her beer. "What else do you have?"

CHAPTER FOUR

Rowan entered the small terminal through the side door and glanced around the room. By the time she'd gotten everything packed back into the plane and made the flight over to Ugruk, she'd arrived an hour later than she had hoped. She felt terrible about the delay, but it was unavoidable. They would already be hard-pressed to make it to the beach where they were to set up camp for the night. She'd expected to find Dr. Martin waiting for her in the terminal, but the only person she saw was the terminal clerk at her desk.

"Hey, Janet," Rowan said. "Did you talk to a Dr. Martin yesterday?"

Janet rolled her eyes as she shuffled papers on the desk and put them in neat stacks to the side. "She's a handful."

"Crap, that bad, huh?"

"Let's just say you're not one of her favorite people, and she gave me an earful about it, so you owe me big time."

"I promise to make it up to you," Rowan said.

"Oh, really?" Janet's suggestive smile and wiggle of her eyebrows made Rowan laugh. She'd known her for many years and had always enjoyed their flirtatious relationship, even though Janet was happily married to a local fisherman.

"Chocolate?" Rowan offered.

"It's going to take more than chocolate to make up for that experience, but it's a start. I want the kind with the raspberry centers like you got last time."

"Roger," Rowan said, then leaned over the counter to kiss Janet on the cheek.

"I assume Dr. Martin will be here any minute now. I said you'd be here by noon," Janet said before picking up the ringing phone on the small desk behind the counter.

Rowan silently waved good-bye to Janet as she walked out the terminal door into the crisp midday air. As she waited for Dr. Martin to arrive, she noticed an attractive blond woman loaded down with bags making her way toward the terminal. "Let me help you with that," she said as she jogged over to take the two heaviest bags.

"You're very kind," she said with a relieved look.

"What brings you out here with all this stuff?" Rowan asked as she set the bags down in the terminal's waiting area.

"I'm scheduled to meet my guide if he even bothers to show up. Are Alaskans always late? Is that just what happens when you live in the middle of nowhere?"

"Maybe your guide had something important come up and wasn't able to make it?" Rowan knew this must be the Dr. Martin she was to meet but was so irritated by her attitude she messed with her a little.

"I'm not sure Ranger Fleming understands the importance of my trip, or he would have met me yesterday. I have a tight schedule to accomplish something that could be a significant discovery in my career. There isn't time to wait for him to decide to stroll in a day late." She took a deep breath and let out a sigh. "I'm sorry. I don't mean to complain to you about this."

"I—"

"Jamie?"

Rowan watched as Caroline Hill jogged across the street toward them. "You left your eye mask on the nightstand." She handed a padded gray mask to Dr. Martin, then gave her a gentle kiss on the lips. "I hope it helps you sleep on those long summer nights without me. Look me up when you're heading home. I'd love to have a drink before you leave." Caroline turned to Rowan and caressed her cheek. "Rowan, you're handsome as ever."

"Caroline, you look lovely." Rowan had to bite her lip to hold back the laughter at seeing the embarrassed look on Dr. Martin's face. She'd have to thank Caroline for her perfect timing the next time she was in town.

They both watched Caroline jog away. Once she was back inside the bar, Rowan turned her attention to Dr. Martin, whose anger seemed to have somewhat deflated after Caroline's disruption. "You must be Dr. Martin. I'm Rowan Fleming, your guide." Rowan picked up several bags and walked toward the terminal doors, leaving Jamie in her wake. "You coming? You have an important schedule to keep."

Rowan found an empty table inside the terminal and set the bags down on one end. Janet had brought the rest of Dr. Martin's things from storage and piled it next to the table. There was no way they'd be able to hike all this into the cabin, so Rowan steeled herself for what she was sure was going to be an uncomfortable conversation. From her previous experience on research trips, she knew the researchers always believed they needed much more equipment than was required for whatever they were studying.

"Can you slow down, please?" Jamie gasped, dragging the rest of her luggage along behind her.

Rowan sighed and took the remaining bags from her. "How much of this stuff do you need?"

"What do you mean?"

The bags made a thud when Rowan dropped them on the floor. "Whatever we take, we not only have to fit in the plane but also pack it to the cabin. There's no way I'm going to carry the equipment you'll need and these bags. You're going to have to pare this down."

"I need all this stuff."

"Do you?"

"Well, what am I supposed to do with anything I don't take? Where would I leave it?"

"Janet will store it in my locker here in the terminal. It'll be safe."

"Look, Ranger Fleming—"

"Rowan."

"What?"

"My name is Rowan. Please call me Rowan, Dr. Martin."

"Oh, Jamie, call me Jamie." Jamie looked so thrown off balance that Rowan had to suppress a smile. "Rowan, I can't be sure what I'll need until I'm there. If I leave something behind and realize later that I need it, I'm screwed. I already thought I'd only brought the things I would need. I'm pretty sure I need all this stuff."

Four of the boxes on the floor were heavy-duty plastic cases that Rowan suspected carried video and audio equipment. The equipment itself would be heavy enough, but add the weight of the cases, and it would be almost impossible to hike it all into where they needed it. She'd need to get creative to keep the equipment safe while leaving the heavy cases behind.

Rowan unzipped the first bag on the table but stopped to look at Jamie before opening it. "May I?" Jamie hesitated, then gave a nod of permission. Rowan emptied the bag's contents and then moved to the next until she'd opened them all on the table. She took a minute to survey what was there and then sorted the items into separate piles. She was thankful Jamie only silently watched. Once she was satisfied, she invited her closer so she could explain what she'd done.

"Okay, I've separated everything into piles. This pile," Rowan indicated the pile of research equipment, "I don't know what you need or don't need from this pile since I don't know what you can live without when you're in the field. I'm hoping you might try to narrow this one down, but that's up to you. We're going to have all kinds of stuff to carry already, and the more unnecessary stuff you have, the more trips we're going to have to take to get it from one place to the next."

Jamie stepped up to the table and sorted through the things in the pile, pulling out several more oversized items and setting them aside. She'd cut the weight of what she would take down by about a third. Rowan could live with that. "Okay, this pile is your clothing. You'll need mostly warm items, but it will be good to have a few short-sleeved shirts. You won't need separate pairs of shorts. I can see you have a couple of pairs of convertible pants, so if you feel you need shorts, you can unzip those bottoms. No use in packing extra things you won't need. Which leads me to your socks and skivvies." Rowan felt terrible when she saw Jamie blush. She wasn't trying to embarrass her, but when they were out on the trail, she'd appreciate not having the extra weight. "You won't need over three or four pairs of each. You'll only need two bras at the most."

"We'll be out there for three months."

Rowan sorted through the socks on the table, pulling out the ones she thought would be the most appropriate for the trail, with one extra thick pair to wear at night. "We'll wash what we have. Trust me, you will thank me when we're out there."

Jamie grumbled but pulled out the clothes she would take and pushed the rest to the side. "What now, boss?"

"Now, the pile of frivolous stuff you have no business taking with you."

"What?" Jamie looked at the assortment of entertainment items she'd brought. "We're going to be out there for a long time. I need something to entertain myself with."

"Jamie, there are four enormous books. Do you think you're going to read four enormous books?"

"I'm a fast reader, and they're only paperbacks."

Rowan rolled her eyes. "One book at the most, and even that will end up as kindling for the fire once you think about having to carry it back to the plane at the end of the trip." Jamie ran her delicate fingers across each book. The way she caressed them stirred something Rowan hadn't expected.

She cleared her throat and did her best to push her attraction aside. Crushing on her would make for a very uncomfortable three months. "They all look pretty worn out," Rowan said. "Which one have you read the most?"

"Probably this one." Jamie held up one book. It wasn't the smallest of the options, but it wasn't the largest either.

"Okay, let's pack that one. It's obviously your favorite. The others will wait for you when we're back."

She didn't look pleased, but Jamie nodded and placed the other books back into a bag staying at the airport. "Is that it?" Jamie asked.

"The rest of that stuff has to stay." Rowan pointed to the remaining items that included travel-sized board games, a deck of cards, and a journal.

"Seriously? None of it?"

"Here." Rowan handed her the journal. "That's it."

"Fine." Jamie stuffed the items she would take into two bags.

The last items were the large cases. Rowan stacked the bags into two piles, one for things that were staying and one that they would take with them. Once the table was cleared, she hefted each case onto the surface and opened them to get a look at their contents. They contained field cameras, batteries, audio equipment, a rugged laptop, solar panels, etc. Everything Jamie would need to document her research. Rowan knew these items would be the most important of any other items they took. Unfortunately, they'd also be the heaviest.

"Okay, we're going to have to get creative here," Rowan said.

"I need all of this equipment. That isn't negotiable."

"I know. I'm not suggesting we leave it, only that we get creative with how we transport it. These cases weigh a ton, and I think we can figure out another way to carry everything without the extra weight."

They were both silent for a few minutes as they thought about what to do. Finally, Jamie picked up one bag that would be left behind and checked its tag. "This is waterproof. What if we took some of my clothes and wrapped them around the equipment as padding and put everything in these three waterproof bags we were going to leave? I can store the cases with the rest of the stuff in your locker."

The idea would work perfectly, and Rowan was pleasantly surprised to see that Jamie was willing to be flexible and creative when faced with challenges. Maybe this trip wouldn't be the hell she'd imagined it would be. They quickly emptied the packs they needed and repacked all the equipment they were taking into them.

Rowan took the bags and cases that were staying to Janet and asked her to place them in her locker until they returned. She wasn't proud that they'd already had a minor battle, but she was happy to see Jamie could be reasonable when pressed. She hoped that would hold out when they were alone with no one else to talk with.

When she returned to Jamie, they packed the equipment onto a cart and walked out the terminal's door toward the waiting plane. They had a long few months ahead of them, and Rowan was eager to get it over with so she could get back to her own life.

CHAPTER FIVE

When told she was clear to get out, Jamie almost fell from the plane and kissed the ground below her. She could hear Rowan's deep laugh at her eagerness to disembark, which did nothing to soothe the tension between them. As she bent over to settle her stomach, she heard Rowan radio someone that they'd landed safely. The disembodied voice on the other end confirmed someone would pick up the plane the next day and wished them a safe trip.

"Roger. I'll keep you updated when I'm able to. Over." Rowan climbed into the back of the plane and tossed bags out onto the ground.

"Hey," Jamie said. "Just hand them to me instead of throwing them in the dirt. There's very delicate equipment in here that I'd rather not have broken before we even get to the location."

Rowan continued to empty the plane but handed Jamie each bag to stack them into a neat pile. Jamie couldn't help but appreciate the faint outline of muscles beneath Rowan's tight-fitting olive drab T-shirt. She hated that the infuriating woman stirred those feelings in her, but she'd have to learn to block them out of her mind for now. She didn't need any distractions from her research, and if she wasn't careful, Ranger Fleming could quickly become an unwanted distraction. Jamie turned away and forced herself not to watch Rowan as she walked toward her carrying the last of their bags from the plane.

"Grab a couple of bags, and we'll come back for the rest," Rowan said, dropping one of Jamie's bags in the dirt next to her as she walked by. "Let's go, Dr. Martin. We're wasting time."

"And there it is," Jamie said quietly to herself as all lusty thoughts left her brain. Damn, she was infuriating. She felt guilty for what she said in frustration at the airport, but Rowan wasn't doing anything to help smooth things over. She took a deep breath to calm her nerves and decided she should probably extend the first olive branch if they would ever make it without murdering each other.

She picked up her bag, dusted off her pants, and quickly jogged to catch up as they stepped into a thicket and followed a narrow trail away from the plane. "May I ask where we're going? They said we were camping near a river this first night."

"That's right."

Jamie waited for more information, but she kept her questions to a minimum when none came. So far, this adventure hadn't been what she had hoped it would be. She wasn't even exactly sure what she expected, but she was sure it didn't involve being delayed a day and pissing off her only companion before they even got started.

"Rowan—" Before she could say more, Rowan stopped abruptly, causing Jamie to run face-first into the backpack in front of her.

"We're here." Rowan slipped her pack off and reached to help Jamie with hers. "We'll lower these things to our campsite below and then go back for the rest. Once we have the equipment taken care of, we'll rappel down to the beach."

"Holy shit, for real?" Jamie gingerly peeked off the edge to see how far down they would have to go. "Holy shit," she repeated, not knowing what else to say.

"You keep saying that. It's not that far down. You aren't afraid of heights, are you?"

Jamie knew she was right, but the unexpected need for mountaineering skills took a minute to sink in. "I've never done this kind of thing before. I never thought I was afraid of heights, but right now, I'm not so sure." She laughed, but the roll of her stomach betrayed her attempt at nonchalance.

"You'll be just fine." Rowan placed her hand on Jamie's shoulder with more compassion than she expected. "I'll make sure you're perfectly safe."

The reassurance helped, but nothing could completely dispel the nervousness that had settled in her gut. "Okay," Jamie said, swallowing past the lump in her throat. Jamie watched as Rowan threaded a rope through the straps of each bag and lowered them down to the beach. The entire process took less than five minutes, but watching the bags descend the rocky cliff made the hairs on the back of Jamie's neck stand up.

Rowan turned and gave Jamie an unexpected wink that oozed confidence and strength. She was such a contradiction that it left Jamie a little confused about how to feel. One minute she seemed distant, and the next, she was warm and kind. The more time she spent with Rowan, the more conflicted Jamie was about her.

"Come on, let's go get the rest of our stuff." Without another word, Rowan turned and walked back down the trail. Jamie watched as the brush swallowed her tall form before she jogged to catch up.

After three trips, they had carried all the bags and equipment to the top of the cliff. Jamie watched as Rowan repeated the same lowering of each item down to the beach. "So, we're spending the night by the river tonight and hiking the rest of the way to the cabin tomorrow?" Jamie tried to recall what the paperwork said about the logistics of everything.

"Yep," Rowan said as she looped the rope around Jamie's body.

"Um, what are you—"

"I'm tying a harness so I can lower you down next."

"Wait, what?" Jamie peeked over the edge of the cliff and back toward Rowan, who was tying an elaborate knot in the rope. "Don't we have a harness for this?"

"We don't need one since we aren't doing any major climbing. This rope will be more than enough for anything we do. Excuse me." Jamie squeaked as Rowan threaded the rope between her legs and made the same knot she'd tied at her waist before doing the same for her other leg. Rowan's hands were dangerously close to the same area Jamie both wanted and didn't want her close to. The anxiety of what was happening, coupled with the gentle brush of Rowan's hand and tightening of the ropes against her center, made Jamie break out in a sweat.

"Rowan, I'm—I'm not so sure about this." Jamie could hear the fear in her voice as the adjustment of the rope jostled her around. Rowan double-checked all the knots and smoothed her fingers between the rope and Jamie's body before pulling a carabiner from her pocket and clipping it to a loop she'd made in the front of the rope harness.

"Okay, I'm going to wrap this rope around that tree for leverage, then slowly lower you down."

"Rowan." Jamie felt her stomach roll like she was going to be sick. "I can't do this." She peered over the edge and down at the beach fifty feet below. She hated to feel this weak, but the idea of stepping off this cliff and trusting someone who was a stranger was more than she could do. "I can't, Rowan. Sorry, but I'll just walk around and find an easier way down."

"Hey." Rowan pulled off her gloves and cradled Jamie's face between her warm hands. "It's okay, Jamie. I know you haven't exactly known me long enough to trust me, but I've got you. I promise I won't let anything happen to you."

"I'm just so scared."

"We've got this. Together." Rowan caressed her cheek with her thumb and smiled. It wasn't a smile that made Jamie feel like she wasn't taking her feelings seriously. It was more of a smile that said, I will take care of you. Jamie stared into Rowan's warm brown eyes and drew from the confidence and comfort she found in them. Without her brain giving permission, her body relaxed.

"What do you need me to do?"

"Attagirl." Rowan slipped her gloves back on and picked up the rope she'd wrapped around the tree. "As I said, I'm going to tie one end of this rope to the carabiner, and the other will be anchored around the tree and wrapped around my waist. I'll use the tree as leverage to slowly lower you down to the beach. You focus on me, and don't worry about the beach, the distance, or anything other than my studly physique."

Jamie snorted a laugh and immediately covered her mouth in embarrassment. "Oh my God, please pretend you didn't hear that." Rowan laughed.

"Let's get you down to the beach, hotshot." Rowan double-checked all of her knots one last time. "Okay, before we get to the edge, lean all of your weight back, like you're going to let yourself fall."

The rope pulled as Jamie leaned back. The move was completely unnatural, but the harness Rowan created tightened around her waist and securely kept her from falling backward.

"Feel that?" Rowan asked. "I'll easily be able to control your descent. When you feel you're ready, back up to the edge of the cliff. This is the only time I want you to look down, but not over the edge. Just look at the ground so you can see when you've gotten to the edge. Once you're there, lean back. I will give you a little slack so your body can lean over the edge, but you won't be falling. I'll have complete control."

"I've seen this before in movies and stuff. I understand the basics. I've just never done it myself."

"Well, let's mark this off your bucket list."

"I can assure you, this was never on my bucket list." Jamie stared at her feet as she walked backward. She peered over and down to the beach fifty feet below when she reached the edge. Rowan specifically told her not to do it, but she couldn't stop herself. Her head spun, and she felt like she was going to lose her balance and tumble to her death. Why did she have to look? Why was she so afraid to do this?

"Hey, Jamie," Rowan called to her. "What's your favorite thing about birds?"

Jamie looked away from the edge and toward Rowan. She was slowly allowing the rope to slide from her grasp. "The rope," Jamie yelped.

"I've got it. I have you. Just lean back. I won't let you fall."

The rope once again pressed against Jamie's waist as she slowly leaned back, never looking away from Rowan's face.

"Excellent. Good job, Jamie. What's your favorite thing about birds?"

The edge of the cliff rose higher and higher as Jamie walked down the rocky surface in front of her. She watched Rowan move forward to position herself where Jamie could still see her. Rowan wasn't wrong. She definitely had a studly physique. Jamie distracted herself by focusing on Rowan's broad, muscular shoulders as she expertly controlled the rope's speed. "They've always fascinated me. My dad was a biologist and my mom an entomologist, so I was raised to appreciate all living things, but I've always been drawn to birds."

"Is the curlew your favorite?" Rowan became smaller and smaller as Jamie descended.

"No, it's hard to choose, but I'd say the Laysan albatross is my favorite."

"Ah, you're a romantic then?"

Jamie laughed. "I wouldn't say that, although that they stay faithfully by their mate's side until death is probably the sweetest thing ever."

"So, if it's not about their sappiness, what do you love about them?"

"Everything, really. The Laysan albatross migration from Hawaii to the Bering Sea in Alaska alone is amazing. That's quite a distance for such an enormous bird. And the way they fly. Have you ever seen one fly? It's called dynamic soaring. They glide low over the waves, rarely flapping their wings until they zoom up into the sky and use the power of the wind to carry them. They're magnificent."

"Jamie?"

"Hmm?" Lost in her own thoughts, Jamie was startled by the sound of Rowan's voice.

"Put your feet down."

"Wha—?" Jamie looked down to find she was only a couple of feet from the sand. "I made it!" She couldn't contain the joy she felt when her feet were back on flat land.

"Can you unclip that carabiner from your harness, and I'll pull it up so I can join you?"

"Sure, yeah." Jamie released the fastener and held it up, so Rowan knew it was safe to pull it in.

"Thanks. My descent will only take a minute."

Rowan stepped out of sight for a moment before dropping over the edge to lower herself down. Jamie gasped as she noticed that the rope was only draped through her legs and over her shoulder instead of the elaborate harness she'd fashioned for Jamie. "Be careful," Jamie said, but before she knew it, Rowan was already next to her on the beach. "That was...impressive."

She gave her the cocky grin Jamie was beginning to be less irritated and more amused by already. "Ready to make camp and have some dinner? I'm starving. We can stack the bags against the cliff face to help shelter us from the wind tonight, and then I'll catch a fish for us."

Jamie looked around at their bags scattered on the beach and then up at Ranger Studly, whom she was begrudgingly starting to like. She wondered if she could handle what the next few months had in store for them. Whatever happened, she was sure it wouldn't be boring.

"Let's do this, Ranger Rowan." Jamie picked up a bag and giggled when Rowan rolled her eyes.

CHAPTER SIX

The late evening sun still clearly illuminated her surroundings as Rowan dropped a fishing line with a hook attached into the river. They'd have proper fishing equipment waiting for them in the cabin, but with the number of salmon in the river this time of year, it wouldn't take more than what she had to catch dinner for them both.

Rowan gently tugged on the line as she watched Jamie gather driftwood scattered on the beach for their fire. It wasn't the best, but she'd used a rain fly and their bags to create a lean-to shelter to protect them from the elements in case it rained during the night. They were only about an hour's hike from the cabin, but they couldn't chance crossing the river with all of their bags so late in the evening. It was safer to stay where they were and then hike the rest of the way the following day. There was enough of a slope from the top of the beach where they were down to the river that they wouldn't need to worry about getting washed away unless there was some major storm that unexpectedly churned up. Greg kept a close watch on the radar and would alert them if anything was concerning.

"Is this enough?" Jamie asked, pointing to a pile of wood near their shelter.

"That should be enough for now. Thanks." Rowan felt a pull on her line, indicating she had a fish. "Dinner is on the way."

An hour later, they were both licking the remnants of their meal from the pan. "I can't believe we ate that entire fish," Jamie said, patting her stomach as if to congratulate it.

"In all fairness, the salmon was on the smaller side. Not to mention, we worked our butts off today. Unfortunately, tomorrow will be more of the same. You think you're ready for this last push?"

"What kind of push do you mean? You won't make me climb down more cliffs, will you? Heads up, there's a chance you'll see the salmon again if heights are on the agenda."

Rowan leaned back against the rock wall they were camping next to and smiled. "I promise we'll have our feet on the ground the entire time. That honestly wasn't even the hard part. Tomorrow we have to get all of this stuff across the river, and then it's about an hour's hike from there to the cabin. With this gear, that should take maybe three trips each. Getting across the river is going to be a pain in the ass. Much more dangerous than that little drop down this cliff."

"That will teach me to ask." Jamie slumped next to Rowan.

"Sorry. We'll work together, and hopefully, it'll go quickly. We should have good weather, so I'll get you across the river first, and we'll tie our rope from that tree over on the other side to the hook you see drilled into the cliff face. People have done this a thousand times before us, so we'll take it one step at a time, and before you know it, we'll be sitting in front of a fire in the cabin."

"This is even more of an adventure than I'd imagined it would be, and we're on day one."

Rowan hoped Jamie could keep her good attitude after realizing how much work these next few months would be. It would be a slog, and even the most enthusiastic people struggled after weeks of hardship. "Once we get everything over to the other side, we can each take a couple of bags for the first trip to the cabin, and then if you don't mind, I'll help you open the cabin up, and then you can get everything squared away for us while I make the last few trips to get the rest of the stuff."

"I hate to leave you to do all the grunt work alone. These bags aren't easy to carry. That's too much for one person." Jamie rubbed her hand along Rowan's arm, and she felt goose bumps erupt on her skin.

"I'll be okay. It will be a relief knowing the cabin will be ready for us to relax at the end of the day. It's going to be a mess. These cabins always are. They're locked up for long periods where dust and bugs have a chance to collect on every surface imaginable, and then when people are staying there, it's almost always big, stinky hunters who don't care if things are clean. Some of them would rather sleep on top of the filth than take the time to clean things up."

"That sounds appealing. At least we'll have a roof over our heads and a bed off of the floor, right?"

"Absolutely. I can't promise the bed will be the most comfortable thing you've slept on, but it will be off of the floor." Rowan suspected that once they'd actually gotten everything to the cabin and could finally lie down to rest, Jamie would be happy with whatever was available. Tomorrow would be the hardest of all of their days there until the last day when they'd need to repeat the process and carry everything back to leave.

Jamie stared at the fire as it sparked and hissed. "I'm sorry for the way I treated you in Ugruk. I acted like a spoiled brat, and that just isn't who I am."

The sincerity of Jamie's apology melted any remaining animosity Rowan may have felt. "Thank you for that."

"Do you mind if I ask what the emergency was that made you late?"

Rowan picked up a pebble from the beach and tossed it toward the water. "Just some kids who'd been rafting and took a spill. One of them had a head injury, so they needed a rescue."

"Jesus, are they okay?"

"I think so." Rowan shrugged and tossed another pebble. She'd always felt a little sheepish discussing her rescues. "I got them to Fairbanks. Someone transported them to the hospital from there. The last I'd heard, the kid had a concussion but would be fine."

"Now I feel like a complete ass. I should have realized an emergency up here is actually that and not some scheduling screw-up being labeled an emergency to make it seem more important than it is."

"Does that happen to you often? Someone tries to pass off something minor as an emergency, so they feel better about screwing you around?"

Now it was Jamie's turn to shrug. "It happens."

Rowan nodded and left it at that. Jamie didn't seem like she wanted to elaborate. Rowan wasn't one to pry, so they sat quietly together for a few minutes and watched the salmon jump out of the water and flop back in on their instinctual drive to reach the place where they would spawn and eventually die. The entire process had always fascinated

Rowan. A salmon's journey was such a solitary one. Even surrounded by others making the same sacrifice, they wholly depended on themselves. Her inclination to emulate that behavior sometimes made it difficult to relate to others. It was something she knew she learned from her father, and it had cost her more heartache in her life than she wanted to admit. She sometimes wanted to be different. Rowan wished she knew how to be different. She could get used to sitting on the beach with an attractive woman, belly full of fresh salmon and a beautiful river in front of them.

"I'm sorry if I was cold to you at first."

"Yeah, why was that?" Jamie nudged Rowan's shoulder in what seemed an attempt to soften what she had said.

"I think…" Rowan considered her following words. She wanted to be honest but didn't want to start an argument now that they were finally on what seemed to be common ground. "I think I expected you to be entitled."

"Okay, well, I wasn't exactly expecting that. Why would you think I would be entitled? You didn't even know me."

The assumptions she'd made about Jamie embarrassed Rowan. Now that she'd gotten to know her, she found her to be so much more than the privileged scientist she'd expected. "You're right. I guess it's because of the way it all went down."

"The way what went down?"

"Them assigning me as your guide. I'm a ranger, rarely a guide. That's just not something I've been asked to do since the early days of my career. When I heard it came from the top, I assumed you must have pulled some strings to get special treatment."

Jamie sat up straight and looked Rowan in the eyes. "What do you mean you thought I'd pulled some strings and got special treatment? They told me you would be my guide because you're the ranger who filed the report and that you knew the area better than anyone else. Is that not true?"

"No, all that's true. I only mean being a guide isn't usually part of my job duties. Combine that with the fact that they told me it came from the top, and that made it pretty clear you had some special pull."

"Oh." A look of understanding crossed Jamie's face, and she stared down at her hands where they lay clasped in her lap. "I guess that makes sense."

Rowan was completely confused. "What makes sense?"

Jamie picked at a stray thread on her shirt. "It's nothing. Should we get some sleep? If tomorrow's going to be as crazy as you say, we'll need all the rest we can get."

"Hey." In a move that surprised even herself, Rowan took Jamie's hand in her own. "What makes sense? You can talk to me."

The feel of Jamie's much smaller, much softer hand sent an unexpected shiver up Rowan's spine. It was a feeling she hadn't experienced in many years, and the shock of it made her release Jamie's hand like it had burned her. "Sorry."

"No, it was nice." Jamie smiled and looked away as if she was trying to figure out what to say next. "I—do you know who Phillip Martin is?"

"The senator who used to have the TV show?"

Jamie stared into the fire. "Yeah, that guy."

Rowan tried to recall what she knew of the famous biologist turned politician. She'd seen his show off and on when she was a kid, but since her mom restricted the amount of television she watched, she wouldn't say she knew much about the man other than the fact that he'd become a politician. Suddenly, a memory of seeing several episodes of him with his daughter came to mind. She was a few years younger than Rowan but close enough in age that she'd been jealous of her. Rowan had imagined what it would be like to have a father as warm and attentive as Dr. Martin seemed to be with his daughter. She pulled up the memory of that little girl in her mind and compared the image to the woman sitting next to her. They both had long blond hair, emerald green eyes, and dimples on either side of an infectious smile.

"Well, that explains why they rolled out the red carpet."

"Hey." Jamie seemed offended, and Rowan felt terrible for her callous comment.

"I just mean it makes sense that they would make special accommodations for you. More than they would for some other scientist coming up to study the possible sighting of a bird that is more than likely extinct."

Jamie hung her head in shame. "Yeah, I guess I owe you an apology. I admit I thought it was strange that they initially denied my request only to come back with approval and even more time and resources than I expected. I didn't ask for any preferential treatment. If

I'd known, I wouldn't have accepted. I try to be very careful to keep my father's identity separate from my career, but sometimes that's difficult. He says he'll respect my wishes when I ask him not to pull strings, but I know he has good intentions."

"It would be difficult to feel you don't know if your accomplishments are your own or because of him." The look of anger Jamie shot Rowan made her immediately regret what she'd said. "I just mean—I'm sorry, that came out wrong."

"Everything I've done has been by my own merit. I graduated at the top of my class and worked my ass off my entire life to get where I am. My father had nothing to do with that other than paying for my education and instilling a work ethic within me that—"

"Hey, I'm sorry. You don't have to convince me. I know we've only just met, but it's clear you're an intelligent, capable woman. I came to that conclusion before I knew who your father was, so please don't think I believe you haven't earned everything on your own." One disadvantage to spending so much time alone was sometimes being a little rusty in her social graces. Rowan had always been a solitary person, and her occasional foot-in-mouth mistakes reminded her she needed to do better at thinking before she spoke.

Jamie folded her arms across her chest in a way that seemed more for comfort than anything else. "I'm sorry, too. I admit I'm a little sensitive about the whole thing. After spending my entire life living in my father's gigantic shadow, sometimes my insecurities get the best of me."

"I get it, Jamie. Relationships with parents are difficult, no matter who they are. You just have the extra burden of having a parent in the public eye. You must feel very vulnerable. I'm sorry if I hurt you. I need to learn to keep my stupid mouth shut."

"Apology accepted." Jamie leaned back into her, and Rowan could feel her body relax against her own. It was strange to have this much physical contact with someone after being alone for so long. Especially someone she'd only known for one day. She'd occasionally hug her mom, of course, but she didn't come from a very affectionate family. That Jamie quickly became comfortable enough to touch her and that Rowan so readily accepted it was a surprise.

Rowan wrapped a comforting arm around Jamie's shoulders. "Let's take care of these dishes and get to bed. I'm sorry we're going to be in such close quarters tonight. I can't say the cabin will exactly be comfortable, but I promise it will be better accommodations than this."

"That sounds great. Don't worry about me, though. I spent my life following my dad around the world. I've slept in much worse conditions than this. As long as you aren't asking me to do any more rappelling, I'm good."

Rowan gave Jamie's shoulder one last squeeze before they stood to get ready for bed. The next few months would be much more interesting than Rowan had expected, and she was almost excited to see what came next. Jamie was turning out to be nothing like she had expected, and Rowan was pleased her initial impression was proving to be wrong.

CHAPTER SEVEN

A cloud of dust billowed through the open door of the small cabin as Jamie swept the surfaces clean for the third time. Rowan had warned her the cabin would require cleaning, but she didn't expect just how much there would be. She had agreed to start the task while Rowan made the last few trips to carry their gear from the beach to the cabin. She would have been happy to help with the heavy lifting, but Rowan insisted it would be more helpful to come home to a moderately clean space and feel like she could relax after such an arduous hike.

Not one to want to feel like she wasn't pulling her weight, Jamie had cleaned like she was expecting a foreign dignitary. She found a clothesline strung between trees on the side of the structure where she could air out all of the curtains and linens. Starting at the top, Jamie dusted her way down to the floor, cleaning each surface as much as possible. She had to repeat the process several times. Each time she swept the floor, the surfaces would need another once-over.

With this final go-around complete, she rested her fists on her hips and surveyed her work. Not bad for someone who despised cleaning. She was thankful the cabin wasn't huge. She didn't think it could be over five hundred square feet. Small by living standards, but plenty for the short time they'd be there. The thought of spending that time so close to a handsome and intriguing woman made Jamie smile.

"What are you thinking about?" Rowan asked.

Jamie turned to find her casually leaning against the doorjamb, looking exhausted but strong and sexy as hell. "Nothing, just daydreaming."

These feelings she was having were such a bad idea, but she wasn't sure she could stop them if she tried. Rowan was one of the sexiest women she'd ever met. Especially after things thawed between them. She was the polar opposite of Jamie. Short cropped, almost black hair, olive skin, and soulful brown eyes. She was taller than Jamie by a few inches, and her broad frame resonated strength and confidence. Dangerous was the best word to describe her. Rowan had the kind of body that could make Jamie lose focus, and that was precisely what she didn't want to do.

Shaking her head, Jamie crossed to the stove where she'd started a pot of water heating for tea. "I used the last of the wood in this bin. If you show me where there's more, I can bring it in."

"I'll have to chop more later. There's a stack behind the cabin that should get us through tonight. We won't need as much this time of year as we would in the winter."

Jamie pulled two mugs from the dish rack where she'd left them to dry. She set one in front of Rowan and held a box of tea in front of her to choose. Rowan watched her intently as Jamie dropped the tea bag into her mug and poured in hot water.

"I'm going to wash my hands first. I'm filthy from the hike, but clean hands will have to do until I can catch my breath a little. Hikes seem to get more difficult the older I get." Rowan poured a little water from the bucket onto her hands and soaped them up. "It looks like you found the water pump next to the cabin?"

"I did. I haven't pumped with a hand crank like that since I was a kid visiting a state park for pioneer days. Is it safe to drink without boiling first?"

Rowan rinsed her hands and dried them before sitting back down at the table to enjoy her tea. "Yeah, it should be fine. We test the water in these cabins once a year just as a precaution and leave notes if we think boiling is necessary."

"Good to know." Jamie sat next to Rowan. She closed her eyes as the warm tea coated her throat and warmed her from the inside out. "I needed this." When she opened her eyes, she found Rowan watching her. The unexpected attention raised goose bumps along her skin. "Tell me about yourself, Ranger Fleming. Have you always lived in Alaska? Does your family live here?"

Rowan ran a long finger along the edge of her mug. "I'm from

Alaska, but I haven't always lived here. I moved back a couple of years ago."

"Where did you live?"

"Southern California," Rowan said.

"That's quite a change from Alaska. What brought you back up here? Not a fan of beautiful weather?"

Rowan sipped her tea and distractedly tapped a finger on the surface of the wooden table. "Something like that."

"What about your family? Are they still up here?"

"You ask a lot of questions," Rowan said.

There was an edge to her voice, and Jamie sipped her tea to hide her embarrassment. "Sorry about that. It's a bad habit," she said.

Rowan cleared her throat and shook her head. "It's fine. My mom lives near me. She's in the early stages of dementia, so I don't like to be far from her."

"Oh, no, I hope I'm not keeping you away from her. Do you think they could send someone else out to help me? I hate to keep you from your mother." Jamie felt even worse about the idea of her getting any special treatment now that she thought Rowan might have been forced to leave her mother alone. "My mom passed away a year ago. I'd give anything for the opportunity to go back and spend more time with her."

"I'm sorry to hear that," Rowan said.

An awkwardness had settled between them, and Jamie wasn't sure what else to say. Talking about her mom still hurt, but it also kept her alive in her mind. It was a double-edged sword.

"Are you close to your mom?" Jamie asked.

"Yes, we're close."

When she didn't elaborate on her answer, Jamie took it as a sign she was done talking about her mother. Jamie could respect that. They'd have plenty of time together to get to know each other more. "Why did you move away from Alaska?"

Rowan cleared her throat and took another sip of her tea. "Thanks for the tea and for cleaning the cabin."

Jamie recognized the intentional change in subject, so she accepted the hint and stopped pestering Rowan with questions. She nodded and looked around the space. It wasn't perfect, but it was certainly better than how she'd found it. "I'm not a big fan of cleaning, but I wanted to make it a nice place for you to relax after all your hard work carrying the bags. Thanks for that, by the way. I'm pretty sure I'd never be able to walk again if I'd had to lift one more bag today."

"Aren't you glad I was mean and made you leave stuff at the airport?"

Jamie rolled her eyes and laughed. "Yeah, yeah, you were right. I knew there'd be an 'I told you so' at some point."

Rowan set down her empty mug and stood. "That hit the spot. Thanks for the tea." She reached her long arms above her head and leaned one way and then the other, stretching her muscles after an already exhausting day. "I'm going to set traps so we'll hopefully have something fresh to eat tomorrow. If you don't mind, we can do soup for dinner tonight. I noticed there were cans in the pantry. I can make something for us."

"Let me do that." Jamie picked up the cups from the table and took them to the sink to wash. "It's the least I can do after all the work you've been doing already. I like to feel helpful, and this seems like the easiest way for me to do that right now."

Jamie turned away from the sink and was startled to find Rowan standing next to her. "Oh, sorry, I—" Before she could finish her apology, Rowan gently touched her face. Jamie held her breath, unsure what she was doing or how she should react. For a moment, she thought Rowan might lean down and kiss her, but instead, she gently swiped her finger across Jamie's cheek. When she pulled her hand away, Jamie could see a tiny feather balanced on the tip of her thumb. "It looks like you picked up a hitchhiker when you were airing out the bedding."

"Thanks." Jamie's voice came out in a croak, and she cleared it before trying again. "Thank you."

"Please don't feel you aren't pulling your weight. The cabin looks amazing. If you can scrounge together a warm meal for this evening, you'll be my hero. While we're here, my job is to keep you fed, warm, and assist you with your work. Your job is to do all the bird stuff. We'll go out to the area where the hiker said he saw your bird tomorrow morning. We can do a little foraging along the way, and with any luck, our next dinner will be something more exciting than soup."

Rowan pulled a jacket from a coat rack near the door and slipped it on. "I'll bring a little more firewood in for the stove and then go set the traps. I'll be gone for about an hour. Will you be okay here on your own?"

Rowan's question interrupted the lustful haze Jamie hadn't realized she was under. "Yeah, I'll be fine."

"It shouldn't get dark before I'm back." Rowan pulled a lantern from a cabinet and rummaged through a drawer for a new wick. "But just in case, you can use this. There's probably an electric one here somewhere, but I hate to carry batteries in, so I prefer to use these when I can. Do you know how to light it?"

"I do, sure, yeah."

"Great." Rowan replaced the old wick with a new one and ensured enough fuel was in the bowl. "Okay, I think you'll be good for now. I'll bring the rest of the wood in and then be on my way."

"How do I contact you if something comes up?" Jamie couldn't think of why she'd need to reach her, but it never hurt to ask, just in case.

"Yes." Rowan patted the pockets of her jacket and looked around the room. Not finding what she needed, she pulled the kitchen drawers open and searched through them until she found a whistle at the end of a lanyard. "I won't be that far away. If something comes up," Rowan walked over to Jamie and placed it around her neck, "blow as hard as you can, and I'll come running." She smoothed the rope until it lay flat against Jamie's shoulders.

The close quarters of the cabin seemed even smaller than they had before. Jamie realized she might have a crush on the tall, dark ranger. That was what she shouldn't be thinking about right now, but she was unwilling to convince herself to stop. Maybe a bit of a crush wouldn't hurt. As long as she didn't let it impede her work, she deserved to let herself enjoy the company of another woman. Of course, she wasn't wholly sure Rowan would even be interested, but she sure seemed like she felt the same way.

She knew the key would be fighting her urge to overthink things. They were consenting adults. She was pretty sure they were both lesbian, consenting adults. A few months alone in the woods with a gorgeous hunk of a butch lesbian seemed like the makings of a lesbian romance novel she would reread again and again. The trick would be remembering what this was—a casual crush and nothing more.

If things between them escalated, she had to remind herself that it was only ever going to be several months in the woods. That's all. This was where the sappy lesbian romance novel and real life parted ways.

Flirting. Flirting and maybe a little more were going to be the extent of it. She could do that. Jamie wasn't an overly romantic person. She was a professional, a fucking scientist, and she could separate feelings from desires. Who said she'd even ever had feelings? Shit. She was overthinking this.

CHAPTER EIGHT

Shafts of light peeked through wooden shutters as the early morning sun struggled to illuminate the cabin. Rowan missed that sweet spot in the year when the days were regular, like in most of the states in the Lower Forty-eight. Seasons in Alaska meant very little darkness in the summer and very little light in the winter. That was what she missed about California the most. Well, that and the weather. She seldom had to wear a long-sleeved shirt in Southern California, but in Alaska, she needed to keep one available at all times. You'd think, having grown up here, she'd be used to it, but her time in a warmer climate had made her soft.

Jamie mumbled in her sleep a few feet away from where Rowan was curled up in her sleeping bag. The sleepy dream babbling made Rowan smile. After much discussion, Rowan had finally convinced Jamie to take the bed and let her sleep on a pad on the floor. She'd had much worse accommodations, and she suspected Jamie would need a good night's sleep to prepare herself for the day ahead. Besides, Rowan was far too chivalrous to take the only stable bed in the cabin. She'd try to repair the broken bed while she was here or make a note of it so someone else could bring the materials to do it once they were gone. The last thing they needed was someone falling out of a broken bed and seriously hurting themselves. Medical evacuations in an area as remote as this were a nightmare.

Rowan rubbed the sleep from her eyes and stretched her arms over her head to work out the kinks in her back. She was getting too old to sleep on the floor.

"Hey," a soft voice said. Rowan turned to see Jamie's face poking out from below the thick blankets.

"Hey, how did you sleep?" Rowan asked.

"I'm not sure yet. My brain is still booting up."

Rowan yawned and stretched. "I'll make coffee."

"Yes." The resounding agreement was muffled by blankets. "Coffee makes brain work."

Not able to postpone the inevitable any longer, Rowan climbed from her sleeping bag and slid into a coat she'd left draped over a kitchen chair. "I'll get a fire going so it will warm the cabin up before you venture out of your cocoon. Then I'll work on coffee and," she opened the pantry and checked through its contents, "pancakes?"

"My God, how are you not married?"

Rowan stacked wood and kindling in the fireplace and lit it with a match. She sat back on her heels and watched as the flames caught the logs on fire. "I guess you'd have to ask my ex-wife that question."

"Ex-wife?"

"Yep." Rowan stood and gathered the things she needed to start a pot of coffee. She could tell Jamie was waiting for her to elaborate, but she really wasn't in the mood to go into it, so she changed the subject. "I have powdered creamer and sugar. How do you like your coffee?" She waited to see if Jamie would be redirected.

"Creamer, no sugar, please. Do you need help?"

"Nope, you stay snuggled in the blankets for now." Rowan started the pot of coffee and pulled out the ingredients for pancakes. "Sorry, we won't have sausage or bacon...or eggs."

"No worries. I'm pretty low maintenance."

Rowan went through the morning routines and realized how much she missed having someone to share it with now that she lived alone. It had always been her favorite part of the day. It seemed full of possibilities. Now that she spent so much of her time alone, mornings were just another part of her schedule.

Jamie pulled the blankets back and sat up to accept the cup of coffee from Rowan. "Thank you." She blew over the top of her mug and sipped the hot liquid a little at a time. "This is perfect. You're my hero." Rowan didn't want to admit to herself how much Jamie's approval pleased her, but she couldn't deny the happiness it stirred in her.

"So, the sighting location is a couple of hours' hike. Are you up for it?"

"A couple of hours? This is starting to be a theme for you. Everything is a couple hours' hike away."

Rowan held her hand above the pan to see if it was hot enough. "Unfortunately, you'll find that everything up here is going to be difficult. Difficult to reach, difficult to find food, difficult weather…"

"You should work for the tourism department. Alaska, everything is difficult."

Rowan smiled. "Just being honest with you. The next few months are going to be—"

"Difficult?" Jamie filled in.

"Exactly," Rowan said, pointing a spatula at her for effect. "The good news is, you'll see some of the most amazing wildlife and views you've ever imagined, and the best part is you only have to deal with me. It's very doubtful we'll see anyone else until we head back."

"Is that what you like about being up here, the solitude?"

Rowan looked at Jamie, wondering what she would think if she was candid with her and hoping she wouldn't ask more questions than Rowan wanted to answer. "Yes, that's what I like."

Jamie seemed to consider what Rowan said, then nodded. "So if it's a couple of hours' hike, I assume we won't be taking all of my equipment with us?"

"No, you'll need to figure out what you need in the field, and the rest will stay here in the cabin."

Jamie's small hands wrapped around the warm mug as she stared at the liquid inside.

"Something wrong with your coffee?"

Jamie sighed. "No, I'm just thinking about what equipment I'd need to take and what should stay here. I don't imagine I'll be able to store anything at the site, will I?"

"Not really. You're welcome to leave things there, but understand that it will probably be rained on, frozen, and possibly destroyed and carted off by some wild creature. They have no respect for private property."

"Will my cameras be okay? I'll mount them on top of the stakes I brought."

"They should be fine. Some might get messed with, but we'll just have to see how things go."

Rowan poured the batter onto the hot surface and watched as bubbles surfaced when the pancake was ready. They had a big day ahead of them, and she wanted to make sure they both had enough food to give them the energy they'd need for the hike.

"Well, I'm desperate to get started. After we eat, I'll pack what we need to take with us, but the heaviest stuff can stay here. Is there an area where I can set up a workspace? A table or something?"

Rowan waved Jamie over to the kitchen table as she set a plate of pancakes down for her and one for herself. "I saw a couple of sawhorses in the back. I can set them up and place a sheet of plywood over the top for a work surface. It won't be fancy, but it should give you plenty of space to work."

"That would be perfect, thank you. I'll try not to take up too much room."

"No problem." Rowan didn't understand how she had so quickly gone from being entirely annoyed by being forced to accompany Jamie to being so willing to cater to her every need. She supposed it had something to do with the fact that Jamie wasn't at all who she'd expected her to be.

Most of the researchers Rowan had dealt with in her time with the National Park Service had been polite but so focused on their own needs that they would completely disregard any rules and regulations set in place to protect them and the surrounding environment. She'd had to rescue many a careless person who was too worried about what their equipment read or what the thing they were studying was doing and not watching where they were stepping. Rowan's stomach churned at the thought of something like that happening to Jamie.

"Try to stay close to me when we're out there in the field, okay?"

Jamie popped another bite of her pancakes into her mouth and gave Rowan a questioning look. "Why?"

Uncertainty made Rowan pause before answering. She didn't want Jamie to think she didn't trust her, but she also wanted nothing to happen to her. "It's just safer. We should try to stay within a few feet of each other at all times. Situations can go from bad to worse in a short amount of time out here."

"True…okay. You realize I'm not completely new to the outdoors, right?" The irritation in Jamie's voice was evident.

"I do. I don't mean to sound like I don't think you're capable." There was a weighted silence between them for several minutes. Rowan regretted what she'd said, but it was too late to change it now, so she pressed on as if it hadn't happened. "Can I get you any more?"

Jamie sat back in her chair and rubbed her stomach. "No, thanks. I don't think I can even finish what I have." Rowan pulled Jamie's plate over and finished the rest in two bites. "How can you eat that much and look like that?"

Rowan winked at her and gathered their plates. "I'm good at working it off." The blush that reddened Jamie's cheeks made her laugh. "Come on, dirty bird, let's get this stuff packed up and hit the trail. I'll check my traps on the way, and with any luck, we'll have something for dinner tonight."

Once the dishes were cleaned and put away and the equipment was packed and ready, they set off toward the area where the sighting happened. "I'm going to cut off the trail up ahead for a few minutes, but I'll catch up to you. I just want to check my snare."

"Will I be okay without you?" Jamie fluttered her eyes and gave Rowan a damsel in distress look.

"Yeah, yeah, smartass. Don't leave the trail, and I'll be back before you know it. It's only a few feet into the brush. I won't be out of earshot. If you need me, yell, and I'll be right there."

Jamie nodded. "Roger, Captain."

Rowan slipped off the trail and into the brush. When she reached her first snare, she found the trap sprung with nothing caught in it. She reset the trap and hiked the few feet back to the trail where Jamie was waiting for her. "No luck. Let's keep going. I set four of them last night. If we didn't catch anything, I'll head down to the river and see if I can catch a fish for our dinner."

They hiked steadily, and Rowan was happy to see that Jamie was keeping up. They had a lot of distance to cover, and the idea that she'd be able to handle what was ahead helped Rowan relax a little. The last thing Rowan wanted to do was figure out a way to get Jamie and her equipment where they needed to go if Jamie wasn't strong enough to do her part. Rowan had to admit that she'd noticed Jamie seemed plenty strong enough. Not that she was checking her out. Well, maybe she was checking her out a little, but that was to be expected. Right? She was undoubtedly a gorgeous woman. She'd only seen her covered in many layers of clothes, but Rowan thought she had an athletic build. Strong, but still very feminine.

"Rowan?"

"Hmm? Sorry, did you ask me something?"

"I was just wondering how much farther?"

Rowan looked up and scanned their surrounding for the first time in a few minutes. She'd made a rookie mistake of letting her mind drift and not being completely aware of what was going on around her. That was a dangerous thing for both of them. She had to get her mind off Jamie and back on her job. "Let's stop here for a sec." Rowan reached into her pocket and handed Jamie a granola bar. "Do you have your water?"

"I do," Jamie said, holding up her canteen.

"Good. You take a break for a minute, and I'm going to check the second snare. I'll be right back." Rowan stepped off the trail and disappeared into the brush. This time would be farther than before since Rowan had been daydreaming and missed the second snare altogether, but it still wasn't far from where Jamie would be.

A few minutes later, she was back on the trail. "No luck?" Jamie asked.

"No, the third one isn't far. It's the best spot, so let's hope that one fares better."

Jamie handed Rowan the canteen and half of the granola bar she had saved for her. "Thanks," Rowan said, eating the bar in two large bites.

"As I said before, I'm easy as far as meals go. I'm happy to have pancakes again if we need to."

"Not the healthiest of meals." Rowan handed Jamie her canteen back. "I think I can at least forage for something that will make a yummy dinner if this last trap is empty."

"You're pretty amazing," Jamie said. "You're like some mountain man, or woman, as the case may be, who can live off the land. I can't imagine having the confidence to do something like that."

The compliment sent a rush of heat to Rowan's face. "Thanks. I grew up out here, like my mother and generations before her."

"Are you Inuit?"

Rowan didn't enjoy talking about herself but avoiding answering Jamie's friendly questions was becoming difficult the more time they spent together. It was easier to answer questions about her lineage than some of the more challenging aspects of her life, so she played along. "Half. On my mom's side. My dad was from North Carolina. His family is Scottish."

"Of course, Fleming. That makes sense."

The last trap was close enough to the trail that Rowan just stepped a few feet away to check it. "Bingo." She found a small brown hare trapped in the snare. Rowan pulled a bag from her pack and dropped it in. "Got one."

She joined Jamie back on the trail, and they walked in silence until they reached a shallow river. Large boulders were scattered across it, providing a dry path to the other side. Their approach depended on the level of the river, but the drier weather they were experiencing would hopefully afford them a route for most of the time they'd be there.

"What now?" Jamie asked, shifting the weight of the backpack on her shoulders.

"Now I need to field dress this rabbit." She reached into her pack and pulled out an empty plastic container, then removed the knife from its sheath on her hip to check the sharpness of the blade. "Okay, you're going to be my lookout. Keep watch, especially downwind from here since the smell will travel that way."

"Why the plastic container?" Jamie asked.

"It's a BearVault. I'll prepare the rabbit, then stick it inside. We'll need to clean the outside of the container thoroughly. Then we'll bury it in a crevice of a boulder, under the water, surrounded by rocks, and hope a bear doesn't get to it before we come back through on our way to the cabin. They're sneaky suckers, but we're going to do everything we can to stack the odds in our favor." Rowan noticed Jamie looked away when she cut into the rabbit's fur. She didn't blame her. Dressing an animal was a necessary but disgusting part of living off the land. "You doing okay?"

"Yep," Jamie said, scanning the area but not looking down at what Rowan was doing.

"I'm almost done here, and then we'll be on our way."

"Are we going to need to do this every day?" Jamie asked.

Rowan rinsed her hands and the rabbit pieces she prepared in the water before placing them in the container. "Nope, we won't always get rabbits. Sometimes we'll catch fish. Sometimes we'll only be able to forage for plants. If all else fails, we'll eat the canned goods available in the cabin. They're the last resort since we only have a limited stock, but they're there if we need them."

"Who replenishes that stuff when we're gone?"

"I'll probably bring a load of supplies back when we're done." The thought of being back at the cabin without Jamie made Rowan sadder than she expected. She shook her head and smiled at the ridiculousness of that thought. The sooner Jamie was out of her hair, the sooner Rowan could get back to her own cabin and her own life. "Let's get this thing secured and then keep going."

CHAPTER NINE

Jamie's stomach grumbled, and her feet hurt. They couldn't have been hiking for more than a couple of hours, so she was far too embarrassed to mention anything to Rowan, who seemed as fresh and energetic as she had when they'd started that morning. She knew she'd need to stop soon for a break, but the promise of finally reaching her goal was too tempting to put off. The hikes and travel from the previous days had left her sore and desperate for a long soak in a hot tub.

Such pleasantries would have to wait. Jamie was finally going to start her much-anticipated work, and nothing else mattered. Not even her grumbling tummy.

"You about ready to stop for a break?" Rowan asked as they crested a hill and found a small gap in the thick brush. "I'm pretty hungry."

"I mean, if you need to stop, I'm okay with it. How much farther until we're there? If we're close, maybe it's better to push on?" Her question was partially to get an idea of how much more they'd need to go and also an attempt to convince her stomach it could wait until they were there before she accommodated its need.

"When we get there, will you want to sit down and take a break, or will you be like a kid at Disneyland, too excited to do anything other than look for what you've come all this way to find?" Rowan asked.

She had a point. A very irritating but accurate point. "Dammit."

"That's what I thought," Rowan said as she dropped her pack to the ground and helped Jamie with hers. "We'll only stop for a few minutes, and then we'll get started again. It's a deceptively strenuous hike, and our pit stop at the river pushed us even further behind. Our future trips out here won't take as long because we won't be carrying all this heavy equipment, either. This one is the worst of it."

Jamie sat on a boulder and began untying her shoes. Her aching feet would appreciate a few minutes being released from their prison for a little free time in the yard.

"How are your feet?" Rowan asked.

"Um, they're okay. No blisters that I can see. They could use a good soak, though."

Rowan pulled two small packs of tuna, crackers, and two forks from her backpack and handed one of each to Jamie. "Don't get too used to this luxury because it won't be every day, but I think we deserve a special lunch to celebrate our first time at the site. What do you think?"

Tuna had never looked as delicious as it did right then. Jamie usually enjoyed it on toast with a blanket of melted sharp cheddar. Still, sitting down on soft grass after an exhausting couple of days of hard work, she couldn't think of anything that seemed tastier than the packet in her hand. "I would kiss you for this, but my breath is about to smell like tuna."

Rowan's fork stopped midway between the pouch and her mouth, and she smiled. "Isn't it the same rules as garlic and onion? If we're both eating tuna, they'll cancel each other out?"

"Good point," Jamie said with a chuckle. "I'm not sure I could stop eating long enough to do something as frivolous as giving you a kiss, anyway."

"No one has ever thought kissing me was frivolous. So that you know."

Jamie tried to ignore the electricity that tickled her skin at their innocent flirting. Rowan was proving to be much more charming than she'd initially pegged her as. A change in subject was definitely in order before they got too far down this road.

"I know you said you see your mom, but tell me more about the rest of your family. Do you see your dad often?" Jamie regretted the question as she watched the playful smile fade from Rowan's face. "You don't have to answer that. I'm sorry I'm so nosy."

Rowan reached out a hand to take Jamie's trash from her and place it in a smell-proof bag before adding her own. "You aren't nosy. I would just rather not talk about my dad."

"I'm sorry I brought him up." Jamie reached out and squeezed Rowan's hand where it rested on her pack. "People ask about my family so much I forget that not everyone's life is as much of an open book as mine."

"How does that make you feel?" Rowan asked.

"What? People wanting to know things about my family or the fact that my life sometimes feels like public property and not my own?" Having a parent in the public eye had always been difficult, but as she'd grown older and as her father had become more prominent in politics, it had become harder for her to separate her private life from her public life. The line between the two seemed to fade. She hated it.

"I guess that answers that question," Rowan said. "I'm sorry."

"It's fine. I have a good relationship with my dad, despite everything."

Rowan nodded, stretched out her legs, and leaned back against her pack to rest. Her body was so long and lean that Jamie found it difficult not to stare at her.

"What about your mom? Were you close when she was alive?"

Jamie scooted toward her and leaned back, resting her head on Rowan's outstretched arm. "Um, no, I guess not. She wasn't a bad mom or anything. My parents were both very career-driven when I was growing up. They were the stereotypical scientist types, focused on their research, and a kid didn't exactly factor into that equation."

"You and your dad seemed close in the episodes of his show that I've seen you in."

"We weren't close. When I traveled with my dad, and we were on location together, he was everything you'd ever want him to be. He was exciting, engaged, fun. He was my hero. Then school would start, and I'd be left home with my mom or the nanny, and I wouldn't see him for long periods. Then he ran for office, and our time together was almost nonexistent."

"Did your parents have a good marriage?" Rowan asked.

Jamie shrugged. "I don't know. I guess it was okay. They loved each other. As far as I know, they were faithful to each other. I think my mom resented him for going into politics. She hated he wasn't ever around but refused to follow him to DC."

"Really?"

"Really. My dad put his career before his family, and she never really forgave him for that. When he was home, and they were together, I could tell that they loved each other deeply, though."

"Wow." Rowan rubbed Jamie's arm to comfort her. "I'm sorry."

"Me, too. Let's get back to neutral ground. Dads are off the discussion topics list for now. Sound good?"

"Sounds perfect," Rowan said as she stood and lifted her pack over her shoulders.

Jamie quickly put her socks and shoes back on and accepted a helping hand to her feet. "Okay, how much farther?" she asked as she settled her pack on her shoulders again.

"Fifteen minutes, maybe a little more?"

"Seriously? I can't believe we were that close, and we stopped."

"I'm glad we did. Now our bellies are full, and you can focus on your work. No more distractions." Rowan carefully guided Jamie down the other side of the hill, and they started the last few minutes of their hike.

"I've seen renderings of the northern curlew, but tell me something that might help me identify one. I might as well try to be of some use while we're out here."

Jamie pulled a small cotton cloth from around her neck and wiped the sweat from her brow. "Well, I'm sure if you've seen the drawings of them, you know they're a small, mottled brown shorebird with a thin, slightly curved bill. Their belly is buff, streaked with mottled brown and pale cinnamon wing linings. They're often confused with the juvenile whimbrel, which makes it even more difficult to identify them."

"I remember reading about that. Do you think the hiker saw a whimbrel, or could he have actually seen a northern curlew?"

Even the possibility that he had seen a whimbrel and not a northern curlew made Jamie's stomach churn. The odds were much more in favor of that being the case, but the hope that it wasn't kept her pushing forward.

"I like to believe he knew the difference, but we won't know unless we can confirm it was the curlew, and to do that, we have to find it. If it is the curlew, it won't stay around for all that long. They aren't known to nest in Alaska, but it's highly suspected they did. There were only ever confirmed nests in Canada, but Alaska and even Russia were potential nesting areas. A nest will be a clutch of about four eggs in a depression on the ground, lined with leaves and grass. It's early July, so if there is a nest, I expect the eggs will hatch in the next couple of weeks. They're precocial, so they're able to walk and feed themselves from day one and leave the nest with the parents within the first couple of days."

"That's cool. I'm sure the guy knew what he was talking about. He seemed pretty confident. Let's prove it and celebrate with a beer back in Ugruk unless you have other plans."

"Nope, no plans. A beer together sounds nice. If you aren't already so sick of me by then that you can't wait to put me on that plane and send me home." Jamie hadn't spent this much time with another person since she was a child, and she had to admit that she worried she'd drive Rowan crazy by the time this was all done.

"I'm sure I'll be able to stand you long enough to buy you a beer." Rowan winked at her, and she couldn't help but smile.

"Then it's a date."

Rowan slowed to allow Jamie to catch up as they reached the end of the heavy brush and stepped onto the tundra. This time of year, there wasn't snow this far south, but the icy wind had a bite to it. "Here we are." Rowan checked the coordinates on her GPS and pointed toward a small group of rocks surrounded by a vast sea of grassland. "Near those rocks is where he said he was, and the bird was two yards northwest of his location."

"This is perfect." Jamie's cheeks hurt from grinning. "This could actually be happening."

"This is happening, my friend. Now it's time for you to do your magic and prove this thing exists. Are you ready?"

Jamie let her pack drop to the ground and made a complete turn, taking in the entire scene before her. There was such a rugged beauty to this place. It was like nothing she'd ever seen before, but so familiar after the countless nature shows and books she'd read. It felt like they were on the edge of the world, and it seemed appropriate that this was where they hoped to find the curlew.

"I'm ready," Jamie said. "Let's make this happen."

CHAPTER TEN

Rowan watched as Jamie pulled her camera from where it rested at the end of a strap around her shoulder. She took several photos of the area, then walked toward the rocks Rowan had pointed out.

"So, he said he saw it that morning around zero seven thirty, correct?" Jamie asked.

"Yes, that's correct." Rowan took Jamie's pack from her so she could move more freely.

"Thanks."

The sun never wholly set for very long this time of year, but the light had dimmed enough that it gave Jamie's hair a golden glow. It struck Rowan just how beautiful she was. She'd noticed before, she wasn't blind, but something about seeing Jamie come alive like this in a way she hadn't before made Rowan's skin tingle. Literally tingle. This was a completely new experience, and her mind raced to understand it. Why this woman? She watched as Jamie knelt on the rocks, took several more photos in the direction the hiker had said he saw the bird, checked the screen on her camera, and then took several more. Rowan set their bags down and studied Jamie as she flitted from place to place, documenting every aspect of the area.

"How would you say the light was? Do you know?" Jamie asked.

"Dimmer than it is now since it was so early in the morning, but plenty light enough to see." Rowan lifted her bottle to her lips and took a drink of water to clear her head and push the lump from her throat. "Is there anything I can do to help?"

Jamie stopped for the first time since they'd walked out of the brush and onto the tundra. She looked at Rowan, checked her watch, and sighed. "How much longer do you think we have before we have to hike back to the cabin?"

Rowan looked up at the sky. "Oh, I'd say we have four or five hours, and then we'll want to head that way. Will you need to come back out tomorrow?"

"I guess that depends on how much we're able to get done today. Are you ready for me to put you to work, Ranger Fleming?" Jamie's smile seemed genuine, and Rowan found it impossible not to smile back.

"I'm at your service, milady." Rowan performed her best imitation of a fancy bow.

Jamie knelt next to Rowan and searched through her bag until she found a measuring tape. "Would you mind recording the coordinates of the rocks where he was and the approximate area where he said he saw the bird, then give me a distance between the two?"

"Sure." Rowan took the measuring tape and pulled her GPS unit from her belt. "Just these two locations?"

"Just those for now. Be mindful of where you're stepping. If by some miracle there is a breeding pair, I might have to murder you if you step on the clutch."

"Roger that." Rowan thought she would forage for something to eat with their rabbit dinner while she already had her eyes trained on the ground. She filled a small bag she kept hanging from her belt with arctic blueberries and qunguliit mushrooms. Rowan was no chef, but those additions would make an enjoyable meal for them. She knew it would be a welcome comfort after a long day in the cold. Somehow, the idea of taking care of Jamie had gone from a chore to something that brought her joy. She liked the idea of making Jamie happy.

Caring for someone else had always been in Rowan's nature, but by the end of her marriage, any effort she made toward her ex-wife was met with hostility. She knew deep down there was much more to the story than that she just didn't want Rowan's attention, but at a certain point, it was difficult not to take every rebuke personally.

Memories of her failed marriage snuffed any flame that had been burning for Jamie. Rowan had thought her heart would never mend when she left her life in California and searched for solitude in Alaska. No matter how tempting any feelings she had for Jamie were, it could never last more than a couple of months. Rowan knew that would never be enough for her. She wasn't built for that kind of thing. She'd had a night here or there with a woman, but she understood herself enough to recognize that wasn't what she'd want from Jamie. It was easier to stop herself before she ever started down that road.

"Hey, Rowan," Jamie called from where she was taking notes on the pile of rocks.

"Yeah."

"Do you think you could help me by standing in the spot he thought he saw the bird, and I'm going to take a few photos from where he was?"

"Sure." Rowan picked a few more mushrooms to fill her pouch and walked to Jamie's indicated area. "Here?"

"I think that should be about right. Watch your—"

"I know. Watch my step. I'm being conscientious, Dr. Martin, don't worry." The grass wasn't dense, but it would be easy to miss a small clutch of eggs if she wasn't paying attention. The thought of accidentally stepping on any potential eggs was enough to send chills down Rowan's back. Ugh. Not only the impact to the bird as a species, but the devastation she knew it would cause Jamie was a thought she wanted to scrub from her mind.

Jamie snapped several photos, opened the packs they'd brought, and started laying out the cameras. Each high-resolution trail camera was about the size of a paperback novel and came equipped with its own solar power pack. They were weatherproof and camouflaged to blend into the surroundings. Leaving them unattended would be a risk, but one they would have to take if they hoped to capture the curlew. There was no way they'd be able to watch the site day and night, and these would provide eyes and ears around the clock. The digital recordings of the videos would be stored on small memory cards that they'd need to swap out every two or three days.

"Would you mind helping me get these set up?"

"Sure. Just attach the cameras to the poles and stick them in the ground?" Rowan picked up the first camera Jamie had set down and noticed a notch in the top of the case that would allow the three-foot pole to rest securely.

"Yep. Ideally, you'd bury the pole a foot in the ground, but I'm not sure how deep you'll be able to get it in this rocky tundra."

Rowan used the pole to tap around the area, searching for a softer spot to drive it in. "I think I'll be able to get it deep enough to make you happy." She chuckled when Jamie coughed at her unintended double entendre. "You are such a dirty bird."

"Me? Have you listened to yourself? You have to know what you're saying."

The ground gave way as Rowan repeatedly jammed the pole into the hole she'd started with the small shovel she kept attached to the outside of her pack. "I'll admit that sometimes I do, but I don't always think about what I'm saying before it's already come out of my mouth."

"Yeah, I noticed that, too." Jamie finished placing the cameras where they needed to go and doubled back to set up the ones Rowan had mounted to the poles. "I take it you don't get a lot of practice talking to other people?"

"Is that a dig at me?" Rowan asked. The question cut more profoundly than she wanted to admit.

"Not at all, just an observation. I'm sorry if I offended you."

The comment hadn't offended her, but Rowan was embarrassed to admit how little human interaction she had, especially after moving back up to Alaska. "You didn't offend me." Rowan attached the camera to the fifth pole she'd buried and moved on to the next. "It's not something I'm exactly proud of."

"Does it bother you—that you spend little time with other people?"

Rowan shook her head. "No. It doesn't bother me." Sweat dripped down her cheek as she stopped to remove her outer layer of clothing and catch her breath. "I haven't met many people I cared to spend time with, other than my mom, of course."

"Tell me more about your mom? Is she quiet like you?"

"No, she has no problem letting everyone know what she thinks." Rowan thought about her mom and how much she'd changed over the years. "The only time I ever remember her being anything other than in complete control was with my dad."

"What do you mean?"

Pouring her heart out to an almost complete stranger about her family was the last thing Rowan wanted to do. She hadn't even shared everything with her ex-wife, so there was no way she was going to start now, no matter how much she realized she wanted to. "What's the motion detection range of these?"

Jamie stopped and watched Rowan for only a moment before

seemingly accepting the change in subject and continuing her task of configuring the cameras. "They should pick up movement within 65 feet and have 120 degrees sensing angle."

"Night vision, I assume?"

"Night vision and the solar panels keep the batteries charged for up to six months, even without direct sunlight." Jamie configured the last field cameras and looked around to ensure they were all set up as she wanted them. "They have 256 gigabyte memory cards that I'll need to swap out every two or three days. I'll need to go through the footage in the camera between our trips out here. At some point, can we mount the folded solar panels I have back at the cabin to the roof to charge the batteries I have for my laptop and the rest of my equipment?"

"Absolutely. I can't believe they have gotten those solar panels down to such a small package. I was worried about how heavy they would be when I saw them in your cases at the airport, but they weren't that bad. They weren't great, but it was manageable."

"Good. I was worried you might have been irritated about having to hike all that stuff in from the river."

"Oh, I was irritated, but I got over it," Rowan said.

Jamie stuck out her tongue and knelt next to her pack. "So, I'm going to collect some samples, and then we should be ready to head back. Does that sound okay to you?"

"Sounds good. I'm going to see if I can forage up some more stuff for our dinner while you do that."

"Perfect."

An hour later, Jamie sat on the ground and spread out a small towel in front of her. She pulled out various vials of soil samples from a small bag she had attached to her belt and a notepad she had been writing in while collecting them. Rowan watched as Jamie labeled each vial with the coordinates of where the sample was taken, then meticulously logged the information in a book. Jamie's perfect lips silently mouthed each sample ID as she made her way through them, documenting everything for future evaluation. She was adorable. Something about the way she tackled this task with such care and attention to detail made Rowan's heart warm to her even more, stirring feelings she was so desperate to avoid.

Rowan cleared her throat and checked the time on her watch. "You about ready to head back toward the cabin?"

Jamie looked up from her notebook, then checked the time on her watch. She sighed, then counted each vial, verifying all had been logged correctly. "Yeah, I guess it's about that time."

"Will we need to come back out tomorrow morning, or do you have enough to keep you busy for a few days?"

"Um, I think this will do for a couple of days. Now that I have these samples, we'll mostly watch the video I collect on the SD cards. I don't want to be here every day because I don't want to scare them off if they are here. We'll just have to see how it goes." Jamie carefully gathered her supplies and safely tucked them into her pack. When everything was secure, she reached up to take Rowan's offered hand to help her to her feet.

Rowan could tell her muscles were stiff from days of physical activity and spending so much time hunched over gathering samples. If she weren't already fighting the urge to touch her, she would offer Jamie a massage when they returned to the cabin. She knew that wasn't a good idea. Two lesbians giving each other a massage only ended one way, and that was something Rowan was trying to avoid.

"I have some ibuprofen at the cabin that will help with your sore muscles. I also saw there was some rice in the cabinet. I can put some in a sock and heat it as a makeshift heating pad. I've heard there's a hot spring around here, too. I'll see if I can find out where it is, and maybe we can check it out when there's time." Jesus, Rowan thought, hot springs are also not something you should be offering.

"That would be great." Jamie arched her back to stretch out her muscles. "I feel much older than I should. I thought I was in better shape than this. Hopefully, it will get better as the weeks progress, or you might need to carry me on your back."

Rowan lifted Jamie's bag and slung it over her shoulder. "I'll carry the load for a bit."

"You don't have to—"

"I insist. Carrying your pack is lighter than giving you a piggyback ride." Rowan laughed as Jamie playfully smacked her shoulder. She felt a lightness that she'd almost forgotten could be possible. "Let's get you home."

CHAPTER ELEVEN

Jamie struggled to keep her eyes open as she watched one of the videos they'd collected the day before. After three weeks of hiking out to the site, followed by watching the three days of video they'd collected, then hiking back out to the site to collect more, she was bored out of her mind. They'd caught some exciting footage of ptarmigans, snow geese, bar-tailed godwits, arctic loons, and the adorable golden plover, but there hadn't been one sign of the curlew. The copious notes she'd taken while observing the behaviors of the birds she saw saved their efforts from being a complete waste of time, but she'd hoped they'd have found something by now.

She wouldn't allow herself to get discouraged yet. They'd only been there for a short amount of time, and Jamie knew she needed to keep a positive attitude. She had to admit that the monotony of their days was wearing on her, though. Stiff muscles protested as Jamie stretched her arms above her head and leaned to one side and then the other. In desperate need of a break, she paused her video and logged her progress in the notebook she kept with her at all times.

"Rowan?" she called when she realized she was alone in the cabin. With her headphones on and eyes glued to the screen on her laptop, she rarely knew where Rowan was until she stopped working. When she didn't get a response, she slipped on her sweatshirt and went outside to search for her.

"Rowan?"

"Here," Rowan answered.

Jamie found her sitting on a log outside the shed behind the cabin with a spool of wire. "What are you doing?" she asked as she turned another log upright to sit next to her.

"Making new snares." Rowan pulled more wire off the spool and cut it with her wire cutters. "They get a little wonky after a while and need to be replaced with new ones. How's the research going? Did you find anything interesting today?"

Watching Rowan's nimble fingers turn a strand of wire into a perfect snare was mesmerizing. Jamie imagined what else those fingers would be talented at doing before shaking her head to force herself to focus on their conversation. She rubbed her face with her hands and cleared her throat before answering Rowan's question. "Good. I've seen more footage of the same birds since we set the cameras up. I think there might be some good stuff there that's worth studying more closely, but no sign of the curlew yet."

"I'm sorry," Rowan said.

Jamie shrugged and picked up one of the completed snares she'd already created. "Did your dad teach you to do this stuff?" They hadn't talked much about Rowan's family since the topic got uncomfortable on their first hike out to the site. She hoped bringing him up now wouldn't upset Rowan.

"Nope. I learned most of this stuff from Auntie Yura."

"Is she your mom's sister?"

"Yeah. My dad was an only child, and his parents immigrated to the States from Scotland, so once they passed away, he didn't have any family left here."

"That's sad," Jamie said. "Is your mom's family close?" Rowan handed Jamie a rose she'd created with the wire. "Aw, it's beautiful, Rowan. Thank you."

Rowan nodded and went back to making snares. "My mom's family is very close. We've lived in the same community for generations, so I'm related to most of the people in the village where I grew up."

"I wish I'd grown up with lots of cousins and family around. I had a lonely childhood. It would have been fun to have a big family around."

Jamie left the subject alone when Rowan offered nothing more about her family. "Did you always want to be a park ranger?"

"I thought I'd fly jets in the Navy, like my dad, but my color blindness put an end to that dream."

"Isn't it rare for women to be color blind?" Jamie asked.

"Not rare, but more men are than women, for sure. I guess I was one of the unlucky ones. Becoming a park ranger seemed like a good backup plan."

"How were you able to get your pilot's license if you're color blind?"

Rowan pulled a string from her bag and began threading one end through the snares she'd created to make them easier to carry. "I could pass the FAA test, but not the Class I flying physical required to become a Naval pilot."

"I'm sorry it didn't work out for you. I'm sure you were pretty devastated."

"It's fine. I'm happy enough as a ranger, and it has given me the freedom to be close to my mom, which probably wouldn't have happened if I was in the Navy. It worked out for the best."

Rowan dropped the string of snares into her bag and stood. Jamie accepted her hand when she offered to help her up, and they both walked back to the cabin.

"Did you ever think you wanted to be anything other than an ornithologist?"

Jamie shook her head. "No. Not really. Not anything serious, at least." Rowan wrapped an arm around her shoulders as they walked. On instinct, she wrapped her arm around Rowan's waist. The contact was comforting, and Jamie considered walking slower to draw out the time it took them to reach their destination.

"You didn't have a backup plan?" Rowan asked.

"No backup plans. My dad didn't allow thoughts of doing something other than a career in the sciences." Jamie's dad had always been a very driven person, and he expected the same focus from his only child. It had taught Jamie to work hard and accept nothing other than her very best, but sometimes she wondered what that had cost her.

"If you could do anything else, what would it be?" Rowan directed Jamie to sit on the cabin steps next to her.

"I guess…an artist."

"Really?"

Her dreams of being an artist were something her father had

discouraged since she was very young, so it had always been her little secret that she'd never really shared with anyone else. "I'm not like some amazing artist or anything, but it's something I've always loved to do."

"I'd love to see something you've drawn sometime. As someone who has zero artistic ability, I've always envied people who have a talent for something like that."

"Everyone has some talent of some sort. What's yours?"

Rowan laughed and shook her head. "Does flying count? I'm a damn outstanding pilot."

"I think that counts. I could never learn to fly. Even as only a passenger in a plane, I'm way too freaked out." Jamie had never been a big fan of flying, even though she loved to travel. She realized it was necessary to get to where she wanted to go, so she usually took something to help her fall asleep and hoped they'd arrive at their destination before she woke up.

"I assumed as much when you stumbled out of the plane and kissed the ground when we arrived."

"Yeah, well, that was a super scary flight. Now that I trust you more, I probably wouldn't be as scared." Jamie twirled the wire rose in her fingers. "This is pretty amazing. I think you have some hidden artistic abilities that you haven't realized yet."

Rowan took the rose from her hand and bent one petal to fix an imperfection, then gently bopped Jamie on the tip of her nose with it before handing it back to her. "You think so?"

"I definitely think so."

They both sat quietly for a few minutes and watched a squirrel forage for food on the ground, constantly aware of what Jamie and Rowan were doing. Rowan leaned back on her elbows and stretched her long legs out in front of her, crossing them at her ankles. Jamie fought the urge to lean against her but didn't want to presume that kind of contact would be welcome.

"What squirrel is that? It's huge," Jamie said.

"It's an Arctic ground squirrel. They usually call them parky or parka squirrels up here because their skin was used to line parkas."

"Well, that's sad." Jamie tried not to judge people, especially traditional practices that were done for generations, but killing animals only to be used for clothing or ornaments sickened her.

"Not sad if you consider they were only making use of every part of the animal they killed to feed their family. I realize that wasn't always the case, but most tribes who killed them would not waste something useful. Kinda like the Native Americans who used every part of the buffalo, and then the white man came along and killed entire herds only for their pelts."

"You're right. I'm not comfortable with the whole killing animals thing. We've eaten so much more meat out here than I ever do at home. I eat fish. I've just never really eaten much meat." Thankfully, Jamie's parents never pushed her to eat meat if she was eating a balanced diet, so she'd always leaned more toward fish or vegetarian dishes.

"Living off the land, you learn to eat what's available, and if you're lucky, that includes meat."

Jamie nodded and watched the squirrel stop to listen for any dangers before continuing with his meal of grass and leaves on the ground. He was a cute little round thing, and Jamie hoped Rowan wouldn't try to feed her one someday. If she did, Jamie would rather just not know what it was she was eating.

"Did you know the Arctic ground squirrel is the only squirrel in Alaska that hibernates?"

"No, that's neat."

"They can hibernate for up to nine months. The males are so territorial that they'll sometimes eat the young of other parky squirrels."

Jamie looked at Rowan to judge if she was being serious. "Oh God, suddenly I'm not so opposed to eating one."

Rowan chuckled and stood, reaching down to help Jamie to her feet. "We'll stick with rabbit stew for tonight. We usually do it on our hike out to the location, but I need to replace all the snares on my traps with the new ones I created. Will you be okay without me for a few hours?"

They'd spent pretty much every hour of every day with each other, and the thought of Rowan leaving without her felt strangely uncomfortable. Jamie had always prided herself on being a strong, independent woman, so she pushed the anxious thoughts aside and chalked them up to being alone in such a remote and unfamiliar environment.

"Of course," Jamie said. "I'll hold down the fort while you're gone. Do you need me to help you with any of your regular chores since you'll be out? I'm not the best at chopping wood, but I think I can at least do enough to keep us warm for another night."

"No, no, you're good. We'll be fine for at least three days. I'll make sure you have enough in the cabin that you won't have to go out to the shed on your own. I'd appreciate it if you tried to stay indoors as much as possible while I'm gone. If you leave to go to the restroom or anything, just make sure you're aware of your surroundings. The further along we get in the season, the more likely we'll be to see a bear. I don't expect that one will come near the cabin if it thinks there's a human here, but if it was desperate enough, it's not impossible that it might investigate."

Jamie nodded. "Okay. I'm going to work another hour, and then I'll have to stop. We still need to get the solar panels mounted on top of the cabin. Do you think we might be able to work on that soon? It's working okay where they are, but I think it might help to have them elevated with nothing blocking their access to the sun. What little sun we get, at least."

"Sure thing." Rowan added more logs to the fire and warmed her hands over the wood-burning stove. "I need to fix the antenna so I can check in with Greg anyway, so I'll get all of that done tomorrow. Will that work for you?"

"That's perfect."

"I'll stack more wood in the cabin, and then I'll fetch our dinner." Rowan squeezed Jamie's shoulder affectionately as she walked to the door. The contact warmed her all over. A few hours apart was probably a good idea. It would give Jamie the space she needed to get her attraction to Rowan under control with any luck. She was sure these brief innocent interactions between them meant much more to her than they did to Rowan, and she could only take so much before initiating something she was sure she'd regret later.

CHAPTER TWELVE

Rowan tugged on the rope harness she'd created to help her safely climb to the top of the tallest tree near their cabin. The radio antenna that allowed her to contact the park service and provided them with a connection to the outside world had gotten blown around in the high winds they'd been experiencing. She wasn't a fan of climbing this high into a tree, but the antenna had moved just enough to make it difficult to hear anything over the static.

"I'm halfway there. Just keep that rope wrapped around your body, and if I slip, you'll stop me from falling to my death." The look of pure panic on Jamie's face shouldn't have been as funny as it was, but teasing Jamie a little just never got old.

"Jesus, Rowan, are you kidding me? You're like twice my size. There's no way I can hold you."

"Why did you think you were holding the rope?"

"I—it's—come back down. I'm not comfortable with this situation anymore. We'll have to figure out another way for you to do this. I was nervous enough when you got on the cabin roof to install the solar panels. Now you're totally freaking me out."

The rough bark of the tree scraped across her arms as Rowan pulled herself up another couple of feet. "You're going to be just fine, Jamie. I'm just giving you a hard time. See where I looped the rope around that sturdy limb up there?"

"Yeah."

"I have it rigged where I have to push this knot up as I ascend. That way, if I slip, the knot will tighten, and I won't slide down very far." Rowan indicated where the knot was on the rope holding her weight.

"You're more of an adorable backup safety measure. You can catch me if I fall out of the tree."

"Rowan?"

"Yes?" Rowan pulled herself up a couple more feet and looked down at Jamie.

"Please don't fall out of that tree."

Rowan smiled and pushed the knot up higher on the rope. "Yes, ma'am."

Someone had cut the top of the tree off to allow for the antenna to be attached. As soon as Rowan could reach the metal pole, she called down to Jamie to have her go into the cabin to listen for a better signal. After a few minutes of spinning it around, Jamie finally came out to let her know the signal was crystal clear. The trip down the tree was much faster than the climb up, and before long, Rowan was safely back on solid ground.

"My arms are killing me. I'm not as young as I used to be. There was a time when going up that tree wouldn't have even made me break a sweat. Now my entire body is reminding me I'm not nineteen years old anymore."

"Poor old lady," Jamie teased her. "It's about time to put you out to pasture."

Rowan washed her arms and face in the water they kept by the sink. "That doesn't sound half bad. Lazy days, relaxing on a grassy hill, watching the clouds move by."

"That does sound nice. Can I hang out on your hill with you?"

Water droplets tickled the hairs on Rowan's arms as she paused in drying off to consider Jamie's question. She knew she was only being playful, but the fact was, she wouldn't mind having Jamie with her. A vision of the two of them on their backs, Jamie's head resting on Rowan's outstretched arm as they enjoyed the crisp midsummer air, flashed through her mind. It was something she hadn't realized how much she wanted and also the thing Rowan knew she'd never have.

"You're too much of a city girl to ever be satisfied with a life on that hill." Rowan saw the hurt on Jamie's face and wanted to take back what she'd said. "Jamie, I—"

"It's fine." Jamie raised her hand to stop Rowan from digging herself any further into the hole she'd already created. "I should try to get a little work done."

"Wait just a few minutes. I need to see if I can reach Greg to update him. I can try to be quiet, but it's hard not to be loud on these radios. Is there anything you need me to pass along? He can contact your family or work if you need."

Jamie shook her head. "No, I have nothing they would be interested in hearing. It'll be hard enough to go home with nothing exciting to report, let alone disappointing them before I'm even halfway done with my time out here."

The sadness in Jamie's expression tugged at Rowan's heart. She wasn't sure if it was from what she'd said or the fact that her dad was obviously a buffoon that didn't appreciate what an amazing woman Jamie was, no matter what professional success she accomplished. Rowan knew her mom had to be driving Greg crazy, asking if he'd heard from Rowan. She almost felt bad for him. Her mom could be a force of nature when she wanted something, and Greg had always been just a little afraid of her. That thought made Rowan smile. She'd explained to him repeatedly that she was only like that with people she loved, but Greg was such a gentle soul he still did everything in his power to avoid her wrath.

"I'm going to wait outside while you contact Greg," Jamie said.

"You're welcome to be here."

Jamie shook her head and squeezed Rowan's arm. "I would like to spend some time outside. I'm a little sick of being cooped up in the cabin."

"Sounds good. I won't be long."

"Take your time." Jamie gave her a quick wave before leaving her alone.

The radio crackled to life as Rowan turned the dials until she found the channel she knew Greg would be monitoring.

"Alpha Lima Four Romeo, monitoring." She waited for the transmission to finish and then listened for a response. When there wasn't one for a few minutes, she tried again. "Alpha Lima Four Romeo, monitoring." A minute later, she got the response she wanted.

"Alpha Lima Four Romeo, this is Alpha Lima Three Zed. Good to hear from you, Rowan. How are things with the city girl?"

Rowan glanced toward the door to make sure it was shut. She didn't want Jamie to hear what Greg had said and be offended. "Hey, Greg, she's not so much of a city girl. Things are going well. We're settled into a rhythm with our days, and I think she's gotten some good video footage of the birds that are up there, even though there's no sign of the one she wants."

"Right. Do you think that's going to happen?"

She glanced at the door once more. If they had asked her that question before they'd come out here, she would have thought there was no way in hell. The probability was still very slim, but she hoped the thing would show up for Jamie's sake. Rowan knew the alternative would break Jamie's heart, and she didn't even want to think about how much that affected her.

"We're hopeful. Haven't given up yet." Rowan wanted to change the subject before Greg asked any more questions about Jamie. It strangely felt like private information, and she wasn't willing to invite anyone else into their world just yet. "How's my mom?"

There was a beat of silence on the other end of the line, and it sent the hairs on the back of Rowan's neck on end. "Alpha Lima Four Romeo, come in, Alpha Lima Three Zed, did you catch my last, Greg?"

"Alpha Lima Three Zed, I did, Rowan, sorry. I spilled coffee all over my desk, and it was heading straight for my repeater. Do you have me now?"

"I do. How's my mom doing, Greg?"

Rowan had so much guilt about leaving her mom for this long, but when she'd told her about the trip, she'd insisted Rowan go. There was no arguing with her mother, so she reluctantly agreed to do it. Not that her director had given her a choice, but Rowan could have put up more of a fight if her mom hadn't wanted her to go. Part of her worried she'd return home and her mother wouldn't even remember who she was. She knew that was unlikely this early in her illness, but she would never forgive herself if it did.

"She's quite good," Greg said. "The private nurse you got her seems to have things well under control. I don't know how he does it. She scares the life out of me, but he doesn't allow any of it to faze him. I think putting her in that senior care community, as well as getting her someone dedicated to her, was the right thing to do. I know it was hard for you, but it was the right decision. She mostly has good days, but Steve says she forgets more of the little things."

Guilt blanketed Rowan, and she wanted to pack up and head home right then. She would never get this time with her mother back, and here she was playing house with Jamie in the middle of the woods instead of with her mom where she belonged.

"You with me, Rowan?"

"I'm here." Rowan could hear the anguish in her own voice.

"She's fine, my friend. You won't be gone all that long, and that bird lady needs you. You know there isn't anyone else better suited to what she needs right now."

Rowan sighed. "I know. You're right."

"Besides," Greg added, "your mom would kick your ass if you left early so that you could fuss over her. I won't be held responsible for bringing you back early, and you know she'd blame me."

Rowan could almost imagine her mother scolding a cowering Greg and had to laugh. "You're right. So, you're sure she's okay?"

"I'm sure. I've been checking in with Steve every day, and he's not one to sugarcoat anything. He would tell me if he thought you needed to come home early."

"Okay. I've adjusted my antenna, so I'll be on this channel if you need to contact me. I don't want to use up too much of the battery life from these solar panels since Jamie needs it for her work, but I'll turn it on every day at nine in the morning, noon, and nine in the evening unless it's a day we're hiking out to the site. If you need me, you can reach me at one of those times."

"Roger. Sounds good, my friend. Alpha Lima Three Zed, clear."

"Alpha Lima Four Romeo, clear."

Rowan secured the radio equipment and made her way outside. She found Jamie relaxing in a chair in front of the cabin. They'd had several days of beautiful weather, but work had kept Jamie locked away inside during most of it. She was glad to see her finally allowing herself to enjoy the warmth of the sun while they still had it.

"Hey," Rowan said as she sat next to her with a small chunk of wood and a carving knife. She hadn't carved anything in years, but she'd give it a try in hopes she could make something that might cheer Jamie up.

"Hey, how was Greg?"

The brightness of the sun and olive green of Jamie's shirt enhanced the color of her eyes. Once again, it struck Rowan how beautiful she was.

"Good," she answered. The need to focus her gaze on the wood she was carving helped keep her from staring at Jamie. She wasn't strictly used to spending time with people since she'd come back to Alaska, but especially with someone she was so attracted to. "He's been checking in on my mom for me while I'm gone."

"That's kind of him. How is your mom? I feel bad I dragged you out here, away from her, for all this time."

"She's fine. Greg said the community she's in is good, and her private nurse has been taking good care of her. She's not exactly thrilled with me for putting her there, but it was just too dangerous for her to be alone in the house she was in before."

"How long has she been there?"

A gust of wind blew strands of Jamie's blond hair over her face. Rowan watched her delicate fingers comb it back and tuck it behind her ear. She cleared her throat and looked back down at the wood she was carving, which looked less like a block and more like the shape she wanted.

"Eighteen months, about. When I first moved back, I lived with my mom, but my job kept me busy. Without notice, I might have to be gone for a week. Everything seemed fine for the first few months, but then I noticed little things happening that seemed strange."

"Like what?"

"Like, I found the remote in the cheese drawer in the refrigerator." Rowan thought about the hour she'd spent searching for it before giving up and deciding to make herself a sandwich, only to find it sealed in a bag of shredded cheese. "I know that seems like a small thing that might happen to anyone, but those small things add up after a while. I'd ask her about it, and she'd get angry with me like I was accusing her of something bad. The more her condition progressed, the more we argued."

Jamie squeezed Rowan's knee to comfort her. "I'm so sorry, Rowan."

Rowan shrugged, not comfortable expressing how difficult that time was for them both. "I think I knew something was wrong, but it's like I wasn't putting the pieces together to understand what."

"You were too close to the situation," Jamie offered.

"Yeah, and I think I was in denial. It's difficult to admit the person who had always been your rock might no longer be as strong as they once were."

Jamie nodded and reclined back in her chair. "Same with my mom. She had always been such a powerful presence in our lives that we didn't understand just how serious things were until it was too late. I wasn't around much because I had just gotten my position at the PWCA, and my dad had been in session in Washington for two weeks. She only wanted to be home in her garden, and I can't say I blame her. DC is a toxic place to be on the best of days. I had talked to her a few days before, and she'd complained about numbness in her hands. She wouldn't listen when I told her she should get it checked out. She said she wasn't comfortable driving because her eyesight had been a little blurry. It worried me, but she insisted it was only her prescription and promised to make an appointment with her eye doctor. I told her I could take a day off to drive her to the doctor myself, but she wouldn't budge. When she didn't show up for a board meeting at the Los Angeles Natural History Museum three days later, a friend went to the house to check on her. She'd been gone at least a day when they found her in her garden. I should have checked on her sooner. I should have insisted she go to the doctor immediately."

"It's not your fault," Rowan said.

"Not realizing what was happening with your mom wasn't your fault," Jamie countered.

"Touché."

They were both silent for a few minutes while Rowan focused on her carving. She wasn't someone who enjoyed opening up to people about her life. Sharing her guilt about her mom was so out of character that it left her feeling very raw. Where did they go from here? She knew she should say something to Jamie, but she wasn't sure how a typical conversation progressed after such a serious disclosure.

"What are you making?" Jamie asked, pointing to Rowan's hands.

Rowan held the object up to see, even though she knew it wasn't far enough along for Jamie to understand what it would be. "It's going to be a surprise."

"Is this another hidden artistic talent you failed to mention like the wire rose?"

Warmth heated Rowan's cheeks. "Maybe? I guess we'll have to see once it's finished. It might end up being a fancy block of kindling for the fire." Rowan set the wood down next to her chair and put the knife back in its sheath. "I better get out of here and check the traps before the day gets away from me, or we won't have anything good for dinner."

"I should do a little work while you're gone. Today has been a pleasant break."

Rowan stood and squeezed Jamie's shoulder. "It has. Thanks for the help with the antenna and the chat. It was nice."

"It was nice," Jamie agreed. "Do you need me to do anything while you're gone?"

They'd occasionally spent time apart over the last few weeks, but they were usually near the cabin. It was always strange when Rowan had to leave Jamie alone. She was a capable woman, but Rowan liked the idea of being near in case she was needed. "I think we're good. If you want to gather some wood to hold us off for a bit, I'll bring more from the shed after dinner. Don't forget to keep your bear spray with you."

"Sounds good." Jamie stood and brushed away the few small wood chips from Rowan's carving that had landed in her lap. "I'll get a little work done and then help you with dinner when you get back."

"Right." Rowan didn't bother with a jacket since it was such a beautiful day, and she wouldn't be gone for very long but grabbed her small game bag to hang from her belt in case she caught a rabbit and tucked her pistol into her belt. "I'll be back before you know it."

CHAPTER THIRTEEN

The sound of rustling leaves drew Jamie's attention from the pile of wood she'd been collecting. She stopped what she was doing and listened for any sign it was an animal or, hopefully, Rowan, and not only the wind. When she was satisfied it wasn't anything to be concerned about, she continued collecting branches for their fire.

Rowan had left the cabin to check her traps three hours before and hadn't returned. Three hours was longer than her usual trip away but wouldn't have concerned Jamie as much if the skies hadn't turned so ominous an hour before. They'd weathered a few rainstorms since they'd been there, but this one seemed different. This storm scared her, and the thought of Rowan being caught in it without protection had Jamie worried sick.

A thunderous crack startled her, and she quickly gathered the pile of wood in her arms and headed for the safety of the cabin. The only thing she could do at this point was to make sure that there was a warm fire burning and dry clothes ready for Rowan when she returned. The fleeting thought that she might not return at all was quickly pushed away. Jamie didn't know what she'd do if Rowan didn't return. Should she go after her?

She entered the cabin and stacked the branches she'd collected into as neat a pile as possible and carefully opened the door to the stove. Thankfully, it hadn't burned out entirely while she was outside, so she could add wood to its belly and wait for it to catch. There was a slight chill in the room, but she knew it wouldn't take long to be warm and cozy again. That was an advantage to having a small cabin. Small spaces heated quickly.

Once the fire was roaring, she searched for dry clothes for Rowan. She assumed she'd likely be wet and cold and would appreciate something warm to put on when she returned. The cabin only had one chest of drawers and no closet, so they'd divvied up the drawers when they'd first arrived, each taking two. Jamie pulled one of Rowan's drawers open to find neatly folded T-shirts, flannels, and a pair of jeans. The second drawer contained socks, boxer briefs, and a thermal underwear set. She wished she could offer her a warm pair of sweats to snuggle into, but the thermals would have to do. She added thick socks and a pair of boxer briefs to her stack and laid them on a chair near the stove to get warm.

With the clothes taken care of, Jamie found Rowan's towel she'd been using and set both it and a blanket with the clothes near the fire. She checked out the window again but only found that the clouds had gotten darker, and the wind was picking up. Trees swayed from side to side as branches crashed to the earth below. "Where are you, Rowan? Please be okay."

She decided to give Rowan another five minutes before thinking about bundling up and braving the storm to look for her. She knew that was a ridiculous thing to do and that Rowan would likely kill her if they both made it back to the cabin alive, but she couldn't sit any longer, knowing Rowan might be out there injured and unable to get home.

Rain pelted the roof of the cabin as Jamie paced. She filled a pot with water and set it on top of the stove to heat before looking out the window once more. Through the darkness, she thought she could just make out the silhouette of a figure running toward the cabin. Jamie quickly opened the door and stepped out onto the porch as Rowan ran up the stairs, soaked to the bone and shivering from the cold.

"Oh, thank God," Jamie said as she guided Rowan into the cabin and shut the door behind them. "Come on, let's get you out of these wet clothes and settle you next to the fire."

Rowan peeled off her shirt and quickly shed her jeans. Jamie absently noticed she wasn't wearing a bra and stored a mental image of her chiseled body for later. They'd both been careful not to undress in front of each other to that point, so Jamie tried to respect her privacy, but the temptation to look was too great.

"I caught a rabbit." Rowan's voice stuttered as she shook from the chill.

"Hmm?" Jamie's brain seemed to have short-circuited as she tried to think of anything other than the beautiful body in front of her. "I— good, rabbit, yes."

"I left it on the porch. Thank you for getting this fire going. It's perfect."

The discarded wet clothes dripped on the floor as Jamie took them to the sink until she had time to hang them to dry. "When you didn't come back, and then the storm came up, I was about to go after you."

Jamie could hear the chattering of Rowan's teeth and used the warm towel to dry her off as much as she could. Once she was at least mostly dry, Jamie grabbed the blanket she'd left to warm by the fire and wrapped it around Rowan's naked body. Jamie knew she should step back now, but she couldn't. She continued to hold on to Rowan until she felt her rest her large frame against her much smaller body.

"I'm sorry, Jamie. I didn't mean to worry you."

Jamie finally stepped back to guide Rowan onto a chair in front of the fire. "Are you hurt? Are you sure you're okay?"

"I'm okay, just cold. The rabbit—"

"I know. The rabbit is on the porch. We'll get to that in a minute." Jamie's heart ached to see Rowan so vulnerable. "I have some dry clothes here for you. Can I help you get dressed?"

Rowan nodded and pulled the blanket tighter around her body. "Socks first, please."

Jamie unfolded the socks and slipped them on Rowan's feet. "Want help with the rest?"

"Um…" Rowan was hesitant to answer. "Sure, if you don't mind."

The clothes Jamie had set by the fire were warm as she picked up the boxers and held them to be put on. Rowan placed her hands on Jamie's shoulders for balance as she slipped first one and then the other leg in so Jamie could pull them up and over her butt. Jamie slipped her fingers under the waistband to smooth it flat against Rowan's body without thinking about the fact that she would be touching her in such an intimate place. Rowan's skin was still cool to the touch, but the firmness of her muscular body sent wetness to Jamie's center. She wanted to run her fingers down the chiseled definition of her abdomen and explore all the areas of Rowan's body she'd only briefly seen. Jamie recognized the hunger in Rowan's eyes when she looked up from her task. She wanted this, too. The urge to kiss her was so overwhelming, Jamie had to force herself to look away.

"I—" Jamie's voice came out as a croak as she picked up the shirt and handed it to Rowan.

Rowan cleared her throat and took the shirt from Jamie, gliding her fingers across her hand as she took it. "I think I got the rest. The rabbit—"

"Yep, on it. Rabbit stew coming right up." Jamie found a bag containing the cleaned and cut rabbit on the porch and added the pieces to the pot simmering on the stove.

"There's wild onion, Eskimo potatoes, and a few mushrooms in the pouch on my belt. You can rinse them and throw them into the pot, too."

Jamie did as Rowan suggested then left the ingredients to do their magic. When she turned back to her, Rowan was dressed and once again wrapped up in the blanket. It was both a relief and a disappointment to see she was covered.

"How are you feeling?" Jamie asked.

"Good. Better." The shivering had stopped, and Rowan seemed more relaxed.

"I'm glad. Once the stew is done, we'll get a warm meal in you, and you'll be good as new." Jamie added salt to the stew and stirred it before replacing the lid. "This is going to take a bit to cook. Did you want to rest, and I'll let you know when it's ready?"

Rowan yawned and snuggled deeper into the blanket. "Yeah, that would be awesome." Jamie watched as she moved toward the pallet on the floor where she'd been sleeping since they'd first arrived. She'd heard Rowan mention fixing one of the broken beds, but they'd been so busy that she'd never gotten around to it. Jamie couldn't allow her to sleep on the floor in this state.

"Hey, sleep in my bed. I can't let you sleep on the floor." Jamie braced for an argument, but she would not let this one go. The more she thought of the sleeping arrangements, the more guilty she felt. She should have at least offered to alternate nights in the bed with her before now.

"I appreciate that, but I'm fine. I've gotten all the lumps in my little mattress perfectly aligned with the contours of my body. That takes work, and I can't just abandon it." The carefree smile on Rowan's face wasn't fooling anyone. Jamie knew she was doing her best to convince her otherwise, but sleeping on the floor had to suck.

"Rowan, please sleep on the bed. I'm not even using it right now. I insist." Jamie squeezed Rowan's blanket-covered arm. "Please."

The room was silent, and Jamie knew Rowan must be doing her damnedest to come up with a counterargument. It wouldn't work. Jamie was sticking to her guns and was determined not to allow Rowan to convince her otherwise.

"Fine, but tomorrow I'm fixing one of the other beds so you aren't kicked out of yours. I should have done it earlier, but I just haven't taken the time."

Jamie led Rowan to the bed and tucked the covers tightly around her. The wood creaked as she sat on the edge and leaned over a now rosy-cheeked Rowan.

"Are you warm enough?" Jamie asked.

Rowan nodded silently. "Thanks for taking care of me."

A lock of still damp hair had fallen into Rowan's eyes, and Jamie combed her fingers through it to push it back and out of the way. "Anytime," Jamie said.

The truth of her admission surprised her. Whatever Rowan needed, Jamie wanted to be the one to be there for her. It was a strange thought, especially considering they hadn't known each other for that long, but it was true. What that exactly meant, she'd worry about another day. For now, she was just happy that Rowan was warm and safe. She was thankful they had each other while they were out here and vowed not to take what Rowan did for her for granted.

Rowan's breathing evened out as she drifted off to sleep. Before getting up, Jamie leaned down and kissed her lips gently. "Sleep tight, my friend."

The rain continued to fall as Jamie checked the stew, then sat down to get some work done. The sight of a sleeping Rowan just a few feet away proved too much of a distraction, so she made herself a cup of coffee and sat on the porch. An occasional burst of wind would push the rain under the overhang, but it had calmed enough that Jamie could sit comfortably and watch the puddles fill. No matter how many rainstorms she'd seen in her life, the ones in Alaska had smelled better than them all. Jamie supposed it had more to do with the remoteness of their location, but the air was almost sweet. If she could bottle it up and take it with her when she had to return home, she would.

For the first time since she'd left home, thoughts of returning made her sad. She couldn't wait to share everything she'd learned while up here, and Jamie would give her kingdom for a dinner that consisted of anything other than rabbit or salmon, but there were many things she would be sad to leave. Not the least of which was Ranger Rowan Fleming. Ugh. The last thing she needed was to pine over someone when there was no chance of it leading to a lasting relationship. She had to get those thoughts out of her head as soon as possible. That path would only lead to heartache.

The clang of dishes pulled Jamie from her thoughts. She entered the cabin to find Rowan still in her thermals and thick socks, stirring the pot of rabbit stew.

"Hey, let me do that. You should be resting."

"No, no, I'm fine now. Thanks for everything you did." Rowan used a hook to move the pot to a cooler area on the stove. "I think this is ready." She found two bowls in a cabinet against the wall and, after a quick rub with a small towel to clean them, she ladled stew into each one. "Are you ready for stew?"

Jamie made her way to the table and sat next to Rowan. She carefully took her first bite of food, cautious of how hot it would be. "This stew is amazing," Jamie said as she savored one of the mushrooms. "I can't believe we threw this together so quickly. I never would have imagined you could forage for all of this amazing food out here."

"Pretty awesome, right? It's much harder in the winter, of course, but there's plenty to eat this time of year. It's all there if you know where to look."

"What happened? You aren't usually gone for more than an hour."

Rowan used her fork to stab a potato and pop it into her mouth. "I took the rabbit down to the river to clean it and heard thunder. I started back right away but wasn't fast enough. Lightning struck not too far from where I was standing, so I found a large boulder to hunker down under until I felt like it was safe enough to move. The temperature dropped quickly, so I had to take more risks than I usually would. It all worked out in the end, though. I'm home, warm, with a full belly and good company. Not a bad way to end the day."

Her words warmed Jamie's heart. She was more content than she'd ever been in her regular life, which was an odd thing to realize. Not something she would have ever expected, but she wasn't ready to overthink it. Right then, she just wanted to enjoy the moment.

CHAPTER FOURTEEN

The following morning, Rowan woke up feeling more rested than she had in days. She snuggled back into her blankets until she remembered why she was so comfortable. Jamie had insisted that Rowan take the bed the night before, and no matter how much she argued, Jamie refused to bend. The sight of her, or at least the pile of blankets she knew Jamie was sleeping under, made Rowan feel horrible that she hadn't repaired another bed before now.

The first order of the day was to remedy their sleeping situation. Rowan had spent most of her time assisting Jamie when she wasn't finding food for them to eat. Living off the land was a never-ending battle to find enough sustenance to sustain them, but she'd been fortunate. The rabbits had been easy to trap, the fish easy to catch, and the rain they'd gotten made foraging productive. Helping Jamie had more to do with wanting to be involved in what was happening with the research. She was sure Jamie would be quite capable of doing it without Rowan's help.

The bed issue hadn't seemed like a priority since Rowan was the only one making the sacrifice. Now that Jamie insisted she join in, fixing another bed moved to the top of her to-do list. She knew there was a larger bed in the shed behind the cabin that needed new legs. There were tools to fix it, but Rowan would need to find the wood to replace the broken parts. Hopefully, someone had left what she needed in the shed, and she wouldn't have to cut down a tree to make her own.

Rowan quietly slipped on her jacket and boots, careful not to wake Jamie on her way out the door. With any luck, she'd be able to repair the bed before Jamie even woke up. The shed was dark and dusty, but

Rowan quickly found the pieces needed to complete the repairs. She'd need to borrow some parts from one of the other broken beds, but she was confident she could make it work.

The repairs were an excellent distraction from the jumble of feelings the day before had stirred up. The rhythm of sawing, the feel of the wood against her fingers, the smell of sawdust, all of it helped push away the memory of Jamie's gentle fingers combing the hair away from her face. Even half-frozen and shivering from head to toe, Rowan luxuriated in the warmth of having her so close.

"Rowan, where are you?" Jamie's voice sounded raspy like she'd just woken up. Rowan couldn't ignore the way her heart lifted when she heard her. Like some lovesick schoolgirl. She had to handle these ridiculous feelings before she did or said something stupid.

"I'm back here by the shed. Do you need something?" Rowan stepped outside so she could see her.

Jamie poked her head around the cabin and held up two mugs of coffee. Rowan watched as she stepped off the porch and walked toward where she stood. "I couldn't find you when I woke up, and the pots were cold, so I thought wherever you were, you probably needed a warm cup of coffee." Jamie handed Rowan her mug, then took a sip from her own.

The rich aroma tickled Rowan's senses, and she was very thankful Jamie had thought of her. "You might be the perfect woman." Jamie looked pleased with the compliment but didn't respond.

"What are you doing out here so early?" she asked as she looked over the work Rowan had been doing.

"I decided it was high time I fixed up another bed. I'll give you this bigger one, and I'll take my old one back." Rowan took another sip of coffee and set the mug on a table near her work area.

"Oh. I'm fine sleeping on the floor. Don't do this on my account."

The words said one thing, but her expression said another. Rowan could see Jamie's night on the floor hadn't been a restful one. She looked more tired than Rowan had seen her since they'd been there, and it only made her more certain she'd need to finish another bed before nighttime.

"So, you were fine sleeping on the floor?" Rowan teased her.

"Yeah, of course. I slept just fine."

"Mm-hmm." Rowan dodged the swipe of Jamie's hand.

"I was fine. It wasn't exactly comfortable, but I made it work. I insist you take the bigger bed, dork. You're like twice my size. I'm fine in the bed I have, and you take the large one so you can stretch out your long legs."

"That's really not—"

"Rowan, seriously, you're being ridiculous. You take the bigger bed."

"I won't argue," Rowan said before pulling a chair from where it hung from a peg on the shed wall, dusting it off, and offering it to Jamie. "Would you like to chat while I work?"

Jamie glanced back at the cabin but eventually sat down. "Only for a minute. I have so much to do today. Did you sleep okay last night?"

"Like a baby. Thanks for letting me take the bed," Rowan said as she resumed her work.

"Of course. I hope you didn't mind me tucking your blankets in around you like a five-year-old. Seeing you like that worried me, and I wanted to make sure you were warm. I realized after I walked away that it might seem a little strange, like I was treating you like a child or something. That wasn't my intention."

Rowan ran her hand over the surface of the wood, then flipped the bed rail over so she could work on the other side. "No, it was nice. I was pretty restless and needed to calm down."

"Did I make you restless, or did I help calm you down?"

Sawdust billowed through the air as Rowan blew it off of the wood. Rowan could see Jamie's sly smile as she sipped her coffee. She knew what she was doing to her. "Both."

"Interesting."

"Why interesting?"

Jamie shrugged and set down her mug. She leaned back in her chair and crossed one leg over the other. She looked so relaxed and confidently feminine that Rowan had difficulty focusing on her task. "I guess I assumed you would have plenty of women tucking in your blankets."

That couldn't be further from the truth, but Rowan was hesitant to admit just how far for fear of looking like some weirdo hermit who never talked to the city folk. She already suspected Jamie might think that, and it wasn't how she wanted Jamie to see her.

"I've dated women."

"I'm sure you have. There's no way you don't have the ladies lined up when given the opportunity. Like Caroline for instance."

Rowan's brow furrowed in confusion. "Caroline?"

"From the bar. The hot waitress that seemed very fond of you."

"Oh, Caroline Hill." Rowan picked up the wood planer and used it to shave off part of the wood. "She's just a friend."

"She seemed like a friendly friend."

She couldn't be sure, but Rowan thought she detected a hint of jealousy in Jamie's tone. "We haven't been as friendly as the two of you were, but we're friends."

"Really?" Jamie's foot rocked up and down to a silent beat, once again drawing Rowan's attention to her jean-clad legs and the curve of her hips. "And how friendly do you think we were?"

"Are you telling me you didn't sleep with her the night you were in Ugruk?"

"No, I slept with her. I was alone and irritated that my pilot stood me up, and she was a beautiful woman who I knew wouldn't expect anything more than a night of fun. I'm an adult, and I'm not ashamed of taking care of my needs when the opportunity arises."

Caroline Hill was the last person Rowan wanted to think about, especially after what she and Jamie might have done when Rowan was supposed to have been there. "I'm sorry I was late picking you up."

"Sorry because you were late, or sorry because I slept with Caroline?"

"Can we stop talking about Caroline Hill?"

"Sure." Jamie folded her arms across her chest and looked at Rowan curiously. "So, if Caroline isn't your type, what is?"

"What is what?" Rowan stopped sanding the bed leg she was working on and wondered if she could just convince Jamie to let her go back to sleeping on the floor. Anything to get out of this conversation as quickly as possible.

"What type of women are you attracted to?"

"I don't think I have a type. I'm almost done with this if you want to go back to the cabin. It shouldn't take me much longer to finish."

Jamie pulled her jacket tighter around her body. "I'm good. Everyone has a type. Tell me about some of the women you've dated since you moved back to Alaska. I'm sure there are plenty who would love to keep the handsome Ranger Fleming's bed warm."

"I haven't been with another woman since my wife left me." Rowan knew her answer would take the wind out of Jamie's sails, and that's what she wanted, but she felt terrible for being so blunt about it.

"I'm sorry, Rowan." Their playfulness was gone. Jamie leaned forward and grasped Rowan's hand. "I didn't mean to be insensitive."

This hadn't been the first time they'd held hands, but it still made Rowan's breath catch all the same. Every time they touched it was like a burst of electricity ran through her body. She understood she was attracted to Jamie, but this felt like something else. Before she allowed herself to linger too long, she squeezed Jamie's hand and let it go.

"No apology needed. You weren't insensitive. I didn't mean to bring the mood down."

Jamie returned her hands to her jacket pockets to warm them up. "No, I was being nosy, and I know you aren't a big fan of that kind of thing. Do you mind if I ask how long you've been back in Alaska?"

"Nope. Three years. I tried to make things work in the Lower Forty-eight for as long as possible, but I didn't belong there. I never belonged there."

"Why is that, do you think?" Jamie asked.

Rowan checked the board once more and leaned it against the shed before picking up another one. "Don't know. I've just always been this way. I prefer the trees, the weather, and the bears to car horns, microwaves, and streetlights. The constant noise of city life is enough to drive me mad."

"No microwaves?"

Rowan laughed. "Nope. Rowan like fire. Fire good."

"You're a dork."

"What about you? Are you a city girl, through and through?"

Jamie sighed and pulled her jacket tight around her shoulders. "If you'd asked me that question a few weeks ago, I would have said that I love being outdoors but could never live as simple a life as this."

"And now?"

"Now, I'm not so sure." Jamie brushed blond curls from her face and tucked them behind an ear. The gesture was so wonderfully Jamie. Rowan fought the urge to lean down and kiss the newly exposed skin on her neck.

"How do you feel about that?"

The shed was quiet except for the rasp of Rowan's hand planer as she worked it over a knot in the wood.

"I don't know how I feel," Jamie admitted. "Confused? I thought I knew myself pretty well, but now I'm just not sure."

"Are you going to abandon it all and come live in the woods, like me?" Rowan was only half teasing her. She'd fantasized about making a home with Jamie many times over the last few weeks. The silence between them was deafening as Jamie seemed to consider how she would answer. Rowan stopped what she was doing and watched a million emotions flash through Jamie's eyes.

"I can't."

"You can't?" The irritation in Rowan's voice was purely accidental, and she immediately regretted it. "I understand. It's not the life for everyone. It can be lonely and maddening when you don't have someone to share it with."

"Is that what you want?" Jamie asked. "Someone to share your life. You've seemed pretty content to be alone."

Rowan ran her hands across the board and leaned it against the shed with the other one before looking directly into Jamie's eyes. "Just about everyone wants someone to share their life. It's human nature. The trick is to find someone who wants the same things out of that life as you. You can't force a person to be someone they aren't."

"No, I suppose you're right. Not if you want the person to be happy."

The rhythmic sound of metal against wood filled the room as neither spoke. What else could be said? Any flirtation between them was just that, flirtation, and nothing more. It could never be anything more because they lived very different lives in different worlds. When Jamie didn't get up to leave, Rowan felt like she had to say something to break the awkward silence.

"How's your research going? I see you working away, and you seem satisfied, but I sometimes forget to ask."

"It's good. The conditions are right. The terrain looks good. The weather has been ideal. I think we may need to spread out a bit and widen our search area. Do you know of any patches of crowberries?"

"Sure." Rowan nodded. "It grows in rockier areas than we've been, but there's a lot about two miles from the place we've been looking."

"Really?" Jamie sat up, more excited than Rowan had seen her in days. "That might be exactly what we need. Do you think we could go there tomorrow?"

Rowan looked at the partially completed bed. If she worked into the evening, she thought she'd be able to finish before bedtime, and they could leave early the following day. "Sure." Jamie's smile was contagious. Rowan drank the last of her coffee and shook her head. The lightness she felt from making Jamie happy was becoming habit-forming.

CHAPTER FIFTEEN

The area where the crowberries were growing had been more rugged than Jamie expected, but it was an ideal place to focus her search. The curlew was known to breed in rocky areas like this. It was beautiful in its own way. Thickets of white spruce and green alder surrounded large boulders and rocky patches. A carpet of green crowberry wove its way through the rocks, clinging to the smooth bedrock. Alaska had many landscapes like that—familiar yet alien.

They'd spent the day collecting the recording equipment from the old location and setting it up in the new spot. A few cameras were left at the old site, but most were moved to focus on the crowberries. They'd retrieved three more days' worth of footage from the old location, so Jamie was eager to get back to the cabin to review it. A warm fire and hot meal would do wonders to bring the feeling back to her cold extremities.

"I think I'm ready to head back when you are." Jamie adjusted the last camera and powered it on. "I've just about lost the feeling in my fingers at this point."

Rowan packed up the last of the equipment they'd brought and slung her pack onto her back. "I'm ready when you are. You up for a detour?"

The last thing Jamie wanted was to delay her date with a cup of hot cocoa and a warm fire, but Rowan had done so much for her she didn't have the heart to say no. "Sure."

A warm arm wrapped around her shoulders and pulled her close. "I promise it'll be worth the effort." Rowan pulled Jamie along as they headed off the trail they'd made on the way there that morning and toward a thickly wooded area in the distance.

"Are you going to tell me where we're going?" Jamie asked.

"Nope."

"Do I get a hint?"

"Nope. Well, we aren't going to the cabin yet. There's your hint."

Jamie smacked Rowan's stomach and wrapped an arm around her waist to steal some of her warmth. "You're a jerk."

"Yep."

"You and those one-word answers. Have you always been a woman of few words?"

"Yep." Rowan winked at Jamie and laughed when she rolled her eyes.

"You're a pain in the ass. Did you know that?"

The shade of the trees when they stepped into the forested area made it even colder than it had been before. It helped that their branches blocked the wind but not enough to make a huge difference.

"A few people may have mentioned that before."

Jamie looked up into deep brown eyes and remembered why she put up with her. "It's a good thing you're so cute."

"Cute? You think I'm cute?"

The confused look on Rowan's face only enhanced Jamie's earlier assessment. "Of course I think you're cute."

"Is that something an adult wants another adult to think of them, or am I like some niece or nephew where you pinch their cheeks and spoil them with candy? Watch your step." Rowan held out her hand to help Jamie up a steep, rocky hill. When they reached the top, Jamie continued holding Rowan's hand.

"I definitely don't look at you with aunt-type feelings, Ranger Fleming."

Rowan laughed and rubbed her thumb along the side of Jamie's hand. "When you're flirting with me, you call me Ranger Fleming. It's funny."

"Who said I'm flirting with you?" Jamie was absolutely flirting with her. They'd played this innocent little game for days now without calling it as it was. She was curious to know how Rowan felt about it. Jamie was entirely on board with flirting and more, but she wasn't sure where they stood with each other on the subject.

"I've spent a lot of time alone, especially in the last few years, but I can certainly tell when someone is flirting with me. You, Dr. Martin, are a flirt."

"Does that bother you?" Jamie allowed Rowan to pull her to a stop when they came to a small stream that intersected their path.

"No. Here, let me help you." Rowan took Jamie's pack so she could more easily jump over the stream. Once Jamie was on the other side, Rowan tossed her the pack and jumped over. "I'm out of practice, but it's nice as long as we're on the same page."

"What page is that?"

Rowan stopped to help Jamie get her pack back on. In the shuffle to get it situated, the knit cap she'd been wearing fell to the ground. Jamie stared at it and wondered if she could get through the next few weeks without it since picking it up with as tired as her legs already were, wasn't an appealing option. With the ease of someone in much better shape than her, Rowan stooped down with her much larger pack still strapped to her back and picked up the cap. "You're kinda my hero," Jamie said as Rowan pulled it onto her head and down to cover her ears.

"I guess the page where this is all just innocent flirting." With a gloved index finger, she booped the tip of Jamie's nose.

"As opposed to what?"

"Something more, I guess. Something serious."

Visions of a serious relationship with Rowan had sparked a fantasy or two of hers over the last few weeks. Still, she'd never actually considered it as a possibility. It couldn't be. Not only did they live too far apart, but they both had legitimate reasons their circumstances couldn't change. It was fine and hadn't been something that made Jamie sad until that moment. For Rowan to mention it had to mean that the thought had crossed her mind, and apparently, she'd come to the same conclusion that Jamie had. The idea that Rowan agreed they couldn't be together somehow hurt more than Jamie realized it would.

The sounds of the forest and their boots against the earth were the only things they heard as they walked silently side by side. Jamie wanted to reach out and retake Rowan's hand, but she suddenly felt too shy to touch her. This wasn't what she wanted. They couldn't spend the rest of their time together, uncomfortable in each other's presence. Jamie wanted to break the silence but couldn't decide what to say.

"Tell me about where you live?" Rowan asked, obviously thinking the same thing Jamie was.

"You've never been to Monterey?"

Rowan shook her head. "No, I've been to Monterey several times. I love it. I'm talking about your house, apartment, or wherever you live. Do you rent, or did you buy?"

"I rent a little bungalow next to a gigantic home on 17-Mile Drive in Carmel. It's owned by a wealthy couple my dad knows who only spend two weeks there every year. They give me a great deal, and I make sure everything is okay with their house when they're gone."

A sharp whistle from Rowan pierced the air. "Wow-we, 17-Mile Drive is swanky. Do you have photos of it?"

"I think I have a couple on my laptop. I'll look when we get back."

"I couldn't live somewhere that fancy, but I bet you have an amazing view."

Jamie nodded. "The main house backs up to the water, so it blocks the view for me, but I can hear the ocean at night if I leave my bedroom window open. It's amazing. Traffic can be a pain in the ass during tourist season, and don't get me started on what it looks like when there's a golf tournament happening. I try to find somewhere else to stay when that mess is going on. I used to stay with my parents, but I haven't really wanted to spend much time at the house since my mom died. Too many memories."

"Did you grow up in that house?" Rowan asked.

"Yeah. It's in Santa Barbara, so about four hours south of where I live now. Not that my dad spends much time in that house. I'm not sure why he hasn't sold it now that my mom is gone."

The thought of her dad selling her childhood home made her sad, but it might allow her to let go of some of her sadness. Knowing another family lived there, someone else's things filled the rooms, might help bring closure to some of the pain she still felt about losing her mom.

"How much farther until we're at this mysterious place you're taking me?" Jamie realized they'd been following the stream they crossed that was now widening into more of a river. Rocks buried under the water caused it to churn in circles. It looked treacherous but beautiful. She thought she could just make out the sound of a waterfall in the distance, but they were still too far away to know for sure.

"Not too much farther."

"I hope whatever it is, it's worth all this extra hiking."

Rowan slowed to allow Jamie a chance to catch up. Her longer stride left Jamie struggling to keep up.

"I promise it'll be worth it. I'll even throw in a massage."

A vision of Rowan straddling a naked Jamie, working her muscles in a deep massage, put a lump in her throat. Her eyes darted to Rowan's powerful hands. There was no doubt in her mind that Rowan could give her a fantastic massage.

"Hey, are you okay?" Rowan reached out and squeezed Jamie's arm.

Jamie cleared her throat. "Yeah, sorry, my mind got lost for a minute." The sound of the waterfall was getting louder, and Jamie noticed the river had quickly grown much larger than it was before. "How are we going to get back? Isn't the cabin on the other side of this river?"

"It is." Rowan took Jamie's hand and pulled her toward a hill to their left. When they reached the top, Jamie looked down the waterfall's face to a gorgeous pool below. Billowy steam floated through the air like fog, rising from the deepest part of the pool.

"What is this? It's beautiful."

"This, my friend, is the hot springs. The river is snow runoff from the mountains over there." Rowan pointed toward an enormous mountain range in the distance. "The cold water feeds this river that pours over the cliff and cools the hot spring below, making it safe for us to swim in."

"You're kidding me?" Jamie had never heard of such a thing.

"I'm not kidding. I've heard of this place, but it's so remote, few people make the hike. You can't land a helicopter near enough to bring lazy tourists in, so this is reserved for those who are willing to sacrifice to get here."

"How are we supposed to get down there? There's no way I will jump off of this waterfall, Rowan. I've learned to trust you, but that's my limit."

Rowan laughed and tugged her back down the hill. "No jumping off of waterfalls for you, got it. It would be too dangerous, anyway. You could potentially dive too deep, and the deeper water will be incredibly hot."

Jamie allowed Rowan to lead her down a steep path that took them along the side of the waterfall. Loose gravel cascaded down the path as Rowan used her sturdy legs to control their descent.

"You have a gift for getting me into harrowing situations," Jamie said as she clung to Rowan's arm like it was the only thing stopping her from falling to her death.

"At least I'm not boring." Rowan grabbed a branch to stop their slide. She held onto Jamie as the rocks and dirt that had been pushing them down the hill slid past them. "Let's stop for a few seconds and let things settle. When everything has momentum, it can sometimes be difficult to keep control. This loose dirt and gravel will sweep us right down with it if we allow it the opportunity."

"Good idea."

"Hold me tight."

"What?"

Rowan pulled Jamie's arms around her waist. "Hold on to me so I can use my arm."

"Okay." Jamie's feet felt like they would slip, and she'd go rolling down the rest of the way, completely out of control.

"This next part is the steepest, so I'm going to toss our packs down ahead of us. The extra weight is causing us to go faster than I'm comfortable with."

Jamie nodded and let go of Rowan with one arm to unsnap the cinch holding her pack in place and slipped her arm from the strap. The bag dangled from one shoulder, so she wrapped her arm back around Rowan's waist and released the other so they could pull the pack free. Rowan tossed it down the hill, and Jamie watched as it stirred up more loose dirt on its way.

"Now mine. You just hold on to me and don't let go, okay?"

"Okay." Jamie stared at the pack that had finally come to rest against a tree at the bottom of the hill.

"Hey." Rowan used her free hand to caress the edge of Jamie's jaw with her thumb. Jamie looked up into those deep brown eyes and drew on the comfort she found there. "I'm sorry I keep getting you into these situations where your fear of heights comes into play."

Rowan unsnapped the cinch around her chest, releasing her pack. She slipped her free arm from the strap and shifted them both so she could hold the tree with her other arm and slip the pack off and toss it down with the other one.

"I didn't realize how much heights bothered me until we came here."

"Isn't it strange for someone who studies birds to be afraid of heights?"

Jamie couldn't help but laugh and squeeze Rowan a little tighter. "I study them when I'm on the ground, smartass."

"Let's get you back on horizontal ground then, yeah?"

After one last glance at what lay ahead of them, Jamie nodded and held on tight.

CHAPTER SIXTEEN

Warm steam rose from the water and created an ethereal landscape around them. Rowan watched as Jamie walked along the shore, peering into the clear blue depths.

"You said we could swim in this water?"

"Yep." Rowan pulled off her cap and jacket before sitting on the sandy beach to remove her boots and socks. "What are you waiting for?"

"Um." Jamie looked down at her body and back up at Rowan. "I didn't bring anything to swim in."

"Sure you did." Rowan stood and unbuttoned her red and black flannel shirt. "Haven't you ever been skinny dipping?"

"What?" Jamie looked around as if waiting for someone to come out of the trees. "Are you kidding?"

"No. Why is that so weird?" Rowan pulled the hem of her thermal undershirt from her pants and slipped it off, letting it drop to the ground next to her. Her breasts were small enough that she seldom wore a bra, especially when she was in the woods under layers of clothing already. "Are you okay?"

Jamie looked away from Rowan's body and unzipped her jacket, dropping it on the beach. "Yeah, I'm fine." The hungry gaze she'd had wasn't lost on Rowan. She knew Jamie felt the same attraction she did, and there was a mischievous part of her that enjoyed teasing her.

Clad only in jeans, Rowan walked over to Jamie and dropped to her knees to untie her boots. Jamie placed a hand on Rowan's shoulder for support as her boots and socks were removed. "Thanks," Jamie said, never taking her eyes off of Rowan's body.

"You bet. Do you need help with the rest?"

"No," Jamie croaked. "No, thanks. I've got it."

Rowan nodded and stepped away to unbuckle her wide leather belt and unbutton her jeans. Once she'd removed the rest of her clothes, she turned back to Jamie to find her folding the last of her clothing and placing it in a neat pile on the beach.

She took the time to admire Jamie's newly exposed body before offering her hand. "You ready?"

Jamie nodded and allowed Rowan to lead her to the water's edge. She'd heard of this place from several people but didn't want to risk Jamie getting hurt before making sure the water temperature was safe, so she motioned for her to wait while Rowan slowly stepped in. The warmth surrounded her as she got deep enough for it to cover her shoulders. Once satisfied, she waved for Jamie to follow her. "Come on in. It's perfect."

Hesitantly, Jamie waded in. "Ow, how in the world did you walk on these rocks so easily. Am I just that delicate?"

Each step she took was obviously difficult, so Rowan waded over to her and offered her hand. "Would you like some help, milady?"

"Thank you, my knight. Ow!" Jamie shifted dramatically to her left and fell into Rowan's arms. The sudden closeness of their naked bodies made Rowan gasp as she looked down into equally surprised green eyes.

"Easy there," Rowan said. She wasn't sure if she should continue holding Jamie or step back to give her space. The feeling of her soft skin against her caused her nipples to tighten embarrassingly hard. "I, um, can you stand on your own?"

Jamie looked into Rowan's eyes and smiled. "I'm not sure. Would you mind helping me the rest of the way?"

"Sure, yeah, of course." Rowan shook nervously as she scooped Jamie into her arms and carried her deeper into the water until she could tread and not put as much weight on her feet. "Better?" The water swirled around them as Rowan stepped back to put distance between their bodies. "I'm sorry the rocks were rough. I'm so used to walking around barefoot, I'm sure I've built up more of a resistance to that kind of thing."

Steam circled them as it rose from the water toward the sky. "I'm sorry I'm such a tenderfoot. I realize I spend far too much time in a building and not nearly enough outside."

"I guess I thought you would spend a good deal of time out in nature doing research-type things, considering that's what you study and all."

Frown lines creased Jamie's forehead as she watched the water swirl around them. Rowan was afraid she had said something to upset her. "I'm sorry if I—"

"No, sorry, you didn't say anything wrong. It's something I've been struggling with lately, and I'm honestly not sure how to react to questions about it."

"What do you mean?"

Jamie slipped on another rock, and Rowan reached out to steady her. She hoped the contact was acceptable because seeing Jamie struggle to steady herself was difficult to watch without offering help. "Is this okay?" Rowan asked, indicating their joined hands.

"It's appreciated, yes. You look like this sturdy tree coming out of the water, and I feel like a little fishing float bobbing along with the current. How do you do it?"

Rowan threaded their fingers together and offered her other hand so Jamie would feel more secure. "I spent a good deal of time in the water when I was in California. I did a lot of hikes and wasted many days swimming in lakes and rivers with pretty strong currents."

"Is that when you became so comfortable skinny dipping with random women?"

"Would you consider yourself random? I think we can safely move you past that category." Rowan pulled Jamie closer while still leaving some space between their bodies. The clear water did nothing to hide the gentle slope of Jamie's breasts or the subtle curve of her clavicle, begging to be kissed. Rowan cleared her throat and looked up into Jamie's eyes when she realized she'd been staring. "Sorry."

"No need to apologize." Jamie released her hands and slid hers along Rowan's forearms to grip her biceps. The move placed them even closer but still left space between their bodies. "It's been a long time since someone looked at me so appreciatively."

"You must not leave your office very often, then."

Jamie looked away, and Rowan knew she'd once again said

something that had inadvertently struck a nerve. "I'm sorry. I seem to have a habit of saying things that make your forehead get that cute little wrinkle."

"No, it's not you." Jamie turned back to Rowan and smiled. "Being locked away at the PWCA and not out in the field is something that has bothered me for a while. I think I'm embarrassed about it."

"Embarrassed about what? Isn't your position a big deal? I don't know much about the PWCA, but I used to know the curator of ornithology at the Natural History Museum in Los Angeles."

"Dr. Amyx?"

"Yeah, Janene. She was in a hiking group I belonged to when I lived down there. I know her position was a huge deal, so I have to imagine the assistant curator of such a prestigious aquarium as the PWCA has to be an impressive accomplishment."

Jamie shrugged. "I'm a pretty big deal."

"And modest, I see." Rowan softened the comment with a wink.

"The problem with being a big deal is it includes a lot of paperwork and administration stuff that I don't know if I realized came with the title. I feel like I worked so hard to get where I am, and sometimes, I'm worried I might have made a mistake. There's no turning back now, though."

"Why not?" Rowan asked.

"Because I'm so close to getting what I want."

"What is that?"

"Director of the PWCA. I think I could make a real difference if I had the authority to direct more of the focus to the ornithology department. They rightfully focus the majority of the funds in the aquarium to aquatic creatures. I get that. And mammals like sea otters help bring people in the door, but I think if I was in a better position to advocate for more resources to go toward the research of shorebirds, there's no telling what we will learn."

"So, what's your sacrifice? Not doing the things you want to do?"

"Well, I'm doing things I want to do. I just wish there was more time for me to do research. Like I'm doing now."

Rowan knew she needed to tread carefully. Jamie had already clarified that this subject was a sensitive one for her and the last thing Rowan wanted to do was make her feel bad about her choices, even though it was clear to her that her current position wasn't making her happy. She decided it was probably safer to revisit the discussion at another time.

"Okay, Dr. Martin, we're going to play three questions. You get to ask me three questions, and I can ask you three questions, but they can't be about family members or our careers."

The way Jamie perked up, Rowan could tell this was a game she would enjoy, and Rowan would probably regret suggesting. She hoped by excluding family and careers, they would avoid the things Rowan wasn't ready to discuss. This was probably a huge mistake.

"Question one." Jamie had an exaggeratedly thoughtful look on her face as if she was solving world hunger, and it was taking every ounce of brainpower she had.

"Who said you get to ask the first question?" Rowan asked.

Jamie dismissed her question with a wave. "Question one, how old were you when you came out?"

Rowan's coming-out story was such a boring one that she'd always been a little embarrassed to tell people. Most of her lesbian friends had dramatic stories of self-discovery, and Rowan's experience just wasn't that exciting.

"I don't think I really ever came out. It was something I just always knew, and my mom and family never seemed like it was a big deal. It probably helped that I have a lesbian aunt and gay older cousin. I didn't realize exactly how traumatic coming out could be until I went away to college and heard other people's stories. I've always felt a little guilty about it."

Small hands squeezed Rowan's biceps reassuringly. "Don't feel guilty. I'm glad your family was so supportive of you. That's amazing."

"What about you?" Rowan asked.

Jamie shrugged. "This is getting dangerously close to talking about family."

"You don't have to answer, but I'll remind you that you're the one who asked the question in the first place."

"You're absolutely right. I'll just say that my mom was supportive, and my dad wasn't. We'll leave it at that."

"Sounds good. Sorry about your dad. My turn?"

A soft blond lock fell onto Jamie's forehead when she nodded. Rowan brushed it away before asking her question. "Okay, not including humans, what is your favorite mammal?"

"Easy, elephant."

"Really?" Rowan asked.

"Can you think of a cooler mammal than an elephant?"

"Nope, elephants are amazing. They're probably my favorite, too. I also like the platypus. They seem a little unhinged."

A bright smile crossed Jamie's face, and Rowan had an overwhelming urge to kiss her. She'd never enjoyed talking to another person as much as she did Jamie. It didn't really matter what they discussed. Rowan craved as much attention as Jamie would give her.

"Hey, where'd you go?" Jamie asked.

"Nowhere, sorry, next question."

"What's your sign?"

"As in my astrological sign?"

"Yep."

"I didn't think scientist types were into that kind of mumbo jumbo." Rowan dodged a smack from Jamie.

"Are you refusing to answer my question?"

"Not at all. Capricorn, I think."

Jamie's forehead creased in the adorable way Rowan loved. "Really? When is your birthday?"

"Is that really your third question?" Rowan asked.

"Nope. Never mind. What's your next question?"

"When is your birthday?"

"July twentieth."

"As in a few days from now?" Rowan was suddenly happy she'd asked.

"Yep."

"Cool. Okay, last question?" Rowan asked.

"You go first. I'll save mine for after."

Rowan took her time considering what her last question would be. She wanted to make it a good one. She was enjoying learning more about Jamie. She couldn't remember the last time she'd had so much fun talking to someone about nothing and everything. She wasn't sure she'd ever really had a relationship with another person like that. It hadn't ever been something she thought she was missing in her life, but here she was, craving every little detail Jamie would share. It was a confusing feeling that made her tingle instead of wanting to shut down and close herself off. Jamie didn't feel like a threat, which wasn't something Rowan was accustomed to feeling.

"Are you going to ask me a question, or do I get an extra one?" Jamie asked.

"Okay, okay, hold your horses. Was your first kiss a girl or a boy?"

"Wow, that's why it took you so long to ask. Okay." Jamie tilted her head and studied Rowan's face. Her expression worried Rowan; maybe she shouldn't have asked such a personal question.

"You don't have to—"

"No, I'll answer. I'm just trying to decide if you'll judge me for my answer."

"Why would I judge you for your answer?"

"I don't know. People can be judgmental," Jamie said.

Rowan pulled Jamie's body a little closer, still leaving a small gap between them. "I promise, no judgment. I hope you know you can say anything to me."

"I do. Boy. My first kiss was a boy, and there were other boys after him. I've mostly dated women, but a few boys were scattered in there. My first experience with a woman was in college, and it didn't end well, which led to a bit of a crisis of confidence. Even though I knew I was attracted to women in my heart, the fear of disappointing my conservative father was always in the back of my mind. I knew what would make him happy, and at that point in my life, it was important to me to be who I thought he wanted me to be."

"You don't feel that way now?"

"About being who my father thinks I should be or my attraction to men?"

"Either. Both." Rowan knew they'd agreed not to talk about family, and she wasn't proud of herself for breaking her own rules, but now that this subject had come up, she wanted to know. If Jamie was willing to share.

"That's question number four," Jamie said.

"You don't have to answer if you don't want to."

"I want my dad to be proud of me. Every kid wants their parent to love and respect them, especially when they only have one parent left, but his opinions no longer guide my life the way they once did. I'm happy when I get his approval, but I don't only consider his approval when making my decisions. I occasionally ask for his advice, but I'm the captain of my ship. No matter how much that frustrates and sometimes disappoints him."

"Is that personally, professionally, or both?"

Jamie shook her head and placed a delicate finger on Rowan's lips to silence her. "That's five questions."

Rowan smiled at the playful tone in her voice. "I'll do all the dishes for the week."

"Fine. Personally, I don't give a shit what my dad thinks. He doesn't ask me about my personal life, and I don't share intimate details. It's been an unspoken agreement between us since I was young. My mom was more of a confidant where my love life was concerned. She was very supportive and a good sounding board when I felt a little lost. Professionally, he pushes me to always reach for more. He wants me to succeed, and as a driven person, I appreciate having a cheerleader in my corner."

The soft curve of Jamie's leg caressed her as she pressed it against Rowan. The movement caught her by surprise. They were close enough at this point that Jamie could feel the gentle pressure of her breasts against Rowan's smaller, firm ones.

"Now, as for whether I'm more attracted to boys or girls, I realized a long time ago that while I'm attracted to all kinds of women, boyish girls are my weakness." Jamie slid a hand behind Rowan's neck and pulled her head down, so their lips were only a whisper apart. Rowan's heart pounded in her ears as her breathing completely stopped. "Are you ready for my third question?"

Rowan silently nodded, afraid that it would somehow break the spell they were under if she spoke.

"Are you going to kiss me, Ranger Fleming?"

All of Rowan's reservations were forgotten as she pressed her lips against Jamie's. Muscular legs wrapped around Rowan's waist as Jamie nipped at her bottom lip, asking permission to deepen their contact. Rowan's hands caressed silky smooth skin on their way down Jamie's sides, coming to rest on the curve of her ass. A moan escaped Jamie's mouth when she rubbed her center against the firmness of Rowan's abdominal muscles. The soft wetness of her pussy was somehow distinguishable from the warm water they were in, as Rowan used her own body to create friction where Jamie needed it. She was desperate to have her. The attraction she'd tried to ignore came rushing through her. It threatened to engulf her in a flood of emotions she realized she wasn't ready to handle.

Things were rapidly getting out of hand, and Rowan knew she should stop it but struggled to find the will to do so. She wanted this. Jamie obviously wanted it, too, yet this was a tiger they wouldn't be able to put back in its cage. It was completely unprofessional, and they still had weeks together, in a remote cabin, alone. The last thing they needed was to get caught up in a situation where they could be at odds with each other with nowhere to go. At the very least, they should have a conversation about what this meant, and what their expectations were before things went any further. Right? Allowing her brain to control her libido once again, Rowan pulled away from the kiss and pressed her head against Jamie's. They both struggled to catch their breath as they clung to each other.

"I'm—that was—"

"Fucking amazing," Jamie said.

"Yeah, and maybe not the best decision."

The look on Jamie's face made Rowan wish she could take her words back. The last thing she wanted to do was hurt her, and it was clear she'd done just that.

Jamie's legs slid from Rowan's waist, and she stepped back, once again putting a space between their bodies. "Okay. I'm sorry, I thought—"

"No, no, no, don't misunderstand me, that was fucking hot. Like short-circuit my brain hot. I think we need to think about this before we do something that will affect the rest of our time here and potentially your work. Do you know what I mean?"

Jamie folded her arms over her chest and nodded. "Sure. Yeah. I completely understand." She looked toward the beach at their pile of dry clothes. "We should probably get going. I assume we have a long hike ahead of us to get back to the cabin." Jamie turned and hobbled toward the beach, trying to navigate her way across the jagged rocks.

"Hey, let me help." Rowan reached out to pick her up so she could carry her back, but Jamie pulled her arm from her grasp. "Jamie—"

"It's okay, Rowan. I get it. You're probably right. I'd just rather not be carried right now."

Rowan lifted her hands in surrender. "No problem. I'm sorry if I upset you." Rowan hadn't moved from her spot in the water, not sure if she should follow Jamie or give her some space to get dressed first. At a loss for what else to do, she turned away to give her privacy. She knew she'd made the right decision to stop things before they escalated, but she regretted the way she'd done it. Now that she knew how Jamie's body felt against hers, it was going to be difficult enough not to want more. Rowan just hoped she'd forgive her.

CHAPTER SEVENTEEN

The pencil Jamie had been holding slid across the page, leaving a dark line in its wake. Realizing she'd nodded off, she leaned back and stretched her cramping arms and back. She still had two hours to finish reviewing the last of the video footage they'd retrieved on their most recent hike to the site, but she couldn't continue without taking a break. Combing through hours of footage, listening, and watching for anything that could even remotely be a curlew had proven to be a frustrating endeavor. Jamie needed to step away and get something to eat, or she might miss an important detail. She stood and stretched again, trying to release the knots in her muscles from a long day of sitting in her work area.

There had been tension between them since the kiss at the hot springs a few days before. Jamie wanted to do or say something that could magically fix whatever they had broken, but she didn't know how to do that. She shouldn't have acted on her attraction to Rowan. She'd thought she was reading the same signals from her, but apparently not. That kiss, though. There was no denying they had chemistry between them. Red, hot, burst-into-flames chemistry that she couldn't get out of her mind. Now that the genie was out of the bottle, there was no putting it back in. She wasn't positive she would if she could. She hated the tension between them, but my God, that kiss was spectacular.

She'd thought she might come right there, rubbing against Rowan's muscular body in the middle of a pool in the remote wilds of Alaska. She had wanted to come. Desperately. Jamie's nipples hardened at the memory of that day. The hike there had been arduous, but the time they spent enveloped in the warm water after so many weeks of sponge baths had made the aches from the extra work worth every step.

Her one regret was pushing Rowan into something she obviously wasn't ready to handle. Jamie was no longer convinced Rowan was even interested in her. She'd seemed very willing at first, but as things escalated, she pulled away. The flirtatious relationship they'd had before that day had all but come to a stop. Things were cordial between them. They chatted about dinner and the weather, but nothing of substance and especially nothing about how they felt about each other. Jamie had never really felt the closeness she had with Rowan with anyone else, and the sudden distance left her feeling colder and more alone than she had since she was a child. She knew they needed to talk. Waiting for Rowan to come to her when she was ready was getting them nowhere.

Jamie moved the mouse to wake her laptop back up so she could shut down her equipment. There was no sense in wasting precious battery life if she took a break. She'd give anything for an internet connection or some other thread to the outside world other than the local bush radio messages they listened to every evening. Most of that information was local weather, which was apparently just a guess since it was only correct about half the time, personal messages from family members of the other people living in remote cabins in the area, and ramblings of the very odd and very bored radio host. Jamie chuckled at how excited she and Rowan were to listen to the radio every evening. It had become an essential part of their routine and something they enjoyed doing together.

She fleetingly wondered what her dad would think of that. She doubted he would understand. Today, he was a very different person than when he led a more adventurous life. The older, politician version of her father wouldn't be capable of disconnecting from the hustle and bustle of the modern, plugged-in life he led today. He had people who catered to his every need and hung on his every word. He told her many times that he wanted that life for her. Maybe not a political one, but a life where her position commanded respect. Where when she spoke, people listened and followed her lead. Jamie had always thought she wanted that, too, but as she looked around the quiet room, she wondered.

Her laptop snapped shut as she pushed the screen down. She took one last glance at the equipment, checking for rogue lights indicating she'd forgotten to power something off, before sliding into her boots and heading outside to search for Rowan.

"Rowan?" Jamie called. "Where are you?" She stepped off the porch and walked back to the shed behind the cabin when there was no answer. When she didn't find her there, she called again. "Rowan?"

"Here," Rowan called back from her left. Jamie walked around to the other side of the cabin and found her digging a large hole in the ground. "Everything okay?" Rowan asked, wiping the sweat from her brow with a handkerchief she kept tucked away in her back pocket.

"Yeah, fine." Jamie cleared her throat and tried not to be too obvious about how good she thought Rowan looked with her muscles rippling beneath her white tank top. "So, um, what's this?" she asked, indicating the hole Rowan was digging.

"Just something I've been working on," Rowan vaguely replied. "How were the recordings? Did you get anything useful?"

Jamie shook her head. "Nope. Still nothing. Would you mind taking a break? I'd love to sit down and chat if you have the time."

Rowan checked the time on her watch, then pulled a tape measure from her belt to measure the diameter of the hole. "Do you mind if we talk this evening after dinner? I really want to get this done."

She wanted to say no. The longer they put off their conversation, the more distance there was between them. "Sure. Are you hungry? I could cook one of the fish you caught yesterday. I think we have mushrooms and onion left, too."

Rowan nodded. "That sounds amazing. Give me a yell, and I'll come in when it's ready."

The light was dimming when Jamie finished making their dinner, and they could finally sit down to enjoy it. She rarely drank wine, but she would have given anything for a glass at that moment. Anything to help break the uncomfortable spell they seemed to be under.

"Hey, Rowan?"

"Dinner is amazing. You're getting good at being creative with the spices we have and putting together something special instead of just the same old thing over and over. I appreciate your efforts."

"Oh, thanks. I try to experiment, and so far, it's been pretty successful."

Jamie took another bite of her food and watched Rowan stack her fork with potatoes and mushrooms before putting them in her mouth. "Do you mind if we talk about what happened the other day at the hot springs?"

Rowan stopped chewing and regarded Jamie thoughtfully. She didn't seem upset, but she also didn't appear to be ready to respond.

"It's just that we haven't discussed it, and I feel you pulling back from me. I would hate to think I did something that upset you."

They sat silently for a minute. Jamie was afraid to do anything that would cause Rowan to pull even further away, so she sat patiently and waited for what seemed like a lifetime.

It surprised her when Rowan slid her hand across the table and took Jamie's in hers. "You didn't upset me. Just the opposite, in fact. It isn't like I hadn't been thinking about kissing you for weeks. I know I hurt you when I stopped the kiss, and I apologize for that. The fear of getting too carried away and doing something we might regret later worried me. I don't want that. Not only do I enjoy working with you, but I also enjoy spending time with you. I'm afraid it will get super awkward if we make things sexual between us."

"I get that, but we're adults, Rowan. I know the score, and I think you do, too. We've been upfront with each other as far as expectations. I think we can handle some flirting." Jamie stood and took both of their plates to the sink to be washed. "Just your classic story of two friends with very relaxed rules regarding physical contact and affection while they're stuck in the wildness alone, together. It doesn't mean we're going to fall in love with each other."

"I know," Rowan agreed a little too quickly. She sat back in her chair and studied Jamie. "Okay. I'll stop fretting over what's going to happen and accept that we're both adults and know what we're doing and what we're capable of."

"Okay. Good."

"I think we should keep things PG-13, though."

"How do you mean?" Jamie asked.

"You know, like flirting, kissing, making out, stuff like that. But not sex. Sex requires an entirely different conversation."

The no sex rule was disappointing, but Jamie understood where Rowan was coming from. She wasn't the type of person who could easily separate casual sex from something that meant more than they could offer each other out here. Jamie respected that and would do her best to be satisfied with the more innocent physical relationship Rowan was suggesting. It would be fine. It wasn't like she needed to have sex with Rowan. She could easily only be her snuggle partner.

Jamie dried her hands on a towel and walked over to the table where Rowan still sat. The light from the fire in the stove cast shadows in the dimly lit room as they stared at each other as if waiting for someone to make the first move. Finally, Jamie leaned down and pressed her lips to Rowan's. The kiss wasn't the passionate, desperate one from the hot springs, but it was nice. Rowan allowed Jamie to place kisses along her jaw and tilt her head slightly to the side so she could whisper to her. "Thank you."

When she pulled back, Rowan smiled and rubbed her hands over the blush on her cheeks. The gesture was adorable.

"I guess I better—"

"Can I show you something?" Rowan asked.

"Sure." Jamie allowed Rowan to guide her to the door, where she pulled Jamie's coat from the peg and helped her slip it on. "What's going on?"

Rowan shrugged and put on her own jacket. "Let's go see."

Jamie did as she was told and allowed Rowan to lead her down the porch steps and into the yard. There was a bite from the cold, but she felt warmth and what sounded like the crackle of a fire after a few feet. The hole Rowan had been digging earlier had been transformed into a firepit. Red bricks lined the sides and were stacked a foot above the ground. There were logs stacked next to it, waiting to be added to the fire, and a handmade bench sat close enough for someone to enjoy the warmth. "You made a firepit?"

"I did. I found bricks in the shed that were probably left over from the old chimney they had before they put the stove in." Rowan encouraged Jamie to sit on the bench near the fire. Once settled, Rowan tossed in more wood to get it going again. "Happy birthday, Jamie." Rowan leaned down to place a gentle kiss on her lips.

"Mm, this is a pleasant surprise." Jamie fanned her hands out near the flames to warm them up. "I can't believe you remembered my birthday and did all of this for me. I thought you were mad at me and avoiding me."

"Nope, sorry, I've been a busy bee. I can sometimes seem a little distant when I'm focused. I was trying not to give anything away."

Rowan sat next to her on the bench and pulled something out of her pocket. "I have one more thing for you." She handed a crudely wrapped object to Jamie before turning away to warm her own hands near the fire.

"What is this?" Jamie turned the wrapped item around in her hands a few times before ripping the paper away.

"I wasn't sure what to carve for you, so I decided to do an albatross. That's your favorite bird, right?"

Jamie felt a warmth that had nothing to do with the fire. She was touched by what Rowan had done but struggled to know exactly how to respond. "Yeah, I can't believe you remembered that."

"You talked about it so passionately when we first got here. How could I ever forget?"

She wiped a tear that threatened to fall and kissed Rowan's cheek. "Thank you so much. I love it." She looked up at the fire and held the carving close to her chest. "All of it. I can't believe you did all this for me."

"Why not? I happen to think you're amazing. I wish I could have done more." Rowan stood to toss another log on the fire, then sat back down next to Jamie.

Jamie took another look at the albatross carving, back at the fire, and finally at Rowan. She couldn't remember anyone ever putting so much effort into doing something special for her, even on her birthday. She usually got a call from her parents, and her friends would take her out for dinner and drinks, but nothing like this. Nothing with so much care and consideration. "This is everything I could have ever wanted. Thank you."

Her heart was so full she was sure it would burst. Jamie rested her head on Rowan's shoulder and snuggled in to watch the fire. There was nowhere in the world she'd rather be for her birthday than on that homemade bench with Rowan. "We're going to be friends for a very long time."

"I hope so," Rowan said. "I hope so."

CHAPTER EIGHTEEN

They'd walked the trail back from the site to the cabin so many times in the last almost two months that Rowan could practically do it in her sleep. In theory, at least. There were still threats she needed to keep an eye out for, so she could never truly let her guard down, but they both had every step of the path memorized.

Initially, they had filled their time chatting, but after weeks of making the trek every three to four days, they'd fallen into a comfortable companionship. Sometimes they talked, and other times they were content to just listen to their surroundings and enjoy each other's presence. It had turned out to be a surprising turn of events. Rowan would never have thought she could enjoy being with someone as much as she did Jamie. She had friends, and her mother, and coworkers. She was around people all the time, but she always thought about when she would be able to escape back into the solitude of her cabin, or the woods, or her plane. It was a strange feeling, and part of Rowan wanted to run from it, to shut down that part of herself she had left open for someone, for Jamie, to creep into and set up camp.

A sound from their left made Rowan stop short and place a finger on her lips to tell Jamie she should be quiet. They were in a dense area of brush, which made it difficult to see what might come their way until it was already upon them. They both stood utterly still, listening for any other noise. Rowan felt Jamie slide her hand into hers. She squeezed it to reassure her she would be safe. As quietly as they could, Rowan guided them farther down the trail, never dropping Jamie's hand.

Rowan's heart pounded as they made their way through the brush.

Sharp branches dragged against her body as she did her best to shield Jamie, who followed closely pressed up against her back. She stopped every few feet to listen for movement, then moved forward when she heard nothing else. Jamie remained glued to her, silently shadowing Rowan's every step.

There was more than a good chance what she heard could have been a bear. The later they got into the season, the more likely an encounter would happen. It wouldn't be the first time Rowan dealt with a bear. It was far from her first experience with this kind of fear, but somehow the stakes seemed higher this time. This time she had Jamie to think about, and the idea of something happening to her made Rowan's stomach turn.

She'd never forgive herself if anything happened to Jamie. She knew deep down her feelings were something different, more than casual feelings one would have for a friend. More than an obligation as a guide or a ranger or any other professional responsibility she might have. She truly cared for her and would do anything to ensure nothing harmed her.

It wasn't love. These feelings couldn't be romantic. Rowan wasn't worried about where they would lead since they were more like a protectiveness for someone important to her. Someone who depended on her for protection. Nothing more than that.

The feeling of Jamie wrapped snugly against her as they walked gave Rowan comfort. She was okay. They were both going to be fine. A half hour after hearing the first noise, Rowan heard another ahead of them and to the left. It sounded like the bear was traveling southeast, and the trail they were on led them directly south. The only problem with that was where it would put the bear in relation to the cabin when they were finally out of the brush.

Rowan could see the edge of the forest ahead of them and held Jamie in place to give the bear time to get ahead. If there was going to be a confrontation, it was better for it to happen after they'd had time to take in their surroundings instead of immediately after they emerged from the brush.

"Listen, I think it might be a bear, and it's pacing us to the east." Rowan spoke close to Jamie's ear to remain as quiet as possible. Bears had very acute hearing, but Rowan knew the bear was aware of their presence already, so there was no use in pretending they could sneak around it. "We're going to hold up here for a few minutes to let it move through the brush and out into the forest. It hasn't come toward us yet, so with any luck, it will move on and not bother with the stinky humans."

"Hey," Jamie said, lifting her arm to smell her armpit. "Speak for yourself, stinky human."

It was nice to see she still had a sense of humor. That spoke volumes to Rowan about how she reacted in stressful situations. The last thing they needed was for one of them to freak out and do something stupid that ended up getting someone killed. Rowan leaned forward and pressed her lips to her forehead. She brushed the hair from her shoulder to expose the area of her neck below her ear and smelled her skin. "Mm...I'm definitely the only stinky one here."

Jamie shivered in her arms and touched the place on her neck. "If you want me to keep it together, you're going to have to stop doing things that make me want to do things to you we really shouldn't do in the woods with a bear present."

"Oh, really?" Rowan was pleased with her response. "Are you ready to move forward?" Jamie nodded. "Good, we're almost at the edge of the forest, so stay as close to me as possible."

They pressed on toward the safety of their cabin, hypervigilant of their surroundings. Once they were clear of the brush, Rowan could pick up the trail of the bear. "Hey, look at this," she said to Jamie, encouraging her to kneel to see the tracks. "I'd say this is a young boar. The impressions aren't that deep, and since it seems to be alone and without cubs, it could be a young sow or a boar, but my money's on a boar."

"Is that good or bad?" Jamie asked, scanning the area around them for any sign of their new friend.

"I'm going to say good, mostly because a sow and her cubs are the worst things you want to mess with out here. That saying about a mama bear is real. They'll mess you up if you're anywhere near their cubs. We want to avoid that situation. I don't see cub tracks this time, so I think we'll be fine if we give it space. We still need to take this slow and be on alert because bears are unpredictable, and you just never know what will set them off sometimes. Mostly, you can scare them away by making yourself seem bigger and scarier than you are." Rowan looked Jamie up and down. "Leave that to me."

Jamie lightly punched Rowan's arm. "Jerk. So, we're okay to keep moving?"

"Yeah," Rowan said. After one more glance at the tracks, she stood and reclaimed Jamie's hand. "Let's go."

Forty-five minutes later, they could see the peak of the cabin's roof poking out of the trees. Rowan felt the tension ease from her shoulders as they got closer. "Are you okay?" she asked Jamie, still pressed closely against her.

"Yep, just ready to get into the cabin. That scared the—"

The sound of the bear only a few yards away stopped them in their tracks. "Rowan?" Jamie gripped Rowan's arm so tightly she wouldn't be able to do anything if the bear came at them.

"Shh, it's going to be okay. Hold on to my belt but leave my arms free so I can protect us if he comes this way."

"Okay."

Rowan felt Jamie release her arm and tuck her hands around her belt. "He wants nothing to do with us, so let's give him a wide berth. You with me?"

"I'm with you." Jamie's voice shook as she gripped onto Rowan for dear life.

"Okay, we'll go around the back so we can put the cabin between the bear and us, then we'll come around the other side and in through the front door." Rowan pulled the bear spray from her belt and unsnapped her holster so she could quickly grab her gun if she needed it. "Here we go." She guided them to the left, around a few trees, and up a slight embankment toward the back of the cabin. The bear kept his eyes on them the entire time but didn't follow.

"Hey, bear, you want nothing to do with us." Rowan had been in situations like this before, but she knew Jamie was probably scared to death. "We're almost there. Are you doing okay?"

"I'm okay," Jamie said. "Reading about bear encounters gave me much more confidence than I'm feeling right now. I'm literally shaking in my boots."

Rowan led them around the back of the cabin, keeping the structure between them and the bear until they could slip inside. Once they were safe, she turned and wrapped her arms around Jamie, who had begun to cry. "Hey, hey, you're okay. We're safe in here." Rowan's heart hurt to see Jamie cry. Her mind frantically searched for something she could do to reassure her they were safe.

"I'll be okay," Jamie said. "Sometimes, I can turn into a blubbering mess when I'm finally able to release my emotions after a stressful situation. I hate it. I cried after every final exam in college. At least I'm able to keep it under control until I'm alone." Jamie buried her face in Rowan's shirt and let the tears flow. "Your shirt is going to be soaked. I'm sorry."

"It's okay," Rowan said. "It'll dry. Don't be hard on yourself. You did well. I'm proud of you. It all could have gone south quickly, but you kept a level head and did what I asked you to do." Rowan cupped Jamie's face between her hands and wiped the tears from her cheeks with her thumbs. "You were perfect."

The smile on Jamie's face made Rowan never want to let her go. Ignoring her old friend, self-doubt, she bent down and kissed her lips. They were slightly salty from her tears but warm and soft. Rowan could get lost in her kisses and never be found. Jamie traced Rowan's top lip with her tongue, asking permission to deepen the kiss. She happily obliged her request and allowed Jamie to take the lead.

The tension, the research, the bear, all the built-up energy between them just flowed out through that kiss, and Rowan never wanted it to end. It was official. Jamie's kisses were perfection. Before Rowan was ready, Jamie pulled away.

"I'm sor—"

"Will you—"

They both spoke at the same time. "I'm sorry, you go," Rowan said.

"I was going to ask if I could sleep with you in your bed tonight?"

Rowan looked toward the beds. Hers was larger than the one Jamie had been using, but neither was very large. "Sure, yeah, of course."

"I'm still a little shaky. Please stay close to me. I'm not sure I'll be able to sleep without knowing you're next to me." Jamie gave Rowan a pleading look, and she knew she'd never be able to deny her request. Truth be told, Rowan would feel better next to her as well. She'd been scared, too, and she wasn't ready to break the connection between them just yet.

"Absolutely." Rowan wrapped her arms around Jamie and pulled her head to rest against her chest. "I think that would be good for both of us. Should we make some dinner first?"

Jamie glanced at the table, then back up at Rowan. "Are you hungry?"

Rowan shook her head. "Not really. That whole situation kind of made me lose my appetite."

"Me, too. Let's get ready for bed."

For the next half hour, they went about their nightly routine in silence. Rowan wasn't sure if it was because of what they'd been through that day or more to do with the fact that they were about to sleep together in a tiny bed with nowhere to go. Rowan rinsed the toothpaste from her mouth, then turned to find Jamie already in bed. She lifted the covers and invited her to lie next to her. Next to this person she couldn't get out of her mind—the one who was weaving her way into Rowan's heart.

CHAPTER NINETEEN

A cocoon of blankets surrounded Jamie as she was pulled from a deep sleep. Rowan's body pressed against her from behind, and her arm draped over Jamie's waist. She couldn't stop the contented moan as she burrowed backward into the comforting heat and security of Rowan. She could get used to this. Sleeping next to someone else had never been something Jamie thought she needed, but she might have to adjust her opinion on the subject. Rowan's body felt perfect next to hers, and the last thing she wanted was to leave the bed and deal with the tasks she knew they'd have to do that day.

At least they wouldn't need to make another trip out to retrieve the video recordings for a few days. After the scare of the day before, she wasn't ready to venture too far from the cabin anytime soon. Jamie shivered when she thought about how scared she was. She couldn't remember ever being that frightened in her life, but she also somehow knew Rowan would take care of her. There wasn't a second during the entire ordeal when Jamie doubted Rowan would do whatever it took to ensure Jamie was okay. She was almost more afraid of what would happen to Rowan, not herself. Her big, brave ranger had put herself between the bear and Jamie, and now that they were safe, it was all rather swoon-worthy.

Jamie reached down and slipped Rowan's hand under the hem of her shirt, letting it rest on the bare skin of her belly. The warmth of their bodies touching in such an intimate way made Jamie immediately wet.

"Are you okay?" Rowan's sleepy voice startled her from her thoughts.

"Mm, yeah, I'm great. Are you okay?"

Rowan grunted a yes and pulled her hand away from Jamie's stomach. Jamie grabbed it and held it in place. "Please, it feels good."

"Are you sure?" Rowan asked.

"Very sure." Jamie grazed Rowan's hand with her nails and pushed her butt back to press even harder against her groin. Rowan rubbed gentle circles across the exposed skin of her stomach. Jamie felt tiny next to her. Their size difference and knowing Rowan would do anything to protect her amped up Jamie's arousal even more.

"Can I talk you into that massage you keep threatening to give me?"

The bed shifted as Rowan changed positions. "Absolutely. Is your back sore?"

"I think coming down from the tension of yesterday is catching up to me."

Rowan nodded and guided Jamie to lie on her stomach. "Let me see if I can help you with that." Warm hands inched under Jamie's shirt and reverently touched her skin. "Is this okay?"

"You can do it harder. I promise I won't break."

The blankets were lifted as Rowan slid under them to straddle Jamie's body. "I hope I did a good job fixing this bed, or we're going to take a spill."

Jamie's giggle turned into a contented groan as Rowan pressed her thumbs along the muscles on either side of her spine. She started at her lower back and inched up slowly toward her shoulders in waves of pressure followed by gentle strokes. It was glorious.

By the time those deft hands reached the area between her shoulders, Jamie felt like her bones were made of jelly. Rowan's warm, strong hands knew precisely how to ease the ache of the miles of hiking and stress her muscles had held on to for the last few weeks.

"I'm going to contact your boss and make sure you get a raise," Jamie said.

Rowan chuckled and leaned down to place a gentle kiss between her shoulder blades. "I don't think my boss wants to pay me for doing something that's making me feel like this."

Jamie's nerve endings felt like they would burst into flames as Rowan's body rocked against hers.

"Rowan, please," Jamie begged, for exactly what she wasn't sure.

Her breath caught when Rowan's fingers grazed the side of her breasts. A million thoughts raced through her mind, but the only one she understood with any sort of clarity was that she wanted Rowan. Jamie needed her to make her come, and she wasn't exactly sure how to ask for it without seeming as desperate as she felt.

"God, I need…"

Rowan's body shifted again as she moved down the bed to rest between Jamie's legs. Strong hands gripped her hips and aggressively pulled her body back as Rowan pushed forward from behind her. A low growl reverberated in Jamie's ear as Rowan's larger frame slid farther over the top of her, pressing her to the bed. Her nipples hardened and became sensitive as they rubbed against the fabric of her shirt with every thrust of Rowan's hips. They were still fully clothed, but Jamie was sure she would come if they continued doing this. Rowan was taking her, using her body for her own pleasure, and the thought was enough to send her over the edge.

"Jamie?" Rowan's voice was almost desperate as her thrusts became more and more frantic.

"Yes, use my body to get yourself off. Don't stop."

There was a rustling of covers as Rowan slipped her hand between Jamie's body and the bed, searching for the wetness Jamie was sure she would find. "Fuck." Jamie's need was driving her to insanity. The weight of Rowan's body over hers constricted her breathing the slightest bit, but that only added to the feeling of being taken. It was like Rowan was desperate to have her, and she was more than willing to give her anything she wanted.

Long fingers slipped into Jamie's panties and found her throbbing clit, swollen and ready to be touched.

"May I—"

"Yes, Rowan. Please take me now."

Another growl from Rowan, and she was driving her strong fingers back and forth across Jamie's hardened clit.

"It feels like I've waited to touch you forever. I want you so fucking much." Rowan's words were flowing from her in a constant stream of consciousness. Jamie gripped the edge of the bed in a desperate attempt not to fall over the side and onto the floor. She'd never experienced anything so raw, so pure in her life, and she wanted it to last forever.

"Fuck. Yes." Jamie's head felt light as she did her best to calm her breathing before passing out. "Don't stop, Rowan. Don't stop, baby."

Rowan drove her body against Jamie's, pulling her against her own need with every thrust of her hips. The bed shifted along the floor with their weight, and the wood creaked with every sudden jolt of Rowan's hips. "Come on my hand, sweet girl. Come for me."

Jamie's body took the words as a command as her orgasm rushed through her. In a desperate effort to make sure it didn't stop before she was ready, Jamie grabbed Rowan's arm and held it in place while she rode the thick fingers that she'd never be able to see without remembering this moment again. Rowan's body shook above her as her own release finally took her. Jamie let out a contented sigh as they both collapsed in a heap, Rowan pushing her body slightly off her so she didn't hurt her.

"Did you…?"

"Yes, yeah, did you?" Rowan seemed as awestruck as Jamie at what had just happened.

"Oh, yeah. That was…" Jamie rolled over, so they were facing each other. She saw satisfaction in Rowan's eyes and something else. Fear?

"Hey, are you okay?"

"Sure." The bed shifted as Rowan almost fell over the edge, pulling away from Jamie. "I better get out there and chop some wood. I can't spend the day in bed." She scrambled to her feet and pulled on her jeans and boots.

"What? Where are you going? What's going on?"

"Nothing. I just—I have a lot to do today. That's all. I'll let you get to your research." Rowan found a flannel shirt to pull on over the undershirt she'd slept in and headed for the door.

"Rowan, wait." Everything had happened so fast Jamie was finding it difficult to process the turn of events. Her pussy still ached to be touched. What had started as the most erotic thing that had ever happened to her now left her feeling cold and alone. She didn't know what was going on, or maybe she did. Jamie sighed and pulled the covers over her head, blocking herself from the world for just a minute. Why did Rowan have to be so goddamn honorable? She was pretty sure that's what sent her running out of the cabin. They'd agreed to kisses and flirting, and as soon as things crept past those boundaries, Rowan ran.

It was probably a good thing they lived so far apart. Jamie could easily see herself falling for Rowan and her tendency to always do the right thing. Falling in love wasn't part of the plan, but thoroughly enjoying each other's bodies while they were here was something she would enjoy. The challenge would be to convince Rowan they could handle a more physical relationship without worrying about emotions getting in the way.

The sound of wood being chopped outside told her Rowan was likely trying to work out some of her pent-up tension. Jamie was more than willing to be an outlet for that energy, but she would have to convince Rowan of that first. She stretched and rubbed the sleep from her eyes.

It was strange to think that this cabin in the woods wasn't their home. She'd gotten so used to the routine and Rowan that she almost forgot they only had a few more weeks, and then she'd be back in the real world. Back to her house and her job, and the hustle and bustle of the city she loved so much. She'd have all those things, but she wouldn't have Rowan. She tried to imagine Rowan in her world but couldn't. It would be like taking something wild and beautiful and putting it in a cage. Rowan belonged to this place, and Jamie was only visiting. She was the outsider, and soon it would be time for her to return to her own life, her own cage.

Jamie wrapped a blanket around her shoulders and walked over to the window. There was already a growing pile of wood to Rowan's left as she stacked a new log on the pedestal and drove the blade down to cut it into pieces, over and over. Sweat dampened her hair and dripped down her face as she almost frantically chopped one log after another. Jamie shook her head and wondered if she should go out to stop her before she hurt herself.

After a few minutes, she finally rested the axe against the shed where they kept the extra wood and started stacking the logs in a neat pile against the wall. Once she was done, she walked to the bucket next to the shed that collected rainwater. Jamie silently watched as Rowan removed both of her shirts. Left only in jeans and boots, she was the perfect specimen of a firm body, male or female. There was nothing overdone about her. She was strong and lean, but not in a way that made her look like she should be on an elliptical commercial. Her body was more like one that should be on the cover of a lesbian romance where the femme girl falls for a lumberjack, or jane, or whatever. Rowan's body was built like someone who worked hard for everything they had, and Jamie couldn't get enough.

Warm breath fogged up the glass as Jamie leaned closer to get a better look. Rowan cupped water from the rain barrel in her hands and poured it over her head to cool off. Clouds of steam floated around her as cold water evaporated from her overheated, hard-worked body. Jamie squirmed, her arousal becoming more and more urgent. Who was she kidding? There was no way she was going to spend the rest of her time ignoring her attraction, her feelings for Rowan. She needed to have a talk with her about how she felt.

It wasn't only about attraction. Jamie knew it. She liked Rowan, probably more than she'd ever liked anyone else. Jamie liked the way Rowan asked her how she slept every morning. She liked that Rowan was always so appreciative of the food she made her. She liked the way she would carry Jamie's bag if they'd had a grueling day and she was struggling to complete their hike home. It was the little things that stood out to her. Rowan was the kindest, most giving person Jamie had ever known.

It was all so very attractive—the entire package.

Rowan shook the water from her hair and put her flannel shirt back on. She turned toward the cabin and saw Jamie watching her. With a smile, she gave her a tentative wave. Jamie crossed to the stove and put on a pot of water for coffee. She didn't want to bombard Rowan as soon as she walked inside but she had to address the situation before things got worse.

CHAPTER TWENTY

H ey."
"Hey yourself." Jamie handed Rowan a towel to dry herself off a little better. "What was that?"

Rowan dried her hair and draped the towel around her neck. "I'm sorry. I kind of panicked."

"Okay, do you want to talk about why you panicked?"

Rowan hung the towel on its hook and pulled open a drawer to find clean clothes to put on. Jamie silently watched and waited for an answer Rowan wasn't sure she had. What had happened? She lost control. That's what happened. Jamie had opened that door, and Rowan shoved her way in without caring about how she would feel after.

"I'm scared I'll want too much." Honesty was the only option at this point. Rowan knew Jamie would see right through any bullshit she might try to feed her.

She took Rowan's hand and led her back to the bed. Without a word, she climbed in and held the blanket up to invite Rowan to join her. It was tempting, but probably the last place she should be. She had already allowed her need to overtake her and now needed to keep distance between them. If things were different and there was a chance at making a relationship work, it would be a completely different story.

"Come on, Rowan. Let's just talk." Jamie waved for her to come closer. "I promise I won't try any funny business."

"I'm not sure you're the one we need to worry about as far as funny business is concerned."

"Come on, silly, let's just talk." Jamie pulled the blankets around them when Rowan finally climbed in next to her in the bed. "Is this okay?"

"Yeah, I'm fine."

"I know talking isn't your favorite thing to do, but I think we need to work this all out so we understand each other better."

"I agree." Rowan couldn't deny being next to Jamie calmed her in a way nothing else did. The fact that she had that much power over her emotions was exactly why the last thing she needed was to be even more vulnerable around her.

"What scares you? Are you sure you wouldn't be able to have a physical relationship without falling in love, or have you just never had that before?"

"What do you mean?"

"I mean, have you ever had sex with someone you weren't in love with?"

Rowan didn't know how to explain that the difference between other women and Jamie was that she already had feelings for her, and none of those other women had meant the same. It had only been sex, and she wasn't so sure she would be satisfied with that kind of relationship with Jamie. It seemed like a disaster waiting to happen.

"I don't want to fuck up the friendship we have."

Jamie sighed and snuggled closer into Rowan's back. "I understand."

Did she understand? Rowan wasn't convinced. How could Jamie understand if Rowan was obviously the only one who had these feelings? Jamie was able to separate the physical relationship from an emotional one because this was all just about sex to her. "I don't think you do understand."

"Okay." Jamie tugged Rowan's arm for her to turn around and face her. "What is that supposed to mean?"

"It means this is all just fun and games to you. You're obviously able to fuck whomever you want without consequences because you aren't brave enough to allow yourself to let someone in."

"Wow, I had no idea that's what you thought about me or about us."

"What does that even mean? There is no us."

Jamie closed her eyes and released a slow, deliberate breath.

When she opened them again, she seemed to have pushed down the anger Rowan was sure she'd stirred within her.

"Look, I'm not going to pretend that I don't have feelings for you. I absolutely do, and if we were in a situation where it would be a reasonable option for us to date, I'd be daydreaming about kids, dogs, and some fantasy life we'd have together. That's not our reality. You can't leave your mom, and I have my career. Those are the facts. I'm so incredibly sorry if I've pushed you into something that makes you uncomfortable. I never wanted to do that. We don't have to do anything you aren't completely sure you want. The last thing I want to do is push you away or make this situation unpleasant. Besides, I'm not willing to sacrifice what I truly hope will be a lifelong friendship for temporary sex."

Jamie combed her fingers through Rowan's unruly black hair. It was such a comforting gesture and helped calm her nerves. As she relaxed, she began to feel a little ridiculous.

"Okay," Rowan said. "I understand that."

"Talk to me about how you're feeling, Rowan. You said before that you don't do casual. I respect that, but then we constantly flirt with each other, and I don't know how to interpret how you really feel."

A shaky breath escaped from Rowan's lips as she covered her face. "You're right. I know I'm sending you mixed signals, and that's a real dick move on my part. You don't deserve to be jerked around like that."

"Hey." Jamie pulled Rowan's hand from her face. "You aren't jerking me around. You have done nothing that I haven't been doing, too. It's obvious that we're into each other. I know my body is very clear about how I feel about you. My brain is the only part that is stopping me from jumping you right now."

"So, you think taking things further is a bad idea?" Rowan asked.

"No, no, no, that's not what I'm saying." Jamie drew delicate circles on Rowan's chest with a finger. "It's completely okay if you don't think you can do this, knowing it's only temporary. I'm just having a difficult time being good and wanted to make sure good Jamie is what you really want."

The rumble of Rowan's laughter made Jamie smile. "I'm not sure 'Good Jamie' exists, but I get your point." Rowan took hold of Jamie's hand and kissed her palm. "I can't pretend I don't want you. I think about you constantly and in a way that isn't only about all the time we're spending together. I want to feel your naked body against mine. I want to know what you taste like and what sounds will escape from your mouth when I make you come with my tongue." Rowan shifted on the bed to look down at Jamie's face. "I can't go to California with you. I know an adult should be able to have a casual sexual relationship with another person and not have that be a thing, but there's a part of me that holds back because I don't want to…I can't fall in love with you. It would break me."

Jamie traced her thumb across Rowan's bottom lip before dipping it into her mouth. Rowan gently sucked. "I understand and will respect your decision, even though I'm quite positive controlling myself is slowly killing me."

The bed shifted as Rowan leaned closer to Jamie and kissed her. Rowan didn't want to read too much into a kiss, but something about this one seemed different. Every other time they'd kissed, she'd felt more reserved. She was finally allowing herself some pleasure but wasn't ready to let go. There seemed to be a shift within Jamie, too. There was nothing timid about this, and Rowan allowed herself to welcome the attention.

"Fuck it." Rowan panted as she pulled away enough to speak. "Denying our attraction and pretending we don't want more is ridiculous at this point."

Jamie's smile warmed Rowan to the core.

"If at any point you feel like it's too much, or you want to pause to talk about things, don't hesitate to speak up. You got it? I'm enjoying this time with you, and the last thing I want to do is fuck that up," Jamie said.

"I agree. I don't want to waste any more time pretending I can spend every day with you and not have you, not be inside of you."

"God, Rowan, I'm aching for you." Jamie pulled Rowan closer and kissed her again.

"Tell me what you want."

"I want it all, Ranger Fleming. For the rest of our time here, my body is yours, and you have my permission to explore and do whatever you would like. In fact, I encourage that kind of scientific endeavor wholeheartedly."

Rowan grinned and kissed the tip of Jamie's nose. "You're so brave."

"I've had all kinds of fantasies about you these last few weeks, and you're fantastic at this sex thing in every one of them, so show me what you got."

"No pressure there," Rowan said as she kissed her way down Jamie's body from her neck to her shoulder to her breast. Jamie gasped when she took her time running her tongue around a painfully hard nipple.

"I want your mouth on me, Rowan," Jamie said as she grazed her teeth across Rowan's chin. "I need you inside me."

Rowan didn't need more direction than that. She quickly undressed and helped Jamie do the same. Confident fingers slid through Jamie's already slick folds, gently circling her opening before sliding back up to brush against her clit. Rowan distantly registered Jamie's moans as she took her nipple into her mouth and sucked it to hardness.

"You feel so good. I've spent the better part of the last few weeks wondering how your mouth would feel on me." Jamie threaded her fingers through Rowan's still slightly damp hair and encouraged her farther down her body.

"Open up for me," Rowan said, settling her body between Jamie's legs. "Drape your legs over my shoulders and let me take care of this ache you were telling me about."

"Yesss…" Jamie hissed when Rowan's tongue brushed against her swollen nub. "Please, Rowan."

"I've got you. Just relax. I'm going to take care of you."

She caressed Jamie's labia with her tongue, sucking each side into her mouth before stroking it again. Rowan's thick finger circled her opening before gently pushing in to the first knuckle. "You feel so good. I need more."

Jamie pressed her heels against Rowan's back and used her body as leverage to ride her tongue. Rowan knew it wouldn't be long before Jamie came.

"I'm so close. I don't want it to stop. I don't—ahhhhh…" Jamie came with a scream, clamping Rowan's head in place with her thighs as she rode out the waves of her orgasm. When Jamie released her head, Rowan climbed to the top of the bed and kissed her with so much passion she thought they both might fall off the side.

"I'm not done. May I still have you? Are you okay?" Rowan asked as she straddled Jamie's thigh and pressed her center against her bare skin.

"Yes, come on me, baby. I want to feel you come all over me." Rowan slipped two fingers back into Jamie's core and rode her thigh like she was desperate. "Oh God, you're going to make me come again, Rowan, don't stop."

"You're a very good girl allowing me to have you like this." The dirty talk wasn't something Rowan had planned, but it felt right. She held her breath, waiting to see how Jamie would respond.

"I want to be a good girl for you."

"I know you do." Rowan felt a flood of wetness coat Jamie's thigh as she moved her body back and forth against it. Her movements became almost frantic as she simultaneously rode her thigh and fucked her fingers into Jamie's pussy. She could feel herself building and knew her orgasm wasn't far off.

"So close," Rowan said as she pinned Jamie to the bed. "I'm so close. Are you ready for me to come?"

"Yes, please, come on me, Rowan. I want you to come on me, baby."

Her orgasm crashed through her like a wave. Her breath caught in her throat, and she could vaguely hear Jamie scream as she found her own release a couple of minutes later.

"Holy fuck," Rowan said as she rolled over to lie next to Jamie on the bed. "Why the hell did we wait to do that? That was amazing."

Jamie turned onto her side and slid a leg over Rowan's lower body. "Because I wouldn't have gotten any work done. You wouldn't have had the energy to find our food, and they would have eventually found us dead in a pool of our own come."

"Good point," Rowan said. "I'm going to close my eyes for just a minute. I'm pretty sure I wouldn't be able to stand even if I wanted to."

"That sounds like an excellent plan," Jamie said.

Rowan pulled the blanket back over them both. With heavy eyes, she allowed herself to luxuriate in the warmth of Jamie's body and drifted off to sleep.

CHAPTER TWENTY-ONE

Several days of storms had limited their ability to do much outside the cabin. When the rain finally relented, Jamie suggested a picnic to take advantage of the sunshine. They'd collected the most recent batch of memory cards the day before, and she wanted a little time to relax with Rowan before she had to dive back into her work.

Even though she had found no signs of the curlew yet, she knew her time there had been productive. The SD cards allowed her to witness the behaviors of several other species of birds during this critical period before they migrated south. Jamie knew there wasn't much time left before her window would close, and her chance to find a curlew would be over.

The idea of returning to California without the results she'd hoped for would be an incredible disappointment. A disappointment for her employer who had funded this trip, her father who believed in her and was counting on her to get the results she would need to guarantee a show of her own, and primarily to herself. Her disappointment would be the hardest to deal with because she'd allowed herself to have hope.

Professionally, it would suck, but she couldn't deny the disappointment over not finding a curlew was compounded by knowing her days with Rowan would soon end. It was hard to believe that only a few weeks ago, she wondered if she'd make it through the summer without wanting to kill her. Now the thought of not seeing her every morning made Jamie want to stretch out each day they had left together to take advantage of every minute. That was new.

Jamie had dated women in the past. She'd dated many people in her twenties, but none had ever left her with the feeling of calm that

Rowan did. She made Jamie feel centered, and it would be agonizing to walk away.

"Are you ready to go?" Rowan asked as she slipped her arms into the straps of her pack and pulled the cabin door shut behind her. "I thought we could head down to the river and catch a fish for our lunch. What do you think?"

"Should we worry about seeing any of our bear friends?" Jamie had been nervous about Rowan going to the river after their last encounter. Everything worked out fine, but she knew there was always a chance another one could show up.

"I haven't seen any lately. I think we'll be fine. Stay close, just in case, and we'll deal with it if it's a problem. The further it gets in the season, the more they're trying to pack the weight on for the winter. There's always a chance we'll come across one. They were here first, after all."

Jamie's short legs sometimes struggled to keep up with Rowan's longer strides. Even with as good a shape as she was in, short legs couldn't cover the same distance. "Slow down, speed demon. We're having a relaxing day, remember?"

"Sorry," Rowan said, allowing Jamie to catch up. "I get focused on where I'm going and forget you're a short stack."

"Shut up." Jamie slipped her hand into Rowan's larger one and threaded their fingers together. "Normally, I work my butt off to keep up, but today is about relaxing. We haven't really taken an entire day to relax since we got here, if you think about it. It's high time we took a day off."

Rowan wrapped an arm around Jamie's shoulders and pulled her close as they continued to walk. "You deserve it. You're doing a physically challenging hike to get the SD cards one day and spending the next few hunched over your laptop, reviewing footage. It can't be easy on your body."

"If only there were someone out there who could give me a massage." Jamie suggestively batted her eyes at Rowan.

"Subtle."

"Hey, if we're going to live out my lesbian romance novel fantasies, there should be at least three times as many massages as are currently happening." It had occurred to Jamie more than once that if she weren't careful, she'd end up falling for the handsome Ranger

Fleming, and her friends at home would never let her live down the fact that she'd basically played out an entire lesbian romance novel in real life.

"No pressure there," Rowan teased her. "I think any good lesbian romance novel would have a much cooler butch character than me."

Jamie wrapped her arm around Rowan's middle and squeezed. "Not true. You're plenty cool enough."

"Really?" Rowan seemed skeptical.

"For sure. First, you're hot." Rowan looked away but seemed pleased by Jamie's comment. "Second, you're very kind and attentive."

"I'm going to have you write my next dating profile."

The comment was a joke, but Jamie felt a jolt of jealousy course through her at the thought of Rowan going on dates. It was ridiculous. Of course she'd go on dates. Even so, Rowan dating wasn't something Jamie wanted to think about when they were on their way to a nice romantic picnic together.

"I think I'd like to keep you for myself for the next few weeks, so no, I'm not going to think about your dating profile right now." She winked at Rowan to soften her words, even though in her heart, she meant them.

The trail they were on opened to a grassy area next to the river. The water was high after the storm they'd had, but the sun had dried out the open area enough for them to not get muddy.

"You spread out the blanket, and I'll see what I can catch. Can you gather some raspberries and blueberries growing around here, and we'll have them with our fish?"

Jamie nodded and dropped her pack to remove the blanket from inside. She had been looking forward to this since she'd suggested it to Rowan that morning, and she wanted to appreciate every second they had together. Once the blanket was spread out, Jamie gathered a few handfuls of berries, eating about a quarter of them before the others made it into her bag. By the time she was done, Rowan was back with a large fish she'd already cut into fillets.

An hour later, with their bellies full, Jamie snuggled into Rowan's arms as they stretched out on the blanket. A sweatshirt served as Rowan's pillow as they silently enjoyed their time together. Jamie couldn't remember ever feeling so content. These last few weeks hadn't been at all what Jamie had expected. Rowan hadn't been who she'd thought she was in the beginning. It was strange to feel you know someone so well but know almost nothing about them. She was almost afraid to ask questions and potentially break the spell they were under, but she wanted to learn more about this person who dominated so much of her thoughts and all of her fantasies.

"Hey, Rowan," Jamie started.

"Hmm?"

"Would you be comfortable talking about your dad?"

Rowan shifted, and Jamie was afraid she'd chased her away, but once she found a comfortable spot, she pulled Jamie back onto her chest and kissed the top of her head.

"Sure. What do you want to know?"

"Whatever you're comfortable sharing with me." Jamie knew Rowan didn't owe her anything and could tell her to mind her own business, but she hoped Rowan would open up to her. Her dad was obviously a difficult subject for her to talk about and she had a feeling Rowan hadn't talked to anyone else about him. She wanted to be that person for Rowan.

"My dad's name was Jack Fleming. He was in the Navy and flew jets off of a carrier in the Persian Gulf. We had a very complicated relationship."

Jamie waited patiently to see if Rowan would continue, but when she didn't, Jamie pushed for a little more. "You mentioned before that he passed away. Did he die in the war?"

"No, he came home from the war." Rowan cracked her knuckles in what was obviously a nervous habit. "Then he committed suicide when I was fourteen."

"Oh, sweetie, I'm so sorry." Jamie wrapped her arm around Rowan's middle and kissed her temple. "No wonder you don't like to talk about it. I'm sorry I brought it up."

Rowan squeezed Jamie's shoulder and shook her head, looking anywhere other than at Jamie. "Don't apologize. I've never really talked to anyone about it. I'm strangely okay sharing it with you, though."

Jamie wasn't sure how to proceed. More questions might upset Rowan more, but if she really felt as if talking about it with Jamie helped, she wanted to keep their dialogue going. "So, you must have been tiny when he left for war?"

"My mom was pregnant with me. She had upset her parents when she got pregnant and married him. Then when he went to war, they pushed her away."

"Jesus, when she needed them the most, they abandoned her? Your poor mom." Jamie couldn't imagine her grandparents ever doing anything like that. They would do anything for her mother, and even though they had completely different political views from her father, they would have never let that come between them and their daughter.

"They eventually came around after I was born. My mom was going to school and trying to raise a baby on her own since my dad was overseas, and it got to a point where they couldn't continue to watch her struggle. I was their only grandchild at that time, so they knew they didn't want to miss out on their chance to be grandparents."

Jamie slipped her hand beneath the hem of Rowan's shirt and pressed it against the soft skin of her stomach. She felt especially protective of her and wanted to comfort her in any way she could. "Were you close to your grandparents?"

"Yes and no." Rowan toyed with a string on Jamie's shirtsleeve. The distraction seemed to help her relax. "I was close to my grandpa, but my grandma was the village leader and wasn't ever able to separate me from the sailor boy who got her perfect daughter pregnant. It only got worse as I got older and not only looked exactly like my father but idolized him as well."

Jamie leaned her head up and studied Rowan's powerful jaw and intelligent eyes. "I look like my mom. I always wanted to look more like my dad, but I take after my mom's side of the family."

"Your mom must have been a beautiful woman," Rowan said and kissed Jamie's forehead.

"You're such a sweet talker." Jamie knew Rowan wasn't perfect by any means, but she couldn't imagine what her ex-wife must have been thinking. She was a catch, and Jamie wished things were different and she could throw her hat in the ring as the future Mrs. Fleming.

"When my dad first came back from the war, my mom said he was different. He was confused about how to feel about being back. He'd served several tours and was shot down at some point and taken as a prisoner of war for a year. They blindfolded him, beat him, interrogated him, starved him, and broke one of his vertebrae. He was eventually rescued but could never fly again. I don't think he knew who he was if he wasn't a pilot."

"How old were you when he came back?" Jamie asked.

"I was five or six when he came home for good. When he first came back, they had him doing rehabilitation for a long time to regain the ability to walk. He never was completely right, but eventually he could get around without help."

"Your poor mom. I can't imagine loving someone and then having to watch them ship off to war, not knowing if they'd return or who they would be when they did." Jamie's father had been a professor during the war and had told her about students he had that joined the service and seemed haunted when they returned.

"Yeah, my mom said he was angrier when he came back. I don't remember him being angry when I was little. He was my hero. Every night before bed, he would tell me stories about the different planes he'd flown and all the crazy things he'd gotten into as a young man. I thought he was amazing, and I wanted to be just like him. It's why I eventually became a pilot."

Jamie smiled at the thought of a little Rowan hanging on every word from her pilot dad. "I bet you were adorable when you were little."

Rowan grew quiet, and Jamie wondered if she would continue. Finally, she raised Jamie's hand to her lips and planted a kiss on her palm before setting it back on her stomach. "I think if you asked my mom, she'd say I was a bit of a hellion. We moved to Anchorage when I was twelve. Having grown up in a tiny village, I went a little wild when I was suddenly thrown into the big, wide world. Things between my mom and dad were volatile by that time, and I fell in with the wrong group of kids to cope."

"I can't even imagine you being a hooligan."

"Yeah, well, hooligan is an awfully gentle word for the person I was. Drugs, drinking, girls in and out of my bed. I was basically on a never-ending quest to find stability and a way to escape the world. I was in a very bad place."

Jamie could see the pain in Rowan's eyes as she remembered that time in her life. It broke her heart to see her like that.

"We don't have to talk about this if you're uncomfortable."

"I guess we've come this far." Rowan blew out a breath. "Things between my parents got worse and worse. Once I began to rebel, my dad didn't handle it well, and I became a punching bag for his frustrations."

"God, Rowan, that's horrible."

"Yeah, well, I gave as good as I got. We'd have knock-down, drag-out fights, and I just pulled further and further into myself. My mom was working all the time to support our family, and my dad and I were doing everything we could to destroy each other. My mom tried to get me to talk to someone, but my dad spent my entire life drilling into me that feelings are a weakness. When you share those feelings with someone else, you're only giving them the tools to break you."

"I don't even know what to say about that," Jamie said as she combed her fingers through Rowan's hair. Knowing Rowan's story helped explain so much about her. Of course she was closed off. Obviously, she wouldn't want to let anyone in.

"Not much to say, really. We fought until we could barely look at each other. Then he took his life. Once I graduated from high school, I wanted to get far away from Alaska, so I moved to Southern California. With a little help from an old Navy buddy of my dad's, I got on with the National Park Service. I lived with him and his wife while I waited to get into the ranger academy. After graduation, my first assignment was the Channel Islands National Park, off the coast of Los Angeles."

Jamie nodded her head. "I know it well. My dad and I have been going there since I was little. It has the only nesting population of California brown pelicans on the West Coast of the United States, and they have the world's largest population of Scripps's murrelets. We filmed an episode of my dad's show there when I was little."

"Oh, yeah," Rowan said excitedly. "They played that episode on repeat in the visitor center on the mainland. You were so adorable in that episode." Rowan's face blanched. "Jesus Christ, I can't associate the person in that show with the person I now constantly have dirty thoughts about."

"You constantly have dirty thoughts about me?"

"Jamie, duh, this can't be a surprise to you." Rowan rolled her eyes, which made Jamie laugh.

"I guess not. You're pretty transparent about what you're thinking where that is concerned."

Rowan covered her face with her hands. "Ugh, that's embarrassing."

"Don't be embarrassed. I'm having the same thoughts about you, so we're even. When did you meet your ex-wife?"

Rowan turned her body, so Jamie had to lie flat on the blanket with her leaning over her. She brushed a lock of hair from Jamie's face and kissed her. "Sweetie, do you really want to hear about my ex-wife?"

"Only if you want to talk about her."

"I never *want* to talk about her, but I will if you want to know." Rowan cleared her throat and took a sip of water from their canteen. "Okay, here goes. A few months after working on the islands, I was leading a group of women on the Point Bennett guided hike on San Miguel Island, and one of them slid down a rock face and broke her ankle. We had no reception where we were, so I had to carry her out on my back."

"That hike is no joke. How the hell did you do that?"

"It was terrible, and it took us hours, but we got her out of there. A couple of months later, that same woman contacted me and asked if she could take me out to dinner as a gesture of her appreciation. My instinct was to say no, but my boss told me she was a journalist who wrote for an outdoor adventure magazine, and he encouraged me to go. I thought it would be one dinner, and then we'd never see each other again."

"I take it that woman became your wife," Jamie surmised.

"Bingo. A year later, Sara Thompson became Sara Fleming, and we bought a house in Santa Barbara where she immediately started making baby plans."

"Wow," Jamie said. "She moves fast."

"She doesn't mess around once she has her mind set on something." Rowan rolled onto her stomach and picked at a thread that was coming unraveled on the blanket. "She wanted to use a donor that we knew, and I didn't have a brother or anyone who could donate, so she asked her ex-boyfriend. They'd broken up five years before but had remained friends. It was a terrible strain on what was essentially a brand-new relationship. Every month that it didn't work, she became angrier and angrier with me, and instead of talking to her and trying to help her through what had to be an incredibly difficult time for her, I shut down and withdrew as I'd always been taught to do."

Jamie slid her hand up the back of Rowan's shirt and gently scratched between her shoulders to comfort her. "It's not your fault. I don't think many people would have handled that situation perfectly."

"Yeah, well, she dragged me to therapy and did her best to put all our problems on me. She wasn't completely wrong. I was a big part of the problem, but I shouldn't have ever allowed that situation to happen. After a year of disappointment, she finally got pregnant. I was working in shifts on the islands at that point. They were seventy-two hours off and seventy-two hours on, which are exhausting. Three hours into my shift, she texted me she was pregnant, followed immediately by a text that she was leaving me for the man who is the father of her child."

There were no words Jamie could think of to say to Rowan that wouldn't sound ridiculous. The only thing she wanted to do was hold her. Jamie's heart broke in two when she heard Rowan sniffle and saw her quickly wipe a tear from her cheek. She wanted to hate this Sara person for putting Rowan in that position, but she knew firsthand how difficult it was to get her to speak about her feelings. It was shocking that Rowan had allowed them to spend the last two hours talking about her life. Jamie pushed Rowan over onto her back and hovered above her. Rowan wiped her eyes with her shirt and gave Jamie a watery smile.

"Sorry I'm such a sad sack," Rowan said. "I can't remember the last time I cried in front of someone. You realize we must part ways and never speak again, right?"

Jamie placed gentle kisses on the corners of Rowan's eyes, brushed her bangs from her face, and kissed her newly exposed forehead. "Fat chance. You're stuck with me forever, now." Jamie had meant forever as a friend, but as she looked into Rowan's brown eyes, she could imagine a different life. One where they were married, and Jamie spent her days showing Rowan exactly how much she deserved to be loved.

CHAPTER TWENTY-TWO

A gentle rain fell as Rowan stacked the last of the logs she'd just chopped on the pile. She winked at Jamie, sitting in her favorite spot in the cabin where she would always watch Rowan chop wood. The first time Rowan had noticed her sitting there, Jamie had been embarrassed and came up with some silly explanation of what she was doing staring out the window at her, but it didn't fool Rowan. She was flattered, if she were being honest, and she looked forward to their little routine at this point.

The best part was always when Rowan would come in from chopping wood, and Jamie would be extra flirty and attentive to her. She knew it should embarrass her by how much the attention thrilled her, but it made her feel amazing. Jamie always made her feel amazing. Especially after opening up to her like she did the week before. It hadn't been something Rowan planned to do. Hell, she'd never shared those details with anyone before, not even her ex-wife. Maybe if she had, things would have been different between them.

Rowan hung her axe on the shed wall and turned to smile at Jamie, still watching her through the cabin window. She lifted the cup of coffee in her hand and pointed toward it, silently asking Rowan if she wanted a cup of her own. Rowan nodded and gave her a thumbs-up. Jamie moved away from the window and into the cabin, presumably to prepare another cup of coffee.

It had been four years since Sara left Rowan and sent her into a spiral of despair and hopelessness. When things had ended between them, she shouldn't have been as shocked as she was. She wasn't the type to walk away from a commitment. They would have remained unhappy for years if it was left to her because Rowan would honor her marriage vows. She realized now how self-destructive and stupid that was. Neither of them was happy, and there's no honor in forcing two unhappy people to stay together when there was no hope for things to change.

The weight that she'd carried around in her heart for much of her life seemed a little lighter after she'd shared her story with Jamie. If things hadn't fallen apart with Sara, she never would have come back to Alaska, and she would never have spent this time with Jamie. No matter how fleeting their time together would be, it somehow seemed worth everything she went through. Jamie was like a gift that had just fallen into her lap, and now that their time was ending, Rowan didn't know how she was supposed to let her go.

In a perfect world, Jamie could stay. Rowan would never ask that of her, but she could imagine a life where that was possible. Rowan could never leave Alaska while her mother still needed her, and Jamie would have to give up far too much to consider leaving her career in California. It's something Rowan would never ask her to do, especially for a brand-new relationship with someone she'd only known for a few months. Ridiculous. Disappointing. There was no doubt it was disappointing.

Rowan toed off her boots on the porch to avoid carrying mud into the cabin. Her thick wool socks cushioned her steps as she walked inside and hung her jacket from the hook near the door. Jamie met her with a warm cup of coffee, and she kissed her cheek to show her appreciation. "You're going to make someone an excellent wife someday, Dr. Martin."

"You think so? Even though some might say, I'm obsessed with birds?"

The coffee warmed Rowan from the inside as she took her first sip. "Your obsession with birds is the least annoying of your quirks."

"What quirks?" Jamie pressed herself against Rowan's back and slipped her hands into the front of Rowan's shirt, stealing whatever warmth Rowan had left for herself.

"Ahh," Rowan exclaimed. "There's one example."

"What, this?" Jamie flattened her hands on the bare skin of Rowan's stomach. "Or this?" Rowan sucked in a breath as Jamie unsnapped the top button of her jeans and slipped a hand inside.

"Uh, that's, I'm okay with that."

"Just okay?" Jamie pulled her hand from Rowan's pants but was stopped when Rowan grabbed her forearm and pushed her arm back down.

"Don't let me, uh," Jamie's fingers slipped into Rowan's already wet folds and circled a quickly hardening clit, "discourage you when you have your mind set on something."

"How noble of you."

Rowan placed her cup on the table and leaned forward, resting her weight on the edge of the sturdy piece of furniture.

"Jamie," Rowan gasped, quickly losing the ability to think. "Maybe we should move to the bed?"

The buttons of Rowan's pants were released one by one as Jamie slid them down to pool at her ankles. "I want you right here. Are you going to let me take you from behind?"

"Yes." Rowan's legs threatened to give way beneath her.

"Yes?" Jamie asked in the sexiest voice Rowan had ever heard in her life.

"This is new," Rowan said. "I didn't know you had a little dominatrix in you."

"If you're very good, that won't be the only thing that is in me today," Jamie said.

"Fuck." Rowan bent over farther and leaned on her elbows to stop from falling to the ground in a puddle. She groaned when Jamie's hands left her body, but she heard her quickly removing her clothes, so she remained in place. A few seconds later, Rowan felt Jamie's naked body press against her from behind, and her hand returned to its position between her thighs.

"You looked hot out there doing your lumberjack thing." Jamie slid a finger into Rowan's core and slowly thrust it in and out.

"I saw you watch—ing." Rowan's voice caught when Jamie slid a second, then third finger inside. "Fuck, Jamie, you feel so good."

"Do you like it when I watch you doing something extra butch?"

Rowan tried to laugh, but it came out as more of a groan. "I didn't realize I was being extra butch." Jamie's fingers pushed deeper while her other hand wrapped around Rowan's body to caress her clit from the front. Rowan knew it was a difficult position for her since she was so much smaller than Rowan. It made the idea of her doing it even hotter.

"That's a lie, isn't it, sweetheart? You were aware of what you were doing, weren't you?"

"I—"

"Now, now, there's no way you can convince me you weren't intentionally showing off when you did that whole stretching routine before your axe ever touched wood." Delicate fingers squeezed Rowan's clit before jerking it off like a tiny cock. "Do you deny you put on a show just for me?"

"I—have—to—stretch—" Rowan choked out, fighting off the embarrassing fact that she was already about to come.

"I've been watching you longer than you realize, and I saw the stretches you did before you knew I was there. I saw how your peacocking tripled when you knew you had an audience."

"Not just—any audience," Rowan said between desperate pants.

"No?" Jamie's fingers were fucking her hard, and Rowan knew her release couldn't be delayed much longer.

"No," Rowan said. "For you."

Jamie's fingers stuttered before she continued. "For me?" Her voice wasn't as confident as it had been.

"For you, only for you," Rowan admitted as her orgasm overtook her, and she crumpled forward onto the surface of the table while Jamie fucked her hard from behind. Once the waves of ecstasy had passed, she took a minute more to catch her breath while Jamie gently slid her fingers from her body. Rowan missed the weight of Jamie's body when she turned to leave.

She reached out and took Jamie's arm before she could walk away. Jamie looked surprised when Rowan lifted her up and gently placed her on top of the table. She was glad she had taken the time to do a few repairs on the homemade piece of furniture soon after they'd arrived. Displaying Jamie across its surface so she could have her way with her hadn't been on Rowan's mind when she made the repairs, but she was glad she'd made them all the same.

"Where are you going?" Rowan asked, leaning over Jamie's body to kiss her.

"I'm—apparently, I mistakenly thought I was in charge." Jamie's fingers threaded through the hair on the back of Rowan's head as she grazed her teeth across soft skin before placing a trail of kisses down her body.

"You can't always be in charge, Dr. Martin. Sometimes you have to let someone else take control." Rowan pulled a chair over and sat between Jamie's thighs. "You are perfect." The muscles in Jamie's legs flexed beneath delicate skin as she rested her feet on the edge of the table, opening herself up for Rowan's intimate inspection.

Rowan used her thumbs to spread Jamie open and watched as wetness glistened on her perfectly pink pussy. "You're so wet." The realization that fucking her had excited Jamie this much sent a rush of moisture to Rowan's own pussy.

"Yes," Jamie admitted. "I'm wet for you."

"Good girl." Rowan knew from the last time they'd had sex that Jamie enjoyed praise. She wasn't usually one to talk much in her day-to-day life, but something about being intimate, so vulnerable, with Jamie made her want to talk to her. Jamie allowing Rowan to have her like this made her want to touch her all the time. As many times as she would allow it for as long as they were together.

She pushed the doubt and emotions from her mind as she focused on the moment. They were together now. Jamie was naked and wet for her now, and that's where she needed to focus. Rowan used her index finger to trace the edge of her core. Her touch caused Jamie to pulse, and a bead of wetness trailed down her labia and along the curve of her ass.

"Rowan?" Jamie asked, reaching down to touch herself.

"Hands off. I'm in control now, and you'll be touched when I'm done looking at how beautiful you are."

Jamie squirmed but pulled her hands away and gripped the edge of the table behind her head. "I just—"

"I know what you need, sweetheart. I promise you're going to get everything you need and then some."

Rowan took her time tracing the edge of Jamie's labia before sucking her clit into her mouth. She could feel Jamie swell as her need increased. Jamie moaned as Rowan languidly studied every inch with her tongue.

"Are you ready to take me inside, Jamie?"

"Yes." The desperation in her voice only made Rowan want her more.

Sweat dripped from Rowan's temples as she stood and pushed the chair back and out of the way. "Wrap your legs around my body, sweet girl."

"Fuck, yes." Jamie reached up to massage her own breasts. The wantonness of her motions left Rowan swallowing around the lump in her throat. She wanted Rowan, and that thought made her breath catch. How had they gotten to this point? What had Rowan done to deserve the attention of such an incredible woman? She would worry about the answers to those questions another time. For now, she only wanted to please Jamie.

Rowan rubbed her clit once more and slipped a single finger inside. Jamie was tight, but she readily took the single digit. On her next thrust, she added a second. Jamie gasped and lifted her head from the table to see Rowan slowly pumping in and out of her.

"You're so big, so good," Jamie moaned, sending Rowan's libido into overdrive.

"Do you like it when I'm inside you, sweet girl?"

"Yes, harder," Jamie begged, still massaging her nipples.

Wetness coated Rowan's hand as she rocked her own body into Jamie's with her fingers between them, fucking her hard and deep. "You're so tight. You feel so good. I can feel that you're close." Jamie's legs squeezed Rowan, pulling her closer.

"Yes, don't stop, so close," Jamie said.

"Come on my fingers, Jamie. I want to feel you come while I'm inside of you. You feel so good," Rowan was panting as sweat dripped down her face. She could see a sheen of sweat on Jamie's skin and smiled, knowing she'd caused it.

"I'm coming, baby, don't stop," Jamie begged as she reached up and pulled Rowan down so they could kiss.

The table rocked back and forth under them, and Rowan said a silent prayer that it would be sturdy enough to hold them both. "Come, Jamie," Rowan commanded as Jamie screamed her release. Rowan slowed a little as Jamie relaxed, but her fingers remained inside her. She wasn't ready to let go, and she hoped Jamie would be okay with that. She questioned whether she'd ever be able to let go.

CHAPTER TWENTY-THREE

The muscles in Jamie's back protested as she committed to one more hour of video review before she'd have to stop for the night. The hike to and from the site had become routine at this point, and since the one bear encounter they'd had, they were reasonably uneventful. Unfortunately, the same could be said for the videos she reviewed day in and day out. She knew it was a long shot. Of course it was a long shot, but she'd still had hope. Just because it was a long shot didn't mean it was impossible.

Rowan's warm hand rested on her shoulder as she leaned around her to set a cup of steaming hot coffee on the desk. "I thought this might help," Rowan said before kissing her cheek.

"Seriously, Rowan, how am I supposed to make it through the day without you once I'm back in the real world?" It had been a rhetorical question, but Jamie noticed a hint of sadness in Rowan's expression at the mention of their time together ending. Surely Rowan was ready to get back to her real life and away from the annoying scientist blabbering on and on about birds and trying to get her to talk about her past.

Their relationship had evolved in a way Jamie had never expected. It had become so much more than anything she had with anyone else in her life. She wasn't sure if that said more about her relationship with Rowan or the ones with everyone else. What did it say that she could become so close to someone she'd only known for a few months? It hadn't ever really bothered her before, but now that she'd had a taste of what it was like to be this close to someone, she wasn't sure she could be happy without it. The question was, could she have that relationship with just anyone, or was this something specific to Rowan? She certainly hoped it wasn't only about Rowan because living without her would be a very lonely life.

Jamie sipped the coffee and closed her eyes as the hot liquid warmed her from the inside. There really was something comforting about such a simple life. She'd never imagined being able to stand living away from the hustle and bustle of her daily life, but she'd settled in nicely. She missed food. This trip might have done her in on salmon and rabbit, but she didn't miss things as much as she expected she would. Living in this cabin was a bit of an extreme. She wasn't sure something this remote would make her happy for long, but occasionally, sure.

Maybe she'd come back and visit Rowan at some point. She'd said something about a truck, so she must not live anywhere this remote. Now that Jamie thought about it, she couldn't believe she'd never even asked. She'd told Rowan all about her life in California and didn't know a thing about Rowan's life other than she had a plane, a truck, and lived alone. Now Jamie felt like an asshole.

"Hey, Rowan?"

"Hmm?" Rowan looked up from the book she was reading. She considered teasing Rowan about being the one to read the one book they brought on the trip instead of Jamie, but she didn't.

"Where do you live?"

She set the book down and walked to the stove to add wood to the fire. "Like my house?"

"Yes, dork, where is your house?"

Rowan poked at the fire a little more and then closed the stove door. "Near Fairbanks."

Jamie shut down her equipment and crawled into Rowan's lap once she'd sat back in her chair. They'd spent more time in this position lately, and Jamie loved being snuggled up into Rowan, resting her head on Rowan's broad chest. It made her feel so safe. "What's your house like?"

"Where are these questions coming from?" Rowan asked. "Are you planning on moving in?"

"No," Jamie sighed when Rowan wrapped her arms around her and squeezed. "I just realized I know nothing about where you live. Maybe I'll visit someday, and I want to make sure we'll be able to have something other than rabbit stew for dinner."

"Well, aren't you fancy?" Rowan teased her. "Nope, I live in the country, but I'm only a half hour's drive from town, and Fairbanks is an honest-to-goodness city. The University of Alaska Fairbanks is there. There are people and restaurants and even an IMAX theater. We're like an actual city. We even use napkins and fancy things like that."

Jamie teasingly pinched Rowan's side. "Shut up, jerk. Tell me about your house. I want to picture you puttering around on a Sunday afternoon in your pajamas."

"Well, first, I don't putter around. I move with purpose."

"Yeah, yeah, you're amazing. Now, tell me about your house."

Rowan shifted Jamie on her lap and slipped a hand up the back of her shirt so she could rub comforting circles against her skin. "It's a pretty basic house. I built it a couple of years ago when I came back from California."

"You built your house? Seriously?"

"Yes, lots of people build their own house."

"I can honestly say you're the only person I've ever met who has built their own house."

"Hm." Rowan shrugged and looked a little surprised by that. "Well, I built my house. It has three bedrooms, two bathrooms, and an office where I keep my ham radio equipment."

"You're so freaking adorable." Jamie kissed Rowan's cheek. She loved that Rowan was a little nerdy with her ham radio and building her own house. She was unlike anyone Jamie had ever met, and she appreciated that. There was something so genuine about Rowan that put Jamie at ease. She was exactly who she said she was.

"My house is two stories, but the top story is a loft with my office space. It's open beam with gigantic windows across three sides so in the winter I can watch the snow falling and, in the summer, I get lots of light."

"Isn't that a nightmare in the summer? You must keep stock in those sleep masks. I never see you wearing one, by the way."

"I don't need one. I've spent my entire life dealing with the seasons. There are blackout shades in the bedrooms, so it's plenty dark when I sleep, but I don't need it. I can sleep in broad daylight, no problem."

"I wish I could do that. I'm going to owe Caroline a beer when we're back for giving me the mask before we left. It's been a lifesaver."

Rowan rolled her eyes and grumbled something Jamie couldn't understand.

"You aren't jealous of Caroline, are you?"

"Why have we spent so much time talking about Caroline Hill?"

Jamie laughed and kissed Rowan's lips. "Poor baby. You know I'm not going to sleep with Caroline when we get back to town, right? I wouldn't do that to you."

Rowan looked at her like she was trying to puzzle something out, then nodded. "I appreciate that."

Silence settled between them for a few minutes. Jamie was warm and content and didn't want to break the spell by asking more questions.

"Do you think you'll ever really visit me?" Rowan asked. The question was quiet, like Rowan was almost afraid to ask.

"Do you want me to visit?" Jamie looked into brown eyes that seemed so vulnerable that it broke her heart. "Of course I'll visit. I'll visit so much you'll tire of me. Now that you've gotten me used to having you around, you're going to miss that solitary lifestyle you're so fond of." Of course, she was joking, but part of Jamie hoped Rowan would want her to visit.

"For the first time in my life, I can honestly say I don't think I could ever tire of spending time with someone. I think I've grown fonder of you than my solitary lifestyle. Let's keep that between us, though. I have a reputation to uphold."

The admission stole Jamie's breath. She wasn't sure how she should respond. She knew admitting that wasn't something Rowan would say lightly. She wasn't the type of person to say something she didn't mean, and the idea that she would want Jamie around, to want her in her life, was difficult to wrap her head around. Maybe she shouldn't be so surprised. They'd been together for weeks, and, for part of that time, they'd basically been in a relationship of some sort. It was an odd, temporary relationship of convenience, but a relationship nonetheless. Maybe it meant more to Rowan than Jamie had thought?

Jamie couldn't pretend that it hadn't meant a great deal to her. She had never been so comfortable with anyone else, ever. She'd never looked forward to waking up next to another person or missed them when they weren't in the room. There were people in her life that she loved a great deal, but she'd felt nothing like this. This, whatever it was, seemed different. That differentness scared her. What the hell was she supposed to do with differentness when their time together was about to end?

Jamie got up from Rowan's lap and walked back to her equipment. "I think I'm going to work a little more before dinner."

"Okay." Rowan watched Jamie walk away. "Did I say something to upset you?"

"No." Jamie regretted causing the look of concern on Rowan's face. "I just want to get through this last video so we can hike out to get new ones tomorrow." Jamie turned to Rowan while her equipment booted back up. "Only two more weeks, and then you'll finally get a break from endless hikes to the tundra."

"Yeah." Rowan stood and walked to the door, taking her jacket from the hook and putting it on. "That'll be a relief. I'm going to go out and chop some wood so we have enough to get us through tomorrow night. Let me know when you're ready for dinner. I think we have one can of soup left. We're almost done here, so we might as well use it."

Jamie wanted to get up from her computer, strip them both bare, and take Rowan to bed. She wanted to feel Rowan's body against hers and pretend like this wasn't as complicated as it was. Like her feelings weren't as complex as they were. She wouldn't do that, though. She needed distance from Rowan if she was ever going to rein in her ridiculous fantasies. Jamie needed to focus on the thing that brought her there.

CHAPTER TWENTY-FOUR

The early morning light illuminated the trail in front of Rowan just enough for her to find her way. She knew Jamie would be sleeping, so she took her time hiking back to the cabin. There was no rush, and having a few minutes to stew on her thoughts and emotions without having an audience was a welcome change of pace. She valued her alone time, and soon enough, it would be her normal again. Rowan tried to convince herself that she would be relieved, but she knew that wasn't true. She'd tried pretending Jamie going back to California would be a good thing, but in her heart, she knew it couldn't be further from how she actually felt. It was going to suck.

No matter how resistant she was, she'd not only gotten used to having Jamie around, but she also craved her company. Even now, when she should bask in her time alone, her only thought was getting back to the cabin to be near Jamie. Good God, it was ridiculous. Jamie's leaving dominated her thoughts, and she wanted to want it to stop, but it didn't. It was like it filled her mind with this belief that she needed to be alone, and she'd hate to have someone in her life, but she knew when Jamie was gone, she'd only feel alone.

Her need to be alone should make her want Jamie to leave, but it didn't. She didn't. Rowan wanted her to stay, but knew that would not happen, so she just pressed on. She did her best to fill her days with projects and busywork, anything to keep her mind occupied and her thoughts off of their time together ending. What else could she do? She knew she should at least talk to Jamie, but she was almost afraid of what she'd say. Their talk the night before hadn't ended as Rowan had hoped. She'd shared how she felt, and Jamie pulled away. The words had escaped Rowan's mouth before she had time to think about them, and Jamie had clarified that she wasn't on the same page.

She didn't blame her. Jamie had a life and a career that she'd spent years working toward, and it would be insane for her to leave all of that to be with someone she'd only met a couple of months before. Insane. If someone told Rowan they were thinking of doing that, she would have thought they were foolish and immature.

The thought of leaving Alaska had crossed her mind, but she knew it wasn't possible. For many reasons, but among them was the fact that she couldn't leave her mom. Even this trip away from her had been difficult. She only had a limited amount of time left before her memories and recollection of who Rowan was were gone forever. Jamie had set up shop in Rowan's heart, but she'd never forgive herself if she walked away from her mother now.

Things were as they were, and she'd just have to get used to the idea that they would not change. Rowan picked up her pace as the cabin came into view. They'd been lucky to have great weather the last few days, and she hoped that would bring good fortune to Jamie's efforts. It was hard to watch her staring at her screen day in and day out, hoping for a one in a million chance the hiker had seen a northern curlew. She knew Jamie was doing her best to stay hopeful, but the cracks in her positive outlook were showing.

Just as Rowan had suspected, Jamie was still sleeping when she entered the cabin. She'd stayed up late the night before to finish reviewing the videos and documenting her findings. There was a slight chill in the room, so Rowan tossed a couple more logs into the stove and sat in her chair to read her book until Jamie woke up. She checked her watch and knew it would likely be at least another hour before that happened. She could clearly see Jamie from her chair near the fire. Her quiet snore made Rowan smile. Part of her wanted to climb back into bed and wrap Jamie up in her arms, but she knew she wouldn't be able to sleep and would only end up waking her. That was why she'd gotten up so early. She'd had trouble sleeping, and her tossing and turning made Jamie grumble in her sleep. Small beds made it difficult for a restless sleeper.

This had been the first night since they'd started sharing a bed that Rowan found herself unable to sleep. Jamie had proved to be a calming presence next to her that helped Rowan sleep better than she could ever remember sleeping. Something else to add to the list of things she'd miss when Jamie was gone. Her ever-growing list.

Rowan opened her book and tried to focus on the story she was reading. The light from the stove illuminated Jamie's face and kept pulling Rowan from her pages. She looked so peaceful and relaxed, snuggled up in her blankets, and Rowan wanted to take a mental picture to carry with her when they had to leave.

When it was clear she wouldn't be able to focus on her book, she tried to help Jamie with some of the video reviews. She'd watched her go through them many times, and if Jamie wanted to rewatch them later, she could, but if Rowan could help her and take some of the burden off of her, she'd call that a win.

Rowan made herself a cup of coffee while the equipment booted up, then settled herself in Jamie's chair. She checked to make sure Jamie was still sleeping, then adjusted the headphones over her ears and pushed play on the video. It was tempting to fast forward, but she knew from what Jamie had told her that it was easy to miss the slightest sound or view of something if she did.

An hour and a half later, Rowan was almost ready to give up. She glanced at her watch and saw that it was a little after eight a.m. She would give it another half hour and wake Jamie up at eight thirty if she wasn't up already. Rowan looked at her empty cup and was about to pause the video to make more coffee when she heard something that she hadn't heard before. She thought it could be similar to the sound Jamie had described when they'd started. The sound of the northern curlew. The empty coffee cup fell to the floor as she pressed rewind and listened. There it was again. It was soft like it came from a distance, but it sounded so much like what Jamie had described and so little like the other birds or sounds she'd heard on the tapes that her heart felt like it would burst from her chest.

She immediately paused the video and pulled the earphones from her head. What if this was a false alarm? What if she was completely wrong, and she pulled Jamie from bed and got her excited only to disappoint her? Rowan knew she had to handle this with care. She took a deep breath to center herself and walked over to kneel next to Jamie. "Jamie? Sweetie?"

"Mmm," Jamie moaned as she pulled the covers over her head. "Five more minutes."

Rowan pulled the covers down and gently kissed the tip of Jamie's nose. "Sweetie? I know you want to sleep, but I think you should get up for a minute. I need to ask you to check something out."

"Can't this wait, Rowan? I'll be up soon, and I'll check out anything you want me to check out." Jamie's voice held a note of irritation, but she also giggled a little at her last comment.

Unsure of what else to do, Rowan scooped Jamie up from the bed and carried her to her chair. "What the hell are you doing, Rowan?" Jamie complained. "Would you like me to murder you? Have you ever successfully picked a woman up from bed, carried her across the room against her will, and not have her murder you?"

It was a rhetorical question, but Rowan felt the need to answer. "If I've made a mistake, and this isn't a good reason to wake you up, you can murder me all you want."

Jamie rubbed her eyes and yawned. "Dead?"

"Yes, totally dead."

She looked at Rowan skeptically and nodded her head as she pulled the blankets tighter around her body. "Okay, what?"

Rowan picked up the headphones but paused before putting them on Jamie's head. "Now that I have you here, I'm full of doubt, but please just listen to this and let me know what you think. I promise to make it up to you with one of those massages you're so fond of if I'm wrong."

"Oh, it's going to take more than that, buddy. I'll make a list." Jamie took the headphones from Rowan and slipped them over her head. "What am I listening for?"

"You tell me." Rowan stepped back and folded her arms over her chest. She held her breath as Jamie rewound the video for a few minutes and listened as it played what Rowan had heard before. When Jamie first listened to the sound, her hands went to the headphones, pushing them against her ears as if that would make it easier to hear. Rowan watched as she rewound the video and turned up the volume to hear better. A few seconds passed, and she rewound, glancing up at Rowan with a look of disbelief on her face.

Jamie listened to those fifteen seconds of video at least a dozen times before looking at Rowan once more with watery eyes. "I think we've done it."

"Yeah?"

She glanced back at the screen, then stood and collapsed into Rowan's arms, tears streaming down her face. "I can't be certain until I see it with my own eyes, but the audio we have is definitely encouraging. Thank you so much, Rowan."

"For what?" Sure, Rowan had listened to the video and woken Jamie up when she heard the bird's call, but it wasn't like she'd spent the exhaustive hours, upon days, upon weeks, scouring the videos as Jamie had. Rowan wasn't the hero here.

"For everything," Jamie said, burying her face in Rowan's shoulder. "For getting me here, for feeding me, for taking care of me, supporting me, protecting me—there's no way I could have done any of this without you, and I won't ever forget it."

Rowan knew what she meant. She knew the bit about never forgetting it was more about Jamie being grateful and not about her needing to remember because they would be apart, but it was impossible for Rowan's mind not to go there, and it was impossible for it not to hurt just a little. "Yeah, well, you're the rock star here. I'm just the roadie, getting you from place to place and making sure you're able to do what you do best. I'm just glad I could be a part of this. It was... something special."

Jamie looked into Rowan's eyes and pulled her down for a kiss. "You're something special, and don't you ever sell yourself short. We're a damn good team, and I'm going to make sure everyone knows it. Well, as long as we're right and we can prove that was the northern curlew you heard."

"How are we going to do that?" Rowan asked, stepping away from Jamie to make them both a cup of coffee. She had a feeling they were going to need it.

"First, is it possible for us to work in the field? I know you mentioned before that we had a tent. Is that still an option?"

Rowan thought about what that would entail. Getting their supplies out there would be challenging, and sleeping in the elements could be dicey. If Jamie needed it, Rowan would make it work. "Pack some thick socks, and we'll figure it out."

Jamie's face lit up with excitement. "Perfect, I lo—love that you're as invested in this as I am."

Rowan rocked her hand from side to side in a seesaw motion. "I'm not sure I'm as invested as you because that could get dangerous. One of us has to be thinking logically."

Jamie laughed and leaned up to kiss Rowan once more before beginning to pack everything they'd need. "I can go through the rest of this video while we're out in the field. I don't want to waste any more time away when we don't know how long it will be there. This tape had to be from at least three days ago. We've already wasted so much time."

"Hey." Rowan stopped Jamie with both hands on her shoulders. "If it's there, we'll find it, and we won't come back until we have the proof we need." Rowan knew they had a long couple of weeks ahead of them, but at least they'd be together.

CHAPTER TWENTY-FIVE

A chill ran through Jamie as she snuggled deeper into Rowan's arms and pulled the blanket over her head. They'd spent the last two nights in a tent on the tundra, and she was questioning her life choices. She could be still sleeping in her climate-controlled bedroom, thousands of miles away from this frozen wasteland.

Of course, the cold would only get worse as they grew closer to fall, but they would be long gone by that time. Jamie would be home, and Rowan would be back in her own life. She wondered if Rowan would miss her when she was gone. She knew Rowan had said she would, but Jamie wondered if that was partly because she'd gotten used to having Jamie around. It would likely be a different story once she was back in her own routine. Before long Jamie would probably be just a distant memory of the few months she spent babysitting an ornithologist, obsessed with finding a bird that was probably extinct.

Although now she wasn't so sure the possibility could be dismissed. Jamie had been through the rest of the video they'd collected. She'd heard the call of what sounded so much like a northern curlew she was finding it difficult to deny it could be real. Now she needed definitive proof.

The last two days had been spent with her sitting alone with her camera a few feet from where she thought the sound on the video originated. When they'd arrived at the site, Rowan had helped her redirect the cameras toward the sound's origin. If she were to guess, it was near a small grouping of rocks. Jamie was reluctant to investigate too closely for fear of startling the bird if it was nearby. They'd just have to be patient.

This was precisely the type of work she'd always dreamed of doing when she was a child. The excitement of the chase, well, the silent and tempered excitement of the chase. Hours alone wholly focused on her surroundings and the nature around her. She was sitting on the cusp of an important discovery that would allow her to make a name for herself. Her name would be known for her own achievements, not her father's.

Rowan stirred behind her and mumbled something unintelligible. Jamie smiled and pulled Rowan's arms tighter around her body. Rowan had been the perfect assistant for Jamie's work these last few days. She'd been invaluable for the entire time they'd been there, but these last few days, Rowan had been extra attentive. Jamie was a little embarrassed by the amount of work she had asked of her. Once she knew there was a chance the curlew was here, Jamie's focus was on finding the proof she needed. Unfortunately, this left most of the grunt work of carrying their equipment from the cabin to the site almost completely on Rowan's very sexy back.

Every time Rowan would return with another load, Jamie would blow her a kiss. It was a simple gesture, but she hoped it expressed just how much she appreciated everything Rowan did. In the evenings, when they were tucked away in the tent they were sharing, Jamie showed her genuine gratitude. Sex with Rowan was unlike anything Jamie had ever experienced. The connection they shared went beyond something she'd had with women she'd known for years. It was as if they clicked together like two pieces of a puzzle. Rowan knew precisely how to coax every ounce of pleasure from Jamie's body, and she was all for it. For a fleeting moment, Jamie wondered if she'd ever experience anything like it again. Had Rowan ruined her for sex with anyone else? If future partners didn't make her feel the way Rowan did, would Jamie be disappointed? She knew the answer to that, and it made her sad. Not about the sex. Well, not only about the sex. She knew saying good-bye to Rowan would be like leaving a part of herself behind. It was something she'd never felt before, and it unnerved her a little.

Jamie turned around in their nest of sleeping bag, so she was facing Rowan. It would soon be completely light outside, and she knew they should wake up. The morning and evening were the most active times for the birds, and she knew they wouldn't wait around for her to get up. The early bird catches the worm and all that.

She studied Rowan's sleeping face for a minute. Jamie loved watching her sleep. When Rowan was awake, she was in constant motion. There was always wood to be chopped, things to be repaired, food to be caught and cooked—a continuous flurry of activity. Except when she slept. She knew Rowan sometimes struggled with insomnia, but she was completely relaxed when she slept. This was one of Jamie's favorite parts of her day. She felt so connected to her and protective of her she would postpone waking her as long as she could.

Sleepy eyes fluttered open as Jamie kissed Rowan's lips. "Good morning," she said.

"Morning." Rowan seemed dazed and unfocused for a few seconds before her eyes settled on Jamie, and she smiled. "Good morning, cute stuff."

Jamie kissed her again, gentle pecks that gradually deepened. She could spend the entire day in bed with her and not regret one minute of it. Jamie realized that this was her happy place. Wrapped in Rowan's arms, snuggled into her warmth, in this wild and unforgiving place, this was where she felt like her most complete self. This was precisely what she would think of and miss when she returned to her life in California.

"You make me happy," Jamie said. She realized too late that it probably wasn't the best thing to say, considering they had so little time left together. "I'm sorry. I know that was a strange thing to say to you, but it's true, and it just came out."

Rowan shifted and leaned on her elbow, suspending herself above Jamie's body. "No, I—it's okay. You make me happy, too. I'll, ugh. We should get…"

"Yeah, sorry, we should get out there. The northern curlew waits for no woman."

The kiss from Rowan that followed was slow and sweet, packed with so many things neither of them could quite put into words. Jamie never wanted it to end, but after a few seconds, Rowan pulled away, and they both slipped out of the bedding and into the cold of the morning.

Jamie watched Rowan struggle into her jeans in the small tent and laughed when she toppled over and slid down the nylon wall.

"Shut up." Rowan playfully scowled. "Not all of us can be as tiny as you."

One boot on and the other in progress, Jamie shrugged. "I thought you liked that I'm tiny?"

"Oh, I do. You're my little pocket-sized friend." Rowan leaned over and kissed the tip of Jamie's nose before fastening her pants and sitting down to put on her boots. "You get out there. I'll be right behind you."

"You know you could always sleep longer? There's no reason you have to get up at the crack of dawn with me."

Rowan unzipped the tent and pushed her outside. "Go. I'll be right out. Someone has to feed you, so you don't waste away."

The chilly wind bit through Jamie's clothes as she finished zipping her jacket and pulled on her knit cap. She wouldn't miss being out in this weather, that was for sure. The longer they were there, the colder it got, and she decided she deserved a beach vacation after this.

She stepped down into the hiding spot she'd been using for the last couple of days and pulled the hood of her coat over her head to help block the wind. She could hear the faint sound of Rowan walking away, probably in search of food for them.

It always amazed her that Rowan had provided for them the way she had. Jamie hadn't missed a meal, and while not every one was something to write home about, she was never hungry. It was incredibly attractive to be with someone you could depend on like that. Jamie wasn't sure she'd ever had that before. Sure, her parents took care of her, and she had a roof over her head, food on the table, clothes on her back, all of that, but it never truly felt like it was about Jamie. She was the beneficiary of her parents maintaining the appearance of a good home.

She probably wasn't being fair to her parents. Jamie couldn't pretend like they hadn't provided her with everything she'd needed, and then some. It was more about how Rowan made her feel while doing those things. Her parents had always made Jamie feel like a burden or responsibility, and after they'd gotten past the uncomfortable part, in the beginning, Rowan had only ever made her feel loved.

Jamie was startled at that thought. She hadn't meant love. It wasn't like she thought Rowan loved her. They barely knew each other. It was more about the way Rowan made her feel. Cared for, not loved. That would be ridiculous.

"Hey," Rowan said as she slid into their hiding spot beside her. "Want some blueberries?"

"Yes, please."

Rowan pulled a clean handkerchief from her pocket and spread it out in front of them. Jamie helped her get it flat, and then Rowan piled the blueberries she'd picked in the middle.

"I'll never get tired of these things," Jamie said. She'd occasionally eaten blueberries at home, but these were on an entirely different level. Sweet and tart, they packed so much more flavor in each little berry than any blueberry she'd ever had before. "My kingdom for a blueberry muffin with these little beauties."

"Mmm." Rowan picked up a berry and held it up for Jamie to eat. "When you visit, I'll make you muffins. My mom used to make them for me when I was little. Raspberry muffins, too."

"Oh man, I bet those are amazing."

"I think I like them even better than the blueberry muffins," Rowan said.

The pile of berries quickly disappeared, so Rowan jumped up to search for more food. Jamie tried to imagine what Rowan was like when she was little. She was sure she was cute as a button. There was no doubt about that. When the adult version of Rowan was feeling playful, she was adorable, so young Rowan must have been extra cute.

An hour later, Jamie was wondering where Rowan had gone. She had heard nothing from her since the blueberries, and she usually would check in now and again to make sure she was okay. Jamie climbed out of her hiding spot but noticed Rowan quietly coming toward her with a bag in her hand. With any luck, the bag would contain food since the berries did little to satisfy her hunger.

"Hey," Rowan said. She slipped in next to Jamie and opened the bag for her to see. "I caught a ptarmigan. I couldn't believe it. I think we surprised each other, but I was quicker on the draw."

Jamie looked at the steaming cooked pieces of the fat little bird and felt guilty. "I don't know if I can eat it. We're desperately searching for a bird, and now you want me to eat another bird right in front of them?"

Rowan laughed and tossed a clean bone toward the forest. "You're a nut. The curlew won't hold it against you. They'll realize you needed food and give you a pass, honey. Besides, you've eaten tons of birds since you've been out here. Why now?"

"Because before, I wasn't eating them in front of other birds. It's weird."

The smell of the food was quickly weakening Jamie's resolve.

"More for me then," Rowan said.

"They'll understand." Jamie took a bite of the plump breast and closed her eyes as flavors exploded in her mouth. "I'll become a vegetarian when I'm back in California."

"How much longer do you think we'll need to be out here?" Rowan asked.

Jamie shrugged and wiped her hands on the handkerchief they'd eaten the blueberries on. "I don't know. I mean, we can't be out here too much longer, but if you can give me a couple more days, I would really appreciate it."

"No problem. I'm going to need to make a trip to the cabin today for supplies if that's okay with you."

"Sure, I'll be okay."

Rowan nodded. "I know. Still, I'll come back as soon as I can."

Soft lips caressed Jamie's before Rowan climbed out of their hiding spot and headed toward the cabin. Jamie had to admit the thought of being without Rowan was a little nerve-racking, but she'd be fine. She checked her watch and hoped Rowan could make it to the cabin and back before the evening. It was still light most of the day, but the days were already getting shorter, and she didn't want to think about Rowan being out there in the dark.

Jamie checked that the camera she was holding still had time left on its battery and room on the memory card before settling back into her spot to wait. Rowan would be back before she knew it.

Chapter Twenty-six

R owan looked around the cabin one last time before hiking back to Jamie. She had been reluctant to leave her alone on the tundra but knew Jamie was a capable woman and had proven repeatedly that she could handle whatever happened. The trip for supplies wasn't something she could have avoided, and asking Jamie to waste her last few days of research hiking back and forth to the cabin wasn't something Rowan could do. She did her best to make it quick and trusted that everything would be okay.

The good news was that they hadn't seen hide nor hair of a bear in weeks. That could either mean they'd cleared out of the area, or it meant they were due to see another one any day now. The further in the season, the more risk there was. The bears would only become more desperate and bolder closer to hibernation.

Not wanting to waste a minute of her precious time, Rowan packed the last items they needed into her bag and closed the cabin. One more week, and they'd need to board everything up and hike out. The plan was to load their supplies into a canoe stored in the shed and float down the river to a designated area where a helicopter would pick them up and take them back to Ugruk. Then they'd say good-bye. Jamie would catch a flight to Anchorage and then home.

Rowan dreaded having to say good-bye at the airport. Her own plane would be there waiting for her, and she'd considered asking Jamie if she wanted Rowan to fly her to Anchorage just so they'd have a little more time together, but she'd decided against it. That would only delay the inevitable, and she suspected that the flight would be uncomfortable. The idea of being emotional while stuck in a plane with someone she was having all sorts of emotions about sitting next to her sounded like torture.

Plans were set in motion, and Rowan just needed to accept them as they were. It wasn't like Jamie would be entirely out of her life. She'd visit, and they could do video calls with each other or whatever. They would make it work. It had to work; they were friends now. This trip had turned out to be an epic adventure that they'd shared, and that was something they would always have.

Her pack seemed to only get heavier with each step she took. The path they used to go between the cabin and the site had become more and more worn every time they took it. Unfortunately, that meant water would collect in areas after rain. Rowan hated soggy boots, and being soaking wet reflected her mood. She knew she needed to pull herself out of this funk, or she wouldn't enjoy the rest of their time together.

When Rowan stepped out of the brush and onto the tundra, she was immediately pulled down to the ground. It startled her at first, but when a soft voice whispered in her ear to be quiet, she got her bearings and relaxed.

"What's going on?" Rowan could feel a slight tremor in Jamie's body as she leaned into her to be heard. "Is everything okay?"

Silently, Jamie pointed to a bird in the distance before raising her camera and taking photos. Rowan retrieved the binoculars from her bag to get a better look.

"Holy fuck," Rowan whispered. "You did it. This is really happening." The northern curlew's head turned from side to side before it leaned down to feed three tiny hatchlings. The gravity of the moment wasn't lost on Rowan, and her chest swelled with pride. Jamie had done this. She'd accomplished what so many thought was impossible.

Rowan set the binoculars down next to her and focused on Jamie. She wanted to remember this forever. The zipper on her bag clicked as Rowan slowly opened the front pocket where she'd stored one of their video cameras earlier in the day. She said a silent prayer that there was, in fact, some charge left in the batteries as she turned it on and opened the viewscreen on the side. Rowan turned the camera toward Jamie, and with a dreaded "ding," it started recording.

The light reflected perfectly off Jamie's golden hair and gave her an almost ethereal glow. She was gorgeous and perfect. Rowan had not only never met someone like Jamie, but she'd also never imagined someone like her existed. Someone who could challenge Rowan like no one ever had but still left her only wanting more. She didn't think she would ever get enough of Jamie, and that thought scared her. She'd have to learn how to continue with her life without her in it, which left Rowan hollow inside.

Jamie turned to Rowan and smiled into the camera before focusing on the birds. Rowan knew this would be one of the most important moments of Jamie's life, and she was just honored to witness it and be able to share that with her.

"Tell us about the importance of this discovery, Dr. Martin," Rowan said, realizing she wanted to know what was going on in Jamie's mind.

The camera in her hands lowered as Jamie took the time to flip through the most recent photos she'd taken. "I can't express to you how important this is. We have just documented the existence of the *Numenius borealis*, or northern curlew. A bird on the critically endangered list and thought for many years to be extinct. Not only does it still exist, but three hatchlings have also just poked their little heads out so their mother can feed them."

"Have you seen the male curlew as well?" Rowan asked.

Excitement sparked in Jamie's eyes before she turned back to take a few more photos of the clutch. "Yes, absolutely. I've photographed both the male and female. There's no doubt in my mind that they are northern curlew."

"Can you tell me more about the northern curlew and the significance of this discovery?" Rowan continued to record as Jamie talked about the history of the bird, how it was brought to the edge of extinction by being overhunted, and the destruction of its habitat. They were all things she and Rowan had discussed before, but Jamie's passion pulled her in as if it was new information. Finally, she talked about how important this discovery was and the steps that might be taken to help preserve what was undoubtedly some of the last northern curlew in existence. She was thoughtful enough to credit the hiker who reported the original sighting and even talked about Rowan and her involvement. She spoke like a seasoned pro, and Rowan knew without a doubt that Jamie would have a bright future ahead of her.

"So where do we go from here, Dr. Martin? What does the future look like for this incredible bird that, before now, was assumed gone forever?"

Jamie lowered her camera but kept looking toward the birds flying around, caring for their young. Rowan thought she saw a hint of sadness in Jamie's expression, and she wanted to wrap her in her arms and reassure her that everything would be okay.

"Well, it has given us the gift of a second chance. I'll spend the next few days observing these birds, and, with any luck, I'll be able to band them so we can study their flight pattern once they migrate south."

Rowan turned the camera to get Jamie in the foreground with the birds in the distance behind her. They weren't close enough to see any detail with this tiny camera, but she knew Jamie would have plenty of footage from the many other cameras she had set up around the area.

"What does this discovery mean to you, Dr. Martin?" Rowan asked. She knew the answer, but she wanted to hear Jamie say it for the camera.

"It's—" Jamie turned from the birds to look directly into the lens. "It's absolutely everything. This means everything to me, both personally and as an ornithologist. We've accomplished something few thought possible, and this research will impact the entire story of this beautiful species of bird." She turned back to look at the birds in the distance. "This discovery will change my life forever. These birds have changed my life forever. I'm eternally grateful to them—" Jamie turned back to Rowan. "And to you, Rowan, for this honor. I will never be the same."

Rowan stopped the recording and lowered the camera to her lap. Jamie silently held her gaze before leaning in to kiss Rowan with more passion than she'd ever known existed. Rowan deepened the kiss as the curlew flitted around their young in the distance. She knew both of their lives were changed forever.

CHAPTER TWENTY-SEVEN

"B est day ever?" Rowan asked as they finally crawled into bed.
Jamie gave her question the consideration it deserved before answering. There had been many great days in her life, and several of those had been over the last three months. The time she'd spent in the field with Rowan had been something plucked right from her dreams. All her childhood visions of her future come to life. Well, not the Rowan part, although if she could go back and tell young Jamie about her, she was sure she'd include Rowan in those dreams of her future. This day was by far the best of them all.

"Without a doubt, best day ever." The grin she'd had the entire day was straining her cheeks, but it was useless to try to stop smiling. She'd documented the existence of a species of bird others had completely written off and declared extinct. She'd found the same bird that meant so much to her and her father. Her name would be attached to the sighting, and she was sure she'd be interviewed by all the ornithological publications and maybe even some of the national news agencies. This was her discovery, and her career would never be the same. Her life would never be the same.

"Good night, sweetheart," Rowan said, wrapping her arms around her and placing a kiss on top of her head. "I'm so proud of you."

Jamie had thought about what this would mean a million times since she'd first heard about the sighting, but there was always a part of her that wouldn't allow her heart to believe they would find it. Why would she? People had been looking for the northern curlew since the last sighting in the 1960s, and there wasn't documented proof it still existed. That was a long time not to see a species of bird whose habitat was so out in the open and one with a migration path that was so vast. It should have been extinct.

When Jamie first heard its call that morning and then made her way around from where she was toward the sound, she was mentally trying to keep her expectations in check. Maybe she'd misheard it. There was always a chance she'd manifested the northern curlew call in her mind after spending months searching for any inkling of a sign out here on this barren landscape. It would be a reasonable thing for her mind to do. She was desperate. Her time there was ending, and finding this bird meant everything to her. Everything.

The moment the pair came into view, and she could see them up close through the lens of her camera, Jamie knew she'd found them. Her heart was beating loudly in her chest, but all she could think about was that Rowan wasn't there to share this with her. It was the one disappointing thing about the entire day.

She'd never missed someone's presence like that before. Of course, she missed her family or friends when they were apart, but this was different. This wasn't about being fond of someone and wanting them there. The most significant experience of her life was missing the one person with whom she wanted more than anything to share it. Jamie had convinced herself it was because Rowan had been such a massive part of this entire process, and it was only fitting that she was there for the discovery, but deep down, she knew that wasn't the only reason. It was an important moment in her life, and she wanted to share that with the one person in the world she felt closest to—the same person who had become the most important person in her life in a very short amount of time.

That was a lot to unpack. It was ridiculous to think her relationship with Rowan had become that important to her. Jamie knew these feelings were mainly because they'd spent so much time together, and the extraordinary circumstances of what had just happened that day couldn't be discounted. There was a voice in the back of her mind telling her it wasn't about that, though. It was about something Jamie wasn't yet ready to allow to take hold of her—something that would only lead to disappointment.

Exhaustion tugged at her body, but Jamie's mind refused to turn off and allow her to get much-needed rest. She could hear Rowan's soft breathing next to her and pulled her arms tighter around her body.

Sleeping like this, with Rowan cradled around her, was something Jamie was going to miss when they returned to their everyday lives.

These were the exact things she needed to put out of her mind, or she'd only be miserable when she had to leave. Returning to her home would be amazing. She couldn't wait to tell her dad about what she'd found. She knew he'd had his doubts, whether he voiced them or not, and now she'd have proof that would validate her decision to drop everything and take this trip.

She couldn't imagine what the board at the PWCA would say. She knew now that her dad had been at least part of the reason they'd funded this trip, and the notoriety this discovery would bring to her, and them by extension, would only help elevate her position there. Her whole life was going to open before her, and she didn't know what her future would hold. She knew Rowan wouldn't be a part of it, though. Not like she wanted. Tears threatened to fall when a wave of sadness struck her.

"Rowan?" Jamie rolled over to face Rowan and kissed her lips. "Are you awake?"

"Mmm?

"Are you awake?"

There was enough light in the tent for Jamie to see Rowan's sleepy eyes open and her concerned expression. "What's wrong?" she asked, brushing Jamie's hair back from her face and wiping the tears from her cheeks with her thumb. "Are you okay?"

"Yeah, I'm fine. I'm sorry." Jamie was embarrassed. Not only had she woken Rowan up after a long, hard day, but she couldn't even explain to her exactly why she was crying. What could she say? *I want you to come home with me. I want you to leave your ailing mother and live somewhere that will almost certainly make you miserable?* That wasn't an option.

"Tell me what's wrong," Rowan pleaded.

Jamie couldn't tell her. She wasn't ready or willing to acknowledge wishes she knew weren't possible. "Just—" As if she knew precisely what Jamie needed, Rowan kissed her. It was desperate, like the first drink of water in the desert. Jamie tugged her pajama pants down and pushed them off and to the bottom of their sleeping bag. Rowan needed no more direction as she slipped two fingers into Jamie and reached as deep inside as she could. It wasn't enough. For the first time since they'd been together, Rowan's fingers weren't enough. She needed more of her, all of her, for as long as she could have her.

Blankets shifted as Jamie climbed on top of Rowan, straddling her head to hover above her mouth.

"Come on, baby, let me taste you," Rowan said as she guided Jamie down. Rowan's mouth was warm and wet, and Jamie moaned as she rocked her pussy back and forth over her tongue. Jamie's emotions bubbled to the surface as silent tears trailed down her cheeks. How was she going to walk away from her?

Three fingers caressed the edge of Jamie's center as Rowan silently asked for permission to enter her. "Yes," Jamie gasped as she rocked back and took them inside. Rowan's fingers weren't the delicate type most women had. They were long and thick, and Jamie groaned at the sweet stretch she felt when they entered her. Her rocking motion increased as she fucked herself on both Rowan's face and her fingers.

"More." Jamie wasn't sure what she was begging for, but she knew she needed more of Rowan. Rowan turned them over and hovered above Jamie as she slid her fingers back in. The stretch stung, and Jamie halfheartedly pushed on her chest, but Rowan instinctively must have known it wasn't what she wanted. Jamie felt surrounded by her. She felt owned by her, and she willingly surrendered to the submission. There was a part of her that would always belong to Rowan, and she knew that no matter how far apart they were or where their lives took them, that would never change. She desperately wanted Rowan to take that part of her. To claim it as her own and keep it safe.

"I've got you, baby." Sweat dripped down Rowan's face. She slowed her movements to a steady thrust and watched Jamie like she was memorizing everything about this. Jamie understood because it was the same thing she was doing. Cataloging the way it felt to belong, body and soul, to her. She was sure it would fade at some point. The longer they were apart and the further they settled into their own lives, away from this place, these feelings would fade. She'd be able to look back on this memory with fondness and not the sadness that threatened to overtake her now.

"I'm going to come," Jamie groaned. "Don't stop. Please, don't stop."

Her impending release erupted as Rowan pushed as deep as she could and touched a place inside her that made her completely lose control. "Ahhhhhh," she screamed as her walls contracted, squeezing Rowan's fingers in a desperate attempt to keep her inside forever. The tent walls seemed to close in for a minute as Jamie fought against the darkness. She had to focus all her strength not to pass out. When the waves passed, Rowan collapsed forward and rested her weight on her forearms, desperately trying to catch her breath.

"I'm going to pull out," Rowan said, gently pulling her fingers out of Jamie's still-pulsing body. Losing Rowan inside broke the emotional dam that had been holding Jamie together. With a sob, she cried an ugly, gut-wrenching deluge of tears. Without a word, Rowan pulled her back into the blankets and wrapped her up in her arms as tightly as possible without crushing her much smaller body.

"Shhh, it's okay, sweetheart," Rowan soothed as she gently rocked her back and forth. "I've got you. You've had an exciting, super emotional day. Just let it all out."

Jamie realized Rowan thought she was crying because of the curlew, and maybe that was part of it, but she wasn't ready to talk to her about what else she was feeling. She would speak to her before she left. Jamie promised herself she would be honest with her about how she felt, but she would make it clear she completely understood leaving Alaska, and her mother, wasn't an option. She respected that and recognized it was a valid reason to stay. She knew sharing her feelings wouldn't change the reality of their situation, but she respected Rowan enough to let her know how she felt. But not tonight. Tonight, Jamie wanted to stay wrapped up in Rowan's embrace and soak up every ounce of her she could. The rest was tomorrow's problem.

CHAPTER TWENTY-EIGHT

Rowan dropped the last of the equipment on the cabin floor and collapsed into a chair from exhaustion. The curlews had cared for their young for another day before they were up and out of the nest, testing their little wings only a day after hatching from their eggs. Three perfect little northern curlews experienced the world for the first time, and Jamie and Rowan were there to witness the entire thing. Jamie had said there might be other nests and birds in the area, but they commonly believed that nest density was low. That meant if there were others, they might not be in sight of this pair's clutch. Rowan could tell Jamie was itching to explore the area more, looking for others, but knew the best thing she could do was stay where they were and document as much as she could about the pair they knew for sure existed.

They'd observed the birds for another two days while the babies figured out how things like legs and wings worked, and then they were gone. The family of five was on its way south, hopefully meeting up with others of its kind. Rowan liked to imagine them landing on a warm beach somewhere with other northern curlews arriving every minute. This couldn't be the last of them. Surely there were others, and this was only the beginning of what would hopefully be their comeback story. Jamie would be credited with discovering their existence. Her Jamie— well, this Jamie. She wasn't exactly her Jamie, but it was sometimes difficult not to think of her that way. Rowan needed to get it into her head that Jamie would never be hers. They had one week left to wrap things up here, and then they would have to go back to the real world.

"That everything?" Jamie asked as she looked up from her laptop.

"Yep. That's everything. It's as if we weren't even there." Rowan hoped Jamie didn't detect the sadness saying that made her feel.

"Hey, I hate to ask you to do something else, but do you think you might try to catch us a nice fish for dinner? I think we have some mushrooms, Eskimo potatoes, and onions left. I could cook you up a nice thank you dinner tonight. Unless you have other plans, of course." Jamie winked at Rowan for the teasing remark. "I'd like to talk to you about something, too."

Usually, when someone said they wanted to talk to you and didn't just come out and say it, it wasn't anything good. In Rowan's experience, anyway. She wanted to ask Jamie to talk about it now, but since she had asked to do it during a nice dinner she'd planned to make, Rowan didn't have the heart to push her. She'd just have to be patient—her least favorite thing to be.

"Sure," Rowan said. She stood up from her chair and stretched the kinks out of her worn-out muscles. "Maybe I could talk you into one of those fancy massages after dinner?"

Jamie laughed. "Oh, really? That wouldn't be code for anything, would it?"

"I won't turn down that kind of fancy massage, but it certainly doesn't have to go in that direction. If you think you have the will to resist, that is."

Jamie stood from her desk and walked toward Rowan with what could only be described as a sexy gait. Small fingers combed through the hair on the back of Rowan's head before pulling her down for a kiss. Rowan groaned and wished they could just skip to the massage portion of the evening right then. She'd eat some other time when every nerve in her body wasn't on high alert and begging to be touched.

"When you put it that way, why—"

The lips that had only a minute before held her captive were suddenly gone as Jamie stepped back and out of Rowan's reach. "Nope, you have to wait. Fancy dinner and a talk first. Those are the rules. I also wouldn't be opposed to snuggling up on a pallet in front of the fire if you don't think that would be too much trouble."

Rowan turned on her heels and headed toward the door. "Fish, dinner, fire, talk, massage, sex. This is the best plan I've heard in a really long time."

Rowan almost skipped down the trail toward the river with her fishing pole in hand. Other than the back-breaking work of breaking down camp and carrying everything back to the cabin, they'd enjoyed some of the best weather they'd seen in a couple of weeks, and it was a welcome sight. Rowan took in a deep breath of clean Alaskan air and let it clear her mind as she slowly blew it out. She could see herself living like this forever. Maybe not quite this remote during the winter, but she didn't mind the seclusion when there was good hunting and fishing.

She pictured spending her days just like this. Fishing for their dinner, maybe teaching their kids how to hunt and fish, to live off the land, just like she'd been taught when she was young. They'd have a little girl who was the spitting image of Jamie, with long blond hair, green eyes, and a feisty spirit. And a little boy who looked like Rowan but was more bookish like his other mom. Rowan laughed at her ridiculous thoughts, not the least of which was the fact that they wouldn't be able to have children together, in the traditional sense. It was fun to dream about, though.

It was strange that she'd been resistant to having kids with Sara because she felt like they hadn't been together long enough, but the idea of having kids and settling down with a woman she'd only known for three months, seemed completely reasonable. She'd never felt this way about anyone before, not even her ex-wife.

The one certainty she knew was that she and Jamie would be happy. She'd make a comfortable home for Jamie, and she'd never want for anything, especially anything she would have to leave behind in California. Rowan's step faltered as she tripped on an exposed tree root. The reality of the situation fell over her like a blanket and seemed to suck the air right from the sky. They'd never have that life. She'd never be able to have a life with Jamie, no matter how much she wished it could happen. She knew that at some point, her mother would be gone, and she'd be free to leave Alaska, but that could be years. Hopefully, it would be years. What then? Would Jamie just wait for her until that time? It was insane to think someone wouldn't see the same things in Jamie that made Rowan fall for her.

Rowan wiped a tear from her cheek. Falling for Jamie had never been the plan. In fact, it was the exact opposite of what she'd sworn to do when she recognized where her feelings were going. That was a path to heartache that you don't get over. She'd thought her divorce had been difficult. Watching Jamie fly away might just be worse.

The loose rocks on the riverbank slid down the rocky slope as Rowan sat on the edge and dropped her line into the water. The salmon weren't running like they were a few weeks ago, but she'd still be able to catch one without too much trouble. Rowan's mood had declined considerably, and she had the sudden urge to just get the next few days over with. She wanted to rip the bandage off and get on with her heartache.

Over the next few days, her attitude would make their remaining time together a good experience, or it would push Jamie even further away. She knew that. The knowledge didn't quell her desire to throw a fit while she was still alone and wouldn't offend anyone other than the fish. It wasn't fair. None of this was fair. Rowan knew in her heart that they could make each other happy, but the universe had brought Jamie into her life only to strip her away. It sucked.

A fish on her line distracted Rowan's thoughts. It was a decent-sized catch, so she would only need the one for their dinner. After cleaning and cutting it into fillets, she placed it in her bag and turned back toward the cabin. A rustling of bushes from the other side of the river caught her attention, and she turned to find a large mama bear and her two cubs appear out of nowhere. Rowan stopped in her tracks and waited to see what the bears would do. The mother lifted her head into the air, and Rowan knew she'd caught the scent of her fish. With any luck, she would eat the discarded carcass she'd left on the bank and leave Rowan alone.

Slowly and carefully, Rowan backed away from the river. She had about a forty-five-minute hike to the cabin at a normal pace, but if she didn't see any signs of them after twenty minutes, she'd speed up and try to make it there sooner. Once she was out of the bear's eyesight, she turned forward and made her way down the trail, stopping every few feet to listen for any sign she was being followed. Twenty minutes later, she broke into a jog and made it safely to the cabin.

"Did you get the fish?" Jamie asked as she stepped out onto the porch.

"Yep." Rowan knew her answer was short, but she wasn't quite ready for pleasantries yet.

"Okay..." Jamie sounded confused, and Rowan knew she

deserved an explanation but wasn't sure what to say. I'm in love with you, and I want you to stay here and be my wife even though you have this gigantic future ahead that you've always dreamed of, and the only thing I can offer you is the love of someone who until now did not know what love was. Perfect. That would go over perfectly.

Rowan took a deep breath and pulled the bag from her shoulder to hand to Jamie. "Here's your fish. Unless you need my help with dinner, I'm going to head out back to chop some wood for our fire this evening. We're getting kind of low." It was a lie. They had plenty to last through the evening, and the skeptical look on Jamie's face told her she hadn't fallen for the ruse. Fortunately, she didn't question her, so Rowan fled to the woodpile to release some of her frustrations on an innocent log.

An hour later, Jamie called Rowan into the cabin for dinner. She had set the table with the few dishes they had and had even lit a candle to burn. Rowan washed her hands in their bucket of water and took a deep breath. She would not ruin this lovely meal Jamie had prepared because she'd gotten herself in a funk wishing for things that wouldn't happen.

"This looks amazing, Jamie." Rowan held Jamie's chair out for her before sitting in her own.

"It still amazes me how much delicious food is just out there in the wild. I mean, I can believe it because humans have been around a hell of a lot longer than grocery stores, but you know what I mean. I never imagined I'd be making a meal under these conditions. It's fun. I might have to try foraging when I get home. I'm getting pretty good at it."

There was one more stab to the heart. Jamie hadn't meant it that way at all, but in the space Rowan's head was in, it was a gut punch that Jamie enjoyed being out here so much. Rowan cleared her throat and picked at the fish on her plate. "Well, I'm impressed you've taken to it so quickly. It's not a challenge everyone would welcome, and you've mastered it."

"I wouldn't say I've mastered it, but I think it's at least edible. I'm proud of it. You're happy, and that's what matters."

"Yeah," Rowan said, pushing a potato around on the plate with her fork.

"Are you sure you like it? You don't seem like you do. I wish I could offer to make you something else, but this is all we have left unless you think there's something in the traps."

"No." Rowan shook her head and took a big bite of fish. She swallowed and speared a potato and mushroom for her next bite. "I'm sorry. I just have a lot on my mind."

"Anything I can help you with?" Jamie asked, reaching across the table to take Rowan's hand. "Seeing that sad look on your face just breaks my heart."

"Nope." Rowan popped the potato and mushroom bite in her mouth and wished for the meal to end quickly. "How was your research today?"

Jamie hesitated but finally pulled her hand back and continued eating her meal. "It was excellent. I can't believe we're out here in the middle of nowhere, and we have this incredible news to share with everyone, and there's absolutely no way we can share it."

"I could always try to get Greg on the radio," Rowan offered.

"No, no, no, it will be so much more exciting when we're back in—well, when I'm back in California and can see everyone's excitement firsthand. I wish you could come back with me, even just for a little while, so you could get the credit you deserve."

"I've already been away from my mom for months. I can't take the risk of leaving her any longer. Who knows how much more time I have before she doesn't remember me at all."

"I know, I'm sorry. It's selfish of me to ask. I know it's important for you to be here with her. I feel guilty enough about the time I've already pulled you away. I hope you can forgive me."

"There's nothing to forgive. I wouldn't trade this time with you for anything. My mom is still good most of the time, so I'm sure she will be fine when I get home. Greg promised to tell me if there was a problem, and I trust him."

Rowan pushed her plate away and wiped her mouth with her napkin. "That was excellent."

"Thanks." Jamie blushed as she placed her last potato in her mouth and stood to gather their plates. "I hope it was enough for you. You've worked so hard over the last couple of days, and I'm sure you burned a lot of calories."

"I'm good." Rowan patted her stomach and stood to help with the dishes.

"When I visit, I'm going to feed you like a king the entire time I'm here. Feasts every night with lots of wine to wash it down."

"Sounds good." Rowan had her doubts that there would ever actually be any visits. Sure, they'd talk and email back and forth for a while, then Jamie would meet someone, and Rowan would simply drift out of her life. It was inevitable. She looked up and found Jamie watching her intently, a confused look on her face.

"Are you sure everything is all right?" Jamie asked.

Heat warmed Rowan's ears as she tried to tamp down her frustration. "I said it was fine, Jamie. Please, just drop it." Rowan regretted the words as soon as they'd left her mouth. "I'm sorry, I—"

Jamie stacked the last dish on the drying rack and dried her hands on the dishtowel. "Come on," she said, taking Rowan by the hand and pulling her toward a pallet she'd set out in front of the fire.

Rowan tossed two more logs into the stove, then joined Jamie on the blankets. "I'm sorry, Jamie. You didn't deserve that."

Small hands wrapped around Rowan's larger ones as Jamie pulled them into her lap. She stared at them, rubbing her thumb along the knuckle of Rowan's hand nervously.

"Is everything okay with you?" Rowan asked, anger immediately dissipating at the thought that something might be wrong with Jamie.

"Yeah, it's fine, I just—I wanted to talk to you about something, and I'm not exactly sure how to approach it."

Anxiety gripped Rowan's chest as a million possibilities ran through her mind about what Jamie wanted to discuss. It wouldn't be what she wanted. Jamie wasn't about to tell her she was staying in Alaska, but the hopeful thought wouldn't release its hold on Rowan's heart. "Just tell me," Rowan said.

Jamie cleared her throat and continued her caress of Rowan's hand. "I think it's only right that I'm honest about how I feel about you."

"What are you talking about?" Rowan wondered where in the world this could be going. The air seemed heavier as sweat trickled down her face.

"I'm trying to tell you, in a not so smooth way, that I have feelings for you."

Rowan's world came crashing down around her. What did that even mean? Was she trying to tell her she was in love with her? If she was, what was Rowan supposed to do with that information when she would only get on a plane and leave her with these emotions and a broken heart? "What are you talking about?"

Jamie seemed startled by her question. "I'm saying I have feelings for you that are more than ones you'd have for a friend, and I wondered if you might feel the same."

"What does that even mean, Jamie? You're leaving. You're going home, and I'm staying here, and there's nothing we can do to change the reality of our situation. What exactly do you expect me to do with this information?" Rowan's anger was bubbling over, and she was doing her best to hold it back but failing horribly.

"Jesus Christ, Rowan, I thought you'd be happy. Yeah, I'm going back, and you'll be here, but that won't be forever. I was under the misguided impression that you possibly felt the same and thought that maybe we could try to make things work remotely until we could be together."

"Really?" Rowan wanted to be anywhere other than in that cabin in the middle of nowhere with someone she wanted to hold on to and never let go of.

"Really," Jamie said. "What do you want me to say, Rowan? Do you not care for me? Would you not even consider trying to make something work?"

"It's not possible, Jamie." Rowan pulled her hand from Jamie's lap and stood to pace back and forth across the floor. "You're going to go home, and the last thing you need is to force a relationship with someone thousands of miles away, in a place you would never be happy living."

"Don't you dare tell me what would make me happy and what I need. You obviously don't know who I am. Tell me you don't have feelings for me, and I'll leave you alone. I'll fly home and never bother you again."

Rowan stopped her pacing to glare at Jamie. "That's a little dramatic, don't you think?"

"Argh…" Jamie growled in frustration. She stood and went toe-to-toe with Rowan. "Tell. Me. You. Don't. Love. Me."

"Don't be a child, Jamie." Rowan's heart broke as she said the words she knew would push Jamie away even further. She couldn't bring herself to admit it. There was no way this would ever work, and it was better to break things off now than six months from now when they'd inevitably resent each other.

"Fuck you, Rowan," Jamie screamed through her tears. "You can't even say it and admit how I know you feel. You'd rather give up before you even give us a chance to make it work."

"It wouldn't work," Rowan said.

"I guess we'll never know." Jamie pulled her jacket from the hook near the door and stormed out of the cabin, disappearing into the dim light of dusk. Rowan let her go. Her legs were like stone as she dragged them toward the bed and collapsed in a heap of sadness and despair. She had fucked up. She wished she could rewind to an hour ago and take back everything she said, handle things entirely differently than she did.

"You're a fucking asshole, Rowan Fleming. You deserve to be alone, you miserable fuck." The cabin grew darker as the night approached, and it only brought Rowan down even more. She let out a pitiful sigh, and then it occurred to her that Jamie had stormed off on her own, alone. She was out there by herself in woods that would soon be way too dark to be safe.

A sudden panic gripped Rowan as she stood and jogged for the door. She didn't bother with a jacket as she stepped off the porch and into the night. "Jamie? I'm sorry. Where are you, sweetheart?"

A scream pierced through the otherwise silent forest, and Rowan ran. She had no jacket, no weapon, nothing, but none of that mattered. Only Jamie mattered, and Rowan wasn't there to protect her. She'd never forgive herself if something happened to her. Their last words flashed through Rowan's mind, and she ran through the forest in the scream's direction. Those couldn't be the last things they ever said to each other. They couldn't. She hesitated to call out to Jamie again for fear of startling whatever scared her, but she had no choice. She couldn't keep blindly running through the forest, hoping she was going in the right direction.

"Jamie? Where are you?"

"Rowan?" Jamie's scared voice rose through the night, and Rowan used it to figure out her general location.

"I'm on my way. Don't move unless you have to. Can you tell me what's scared you?"

"Bear. Mama bear and her cubs. Rowan, I'm scared." Jamie's voice cracked as she squeaked out the words.

"Don't be scared, baby. I'm on my way. Everything is going to be okay." Rowan stopped short when she saw the mama bear and two cubs she'd seen at the river. She must have followed the trail of fish scent Rowan left when she hiked back to the cabin. She'd led the bears straight to their door, and now she'd put Jamie in danger. Stupid, stupid, stupid. The mama bear turned when she heard Rowan's footsteps and rose up on her hind legs. She was trapped with Jamie on one side, Rowan on the other, and brush on either side of the trail. This was a worst-case scenario situation. It was something Rowan wouldn't have believed if someone had told her it happened.

"Jamie?"

"Yeah." Jamie's voice was weak, but she was relatively calm despite the situation. God, she loved her.

"I'm going to get them to focus on me, and I want you to back away until you can't see us, then slip into the brush to make a wide circle around and back to the cabin. I'll meet you there."

"No fucking way, Rowan. It's too dangerous. I'm not leaving you here alone." Jamie's voice was suddenly strong and controlled. Rowan knew she'd have to leave her no choice but to follow her instructions.

"Hey, bear." Rowan picked up a stone and tossed it toward the bear. "Look at me, you gigantic beast."

"Goddammit, Rowan." Jamie backed away down the trail. Rowan waved her arms and tossed a few more rocks until Jamie was entirely out of sight. She knew she needed to keep the bear's attention for a few more minutes so Jamie could get a safe distance away. She knew it would be a very fine balance keeping her attention but not so much that she'd feel the need to attack. Rowan could hear Jamie making her way through the bushes to her left. They were thick, and it would take her a few minutes before she'd be able to get back onto the trail and get to the cabin.

"Hey, bear. You don't want her. She's mad at me right now and probably wouldn't taste very good." The bear turned her head toward the noise Jamie made and reared up on her hind legs again. The baby bears took a few steps in Rowan's direction, and she raised her arms and growled, trying to scare them back toward their mom. It worked, but the mama bear lunged toward Rowan and then stopped only a couple of feet from her on the trail. She knew if she ran, it would be over. The bear would run her down and tear her to shreds. Her only option was to back away.

The movement to her left had stopped, so she knew Jamie had probably made her way to the trail. On shaky legs, she backed away. "You stay there, bear. I don't want any trouble with you. A few more days and we'll be out of your hair, anyway. Then you shouldn't have anyone else bothering you before you take a long winter nap." The bear dropped to all four feet and sniffed the air. Rowan was very aware of the fact that she was heading in the same direction as the trail of fish she'd left only a few hours before. It couldn't still be that strong, but what did she know? Bears' sense of smell was something her human brain couldn't understand.

"Stay there, Mama. I'm going to leave you guys alone." Step by step, she backed away, but the bear kept walking toward her. "Go on, bear," she said in her best growl. Once again, the cubs waddled up the trail until they were close enough that Rowan could have reached out and touched them. She knew this wasn't good. Before she could decide what to do, the bear charged her once more and, with her giant front paw, slashed at Rowan, her claws driving deep into her chest. The blow took Rowan's breath away, and she knew she was a goner. As she fell to the ground in pain, she thought she heard a loud bang behind her. She did her best to cling to reality, but the darkness swallowed her whole.

CHAPTER TWENTY-NINE

Jamie's heart raced as she ran back down the trail toward where she'd left Rowan. Her mind was a jumble of thoughts, but she did her best to push the fear aside and focus on what she'd do once she found her. Knowing Rowan had been left to face the bear alone, the hike back to the cabin was one of the hardest things Jamie had ever done. Everything inside her told her to go back, help, not leave her alone to face an animal that could easily tear her to shreds and take her life. The only thing that kept her moving forward was the knowledge that there wasn't much she could do without help. She had to get to the cabin to retrieve the only thing that could put the odds back in her favor, the gun.

The door slammed behind her as she stormed into the cabin, frantically looking for the weapon. She found the can of bear spray she'd brought with her and then found the rifle in its cradle above the door. She pulled back the lever to make sure it was loaded and tossed a few shells in her coat pocket, just in case. When she stepped off the porch and ran toward Rowan, she felt like her body was in free fall. As she ran, she was aware her feet were touching the ground, but the rest of her reality felt like it wasn't in her control. She was scared beyond anything she'd ever experienced before and was functioning on pure adrenaline and instinct at that point.

Her world crumbled away when she finally reached Rowan to see the mama bear charge her. Jamie raised the rifle into the air, but Rowan stood between her and the animal. Out of better options, she fired into the air above them, but it was too late. The bear had already knocked Rowan to the ground. The sound had the desired effect, and the bear and her cubs turned and ran back down the trail, away from them, but her worst fears had been realized. Jamie's heart felt like it had been ripped from her chest as she watched Rowan crumble to the ground, covered in blood.

"Rowan!" Jamie screamed as she ran to her side. There was no response from her as Jamie watched the blood drain from her body. "Don't you dare fucking leave me. Do you hear me?" She checked for a pulse and found it was weak, but she was still alive. Jamie took a deep breath and made a mental checklist of what to do to help her keep calm and focused. "One, I need to put you in a better position." She got behind Rowan's body and slipped her arms under hers so she could gently lower her body flat on the ground. "Come on, baby. We can do this. Two, we have to see what she's done to you." Blood covered Jamie's hands as she tore Rowan's shirt away to get a better look at her injury. Several deep slashes cut across Rowan's chest. There was a steady stream of blood coming out of each gash.

She was going to need help. There was no way Jamie would be able to give Rowan the care she needed on her own. Her only option was to get on Rowan's radio and pray someone would make it in time. She didn't think Rowan could hear her talking to her, but voicing her actions helped calm her nerves. "Three, I'm going to wrap my shirt around you to stop the blood, and then I'm going to see if I can wake you up. If you can find the strength to help me get you back to the cabin, we'll at least have a little more protection than just being out here in the open in case she comes back."

Jamie ripped fabric strips from her shirt and tied them together to create a makeshift bandage. She'd be able to fashion something a little better back at the cabin, but for now, this would need to do. Once she'd done all she could with the shirt, she wrapped her jacket around Rowan's shoulders to keep her warm. There was no way she'd be able to get her much smaller coat on her body, but she did the best she could.

"Okay, Rowan, baby, please wake up." Jamie rechecked Rowan's pulse and found it still weak but steady. "Come on, Ranger Fleming, I need you to come back to me now." She could see the bandage she'd created turning red with blood and knew she couldn't wait much longer before having to leave her there so she could run to the cabin to call for help. Leaving Rowan again was the absolute last thing she wanted to do. "Please, baby, wake up." Tears streamed down Jamie's cheeks as she felt herself giving up hope. "No. No. Wake the fuck up, Rowan. Wake up! I need you to wake up and help me save your damn life. I can't do this without your help, baby."

Rowan's eyes flickered open for a second before she moaned and grabbed at her chest. "It hurts."

"I know it hurts. The bear got you with her paw, but she's gone now. We need to get you to the cabin. Come on, sweetheart, let's get you up."

The confused and painful look on Rowan's face broke something inside Jamie. This couldn't be happening. Not when they'd only just found each other. Not when they still had so much to work out between them.

"Help me stand up," Rowan said. Jamie hurried around to her side and slipped her shoulders under Rowan's arm to help lift her to her feet. "Did you shoot a rifle?"

Jamie nodded and moved a step forward, holding as much of Rowan's weight up with her body as she could. "I did. You were in my way, so I just shot it into the air to scare her off."

"Thank you."

The hike back to the cabin seemed to take a lifetime. Rowan needed to stop every few feet to catch her breath, and then they'd move a few feet more. By the time they were on the porch, Jamie had to drag Rowan's body into the cabin and to the bed. There was a trail of blood in their wake, but at least she was safely in the cabin. Once Rowan was on the bed, she immediately passed out again. Jamie quickly went to the radio and tried to mimic what she'd seen Rowan do in the past.

"Greg, are you there? This is Jamie Martin, over." She only heard static. "Greg, this is Jamie Martin. We have an emergency, over." Jamie turned the radio dial to another channel she'd seen Rowan use in the past. "Greg, please, this is Jamie Martin. Rowan is hurt. Please help us."

"Dr. Martin?" Greg's voice was possibly the sweetest sound she'd ever heard.

"Yes, it's me. A bear attacked Rowan. We need help right away."

"Is she awake?" Greg asked, concern evident in his voice.

"No, she woke up long enough to help me get her back to the

cabin, but now she's passed out again. She's lost a lot of blood, and I can't seem to get it to stop. Her pupils were dilated, and her skin is pale."

Jamie could hear Greg say something into another radio, and then he was back with her. "Listen to me carefully, Jamie. We're going to help her together, but we both have to stay calm if she's going to have a chance, got it?"

"Yes." Jamie felt like she might lose control before refocusing on Greg's voice. "Tell me what to do."

"First, we need to make sure you've bandaged her as tightly as you can with clean bandages. You should find some in a medic bag she must have with her in the cabin."

"Okay." Jamie remembered seeing the bag at one point and searched the area where Rowan kept her things until she could find it. "Got it."

"Good job. Now, where is she injured?"

"Her chest. She swiped Rowan across the chest and knocked her to the ground."

"How deep are the cuts?"

Jamie cleared her throat to push back her emotions. "They're really deep."

"Okay, do you think she has any broken ribs? We have to know before we potentially bandage something too tight and cause even more damage."

Jamie thought about helping Rowan back to the cabin. She'd had her arms wrapped tightly around her and noticed nothing that might indicate she had broken ribs. "I can't say for sure, but I don't think so. It looked like Rowan leaned back at the last moment, so the bear only slashed her chest."

"You saw it happen?"

"I—" Jamie didn't know what to say. Was this entire thing her fault? Yes, it was. She knew better than to run out into the forest alone, especially when it was almost dark. She'd never forgive herself for causing this. Her emotions and anger got the better of her, and this happened.

"Hey, I only ask because I want to make sure there couldn't be other injuries you just don't know about."

"No, this is the only one."

"Right, a helicopter is on its way to get you. We're going to bandage her up to stop the bleeding as much as we can before they arrive. Sound like a plan?"

Jamie searched through the medical bag to figure out what supplies she had available. "How long until they get here, Greg?"

"They're an hour and a half out."

"What?" Now Jamie was panicking.

"Hey, she's going to be okay. Take a deep breath, and let's get her bandage in place."

Greg patiently walked Jamie through cleaning the wounds and wrapping the bandages around her body. Rowan woke a few times and moaned in pain but didn't make any coherent sentences. Finally, the sound of helicopter rudders filled the air, and Jamie stepped onto the porch to watch a medic being lowered from a wire into the clearing in front of the cabin. A long basket was lowered to the ground after her, and the medic unhooked it and carried it to the porch with her.

"Are you Jamie?" the medic asked after raising the visor of her helmet.

"Yes, she's in the cabin."

"Very good, I'm Carrie. Are you hurt or just Rowan?"

"Only Rowan, I'm fine."

"Roger that. Let's get her out of here." Carrie charged into the cabin without hesitation. She took a few minutes to check Rowan's status before hefting her up into her arms and gently placing her into the basket. She tightened several straps around her body and then asked Jamie to lift the basket at Rowan's feet, and she lifted at her head. They gently carried her outside, where Carrie connected cables to the basket and signaled that it was safe to raise it to the helicopter. Once Rowan was safely inside, they lowered another line with two straps that Carrie fastened around Jamie and herself before they were lifted.

Jamie stared out the helicopter door as they banked to the side and watched the cabin fade into the distance. The thought occurred to her that had she been told six months ago that she'd find evidence of the existence of the northern curlew and then leave it all behind without a second thought, she would say to that person they were insane. Something like that, a career-changing, life-altering discovery like that, only came around once in a lifetime if you were fortunate. Jamie looked down at Rowan, eyes still closed but finally looking peaceful, and knew she was where she belonged. Rowan was the only thing in the world that mattered to her. They'd figure out what that meant and what their future looked like later. For now, she couldn't imagine being anywhere else.

CHAPTER THIRTY

Brightness stung Rowan's eyes and made them water as the world took shape around her. She tried to raise a hand to block the light, but she found she was not only connected to tubes but too weak to make any genuine effort to lift her arms. After a minute, shapes formed around her, and she knew she was in a hospital. Contraptions beeped as lines and numbers pulsed across the screens of the monitors. She decided this must mean she was alive. That was good news.

She tried to clear her throat, but the dryness only stung. There were several chairs in the room, but she was the only person there. Panic coursed through her as she realized Jamie might still be in danger, or worse, injured.

"Hey, sleepyhead," Jamie said as she came into the room with a cup of coffee in her hand. "Of course, you would pick the ten minutes I left to get coffee to decide to wake up." She set down her cup and went to Rowan's side.

"Jamie?" Rowan tried to determine if this was real or she'd only conjured her up in her mind. The bed shifted as she sat on the edge and placed a hand on Rowan's arm.

"It's me, baby. I can't tell you how happy I am to see those beautiful brown eyes of yours." Jamie placed gentle kisses around Rowan's eyes and across her forehead. "You scared the crap out of me, Rowan."

Rowan looked up to find tears streaming down Jamie's cheeks. "I'm sorry. I—what happened? Where are we?"

"You're in the hospital in Anchorage. After you passed out, I got Greg on the radio, and he sent a helicopter to get us. A charming lesbian named Carrie showed up. She said she's a friend of yours."

"Carrie?" Rowan's words came out in a croak.

"The doctor said you can have some crushed ice for now." Jamie slipped a little crushed ice into Rowan's mouth and gave it a minute to melt before giving her a little more. "Good?"

Rowan nodded. "Don't get any ideas about Carrie. I'm too weak to kick her ass now."

Jamie laughed and took Rowan's hand in hers. "You have nothing to worry about. She was the perfect gentlewoman, and besides, I only have room in my heart for one cute lesbian at a time."

The events of their last day together ran through Rowan's mind. The hike to the river, fishing, the bears, dinner, Jamie's confession, Rowan's terrible behavior that broke Jamie's heart and sent her running out of the cabin and right into danger. Finally, the standoff on the trail, Jamie's escape, the bear charging, and then a shot from a rifle. "Did you shoot the bear?" She felt like she might have asked this question before, but everything was in such a jumble in her mind she couldn't tell what was real and what wasn't.

Pain clouded Jamie's eyes as she turned away at the mention of the bear.

"Hey," Rowan soothed her. "We're okay now. I'm a little fuzzy on the details, but you saved our lives. You're my hero."

Jamie turned back to Rowan, eyes full of tears, and smiled. "I'm so glad you're okay."

Rowan looked down at her bandaged chest, then checked her arms, hands, and anything else she could easily see of her body. "I am okay, right? I hurt like hell, but I seem to have all my parts still." Eyes wide, she checked her appendages once more. "I do have all my parts, right?"

"You do. Everything is present and accounted for," Jamie reassured her.

"It's all still a little fuzzy. Can you tell me what happened?"

Jamie stood and crossed to the window. She folded her arms over her chest and stared outside, obviously uncomfortable talking about the day before.

"You don't have to—"

"No." Jamie turned back to Rowan with a sad smile. "Sorry, I'm still trying to figure it all out myself. I've never been so scared in my life, and when she charged you, I—" Jamie turned back to the window. "I thought I'd lost you forever," she said in almost a whisper.

"I'm okay," Rowan reassured her. "I'll be up in no time at all, thanks to you."

Jamie turned back to Rowan and busied her hands by straightening the blankets that covered her, tucking them tightly around her feet. "You wouldn't have been out there in the first place if I hadn't run out on you like that. I knew better. God, I was so stupid. I hope you can forg—"

"Hey," Rowan grabbed Jamie's hand and pulled her closer. "We fought. I was being a total dick, and you got upset. I shouldn't have reacted the way I did. Please forgive me."

"Let's agree that we're both at fault and both forgiven."

Rowan tugged Jamie's hand until she sat back on the edge of her bed. "Now, please tell me what happened."

"What do you remember?" Jamie asked.

Memories flashed through Rowan's mind in a disjointed mess, but she clung to the last clear ones she had. "I remember hearing you making your way through the brush. You caught the bear's attention, so I taunted her to get her attention back to me. When I thought you were clear and on your way to the cabin, I started backing down the trail, hoping now that they had an escape route, they'd go the other direction. I could tell she wanted to keep going down the trail in the direction I was going, but I think she'd finally given up when her cubs came so close to me I could have touched them. It all happened so fast."

Rowan tried to touch her chest at the memory of what came next, but the equipment attached to her wouldn't allow it. "She charged, and the next thing I knew, I saw her gigantic paw coming at me. I leaned back to avoid it, but she was too fast. The wind was knocked out of me, and I was gasping for breath, but I could have sworn that I heard a shot from a rifle before everything went dark. I assume that was you?"

A pink blush covered Jamie's cheeks. "It was me. I knew I wouldn't be able to help you without a weapon, so I grabbed your rifle and ran back just in time to see her charge you. I've never been so scared in my life. You were blocking any shot I could have made, so I shot into the air, hoping the noise would scare her away."

"I assume it worked?" Rowan asked.

"It worked. The three of them ran off, and I could finally get to you."

Rowan could see the anguish in Jamie's face, recalling the memory. "I'm sorry, Jamie. I'm sorry you had to deal with that all on your own."

Jamie retook Rowan's hand. "We were a team. I don't know if you remember, but you woke up enough to help me get you back to the cabin before passing out again. After a few tries, I was able to reach Greg on the radio, and he walked me through the rest. There are many people out there who care deeply for you, Ranger Fleming, including me."

"Yeah." Rowan squeezed Jamie's hand and fought to keep her eyes open. "About that—"

"We don't need to talk about it right now. You're exhausted, and we need you back on your feet."

The thought occurred to Rowan that they hadn't discussed her research or the reception of the news of her discovery. "Hey, what did everyone say about the curlew? You're probably going to be heading out of here soon."

A tall older man in a lab coat stepped into the room, followed by three much younger people taking notes. "Hello, Ms. Fleming. I'm so glad to see you're awake. I'm Dr. White, and I've been looking after you since you arrived. How are you feeling?"

Rowan looked at Jamie, who kissed her on the cheek before stepping away to give the others room. "I'll come back later. You get some sleep." Jamie fled the room before Rowan could say anything else to her.

"I basically hurt all over. What's the damage look like?"

The doctor explained her injuries and their long-term effects. She was expected to make a full recovery, but with months of rehabilitation ahead. He explained she would always carry the scars across her body, but it was a small price to pay for her life.

"Thanks, Doc."

"You're fortunate that young lady could help you as much as she did. We've seen many others who have tangled with a bear and didn't fare nearly as well."

Rowan looked toward the door to see if Jamie might be lingering outside. "Extremely lucky."

"Right, well, I'll let you get some rest. Please tell a nurse if there's anything you need."

After one last nod, the doc and his little soldiers filed out and were off to their next patient. Rowan looked again, hoping she might see Jamie waiting outside the door, but she wasn't there. It was just as well, she supposed. She would have to learn not to depend on someone else again, and the sooner she did, the better off she'd be. What a royal mess she'd gotten herself into. All she had to do was meet this scientist and keep her alive. That's all. She hadn't asked or wanted to fall in love. Now she'd have to figure out how to move on without having Jamie in her life.

"Hey there, I'm the day nurse, Roxanne. I'm glad to see you're awake. We were worried about you for a while. You lost quite a bit of blood."

Rowan touched the bandages on her chest again, needing the reassurance that everything was still okay. "That's what I hear. I guess I shouldn't pick a fight with a mama bear and her cubs."

Roxanne snorted and made some notes in her chart. "I'd say that's a good idea. She just about lopped your noggin off. You were very lucky."

Was everyone going to tell her how lucky she was? She got it. Rowan was extremely lucky to be alive. She didn't feel so lucky with a broken heart and a lump in her throat from the fear that Jamie would walk in any moment and say good-bye.

"You didn't notice where the woman who was in here before got off to, did you?"

A sly smile lit up Roxanne's face. "You mean the beautiful Jamie?"

"Yeah, Jamie Martin. Do you know where she is?"

Roxanne shook her head as she checked the monitors one last time. "Nope, but she won't be gone long. That poor girl has hardly left your side since you got here. She's been beside herself with worry. I think you just might have yourself a keeper in that one."

"We aren't together."

The bed shifted as Roxanne sat on the edge and took Rowan's hand in hers. "That girl is completely in love with you, silly. It's plain as day."

She couldn't believe she was talking about this with a stranger, but she was desperate to talk to anyone about the pain she was feeling. "Love doesn't really matter. She lives in California. I live in Alaska—"

"I'm sorry, but blah, blah, blah. That sounds like a lot of excuses to me. If you want it to work, you'll make it work. Or you'll at least try to make it work. It's none of my business, and you didn't exactly ask for my opinion, but don't be a dummy. How that girl looks at you isn't something a normal person could walk away from."

Rowan nodded. This woman knew absolutely nothing about their situation, but she couldn't argue with her logic. The details didn't exactly matter. When Jamie returned, Rowan would tell her she'd be willing to try a long-distance relationship. It could be for a year or several years, but she had to try. Jamie wasn't someone Rowan could just walk away from.

CHAPTER THIRTY-ONE

Rain gave way to the late morning sun when Jamie made her way outside of the hospital. She'd spent the morning with Rowan, but now that she was giving her space to sleep, she craved some fresh air. Jamie shook her head at how much the last few months had changed her. She'd always loved being outside, but now that they were back in civilization, she found the tall buildings, streets, noise, and people annoying. She longed to be back in their cabin in the forest, together, safely snuggled up in front of the fire.

The song of an American robin caught her attention, and she watched it happily hop along the ground, stop to listen, then continue along before digging its beak into the dirt. The worm wiggling in its grasp would soon be a meal for the chicks Jamie could hear complaining of hunger in the tiny nest nestled in the tree branch above her. She took a deep breath to calm her nerves before making the phone calls she'd been putting off.

The old Jamie would have made these calls as soon as she could get a cell signal. Things she had thought were her priorities no longer held the same weight. There had been a seismic shift in what qualified as vital to her, and it not causing her more concern, worried her. She didn't know who she was without her drive to fulfill the goals that had defined her since she was a child. Suddenly, her career felt like something she did, not who she was. This change happening when she was on the cusp of realizing all her wildest dreams confused her.

It mattered, of course. She was extremely excited to share her findings, but the part that came after that, the notoriety, the recognition, none of that mattered as much as it had before. All that she'd been through in the last few days had to play a massive role in her shift in priorities. Knowing that she could have lost Rowan, like really lost her, was a sobering thought.

Walking away from the career she'd worked toward her entire life to stay in Alaska with Rowan seemed like insanity. If they could only make the long-distance thing work, for now, she might divide her time between here and California. That was the only reasonable solution she could imagine, but Rowan refused to listen to reason. She wouldn't even consider it, and Jamie wasn't sure what choice she had but to leave.

Jamie pulled out her phone to call her dad. She suspected she knew what he'd advise her to do, and maybe that was precisely what she needed. Someone should probably talk some reason into her before she walked away from everything she'd worked so hard to achieve.

"Hey, Pigeon, I take it you've made it back to the real world?" Her dad's deep voice wrapped around her like a warm, familiar blanket. She'd missed talking to him over the last few months but hearing him now made her realize just how much.

"Hey, Dad, how are things?"

"Things are good. I'm getting out and walking every evening. It was hard at first because my schedule is already so full, but it's been nice. The fresh air really helps me clear my head."

Jamie smiled at the mental picture of when her parents would walk together when her dad was in town. Both had always had busy careers that kept them away from each other more than she knew they would have liked, but they always enjoyed those walks together. She wondered if he had his life to do over again. Would he make the same choices?

"Dad—"

"Honey, it's okay," her dad said in a soothing voice. "I know things like this can sometimes feel like a blow, but I'm proud of you for putting yourself out there. I think you needed to get this curlew thing out of your system, and now you can honestly say you gave it your all."

It took Jamie time to understand what he was saying. He'd assumed she called to tell him they hadn't found the curlew, and he was trying to comfort her. It was weird that the news of the discovery almost felt like a side note now.

"Oh, no, I found the curlew." Her father's gasp on the other side of the line made Jamie laugh.

"What? Did you see it? Do you have photos? Are you sure it was the northern curlew?"

Jamie leaned back on the bench and watched the robin feeding its young. "Yes, I saw it. Yes, I have photos, audio, video, documentation, everything. Dad, I'm an ornithologist who has studied the northern curlew my entire professional career, not including my obsession and trips with you when I was a kid. I'm absolutely positive they were northern curlews."

There was a pause on her father's side of the conversation. "They?"

"A bonded pair and their hatchlings," Jamie answered.

She could hear the creak of leather as her dad sat in his favorite chair. She could picture the shocked look on his face, and it gave her some satisfaction that she'd exceeded his expectations.

"I don't even know what to say, Jamie. Do you know what this will mean for your career?"

She had imagined this conversation since Patty had first told her of the sighting. Playing out what she'd say to her dad and what his reaction would be. His part in this was much like Jamie had expected, but it wasn't giving her the satisfaction she had thought it would. She was excited, but the need to be near Rowan when she woke up was more substantial.

"I know what this will mean." Jamie brushed away a leaf that had fallen from the tree onto her jeans and looked back toward the hospital door. "Hey, Dad, can we talk about this later? I have some things to do."

"Jamie, what's wrong?"

"Nothing, I'm fine." Jamie had called to talk to her dad about Rowan and hopefully get a dose of reality to help get her mind back on track. Instead, she'd only realized how much she would rather be next to Rowan and put this conversation off with her dad until she'd had some sleep and a good meal.

"Pigeon, I can tell something is bothering you. I won't force you to talk about it, but I'm here if you need me."

"Can I ask you a question?"

"Anything," her dad immediately answered.

"Do you regret having a family?"

"What do you mean by that? Of course, I don't regret having you and your mom in my life."

He seemed defensive, and she realized she could have asked a little more delicately, so it didn't seem like she was asking if he regretted having her.

"No, I know you loved us, and I'm not asking if you wish we didn't exist, but if you had it all to do over again, would you have had a family at all? I know there were many times when you had to choose between your career and your family, and that can be an impossible choice."

Her dad sighed. "Oh, Jamie, I'm so sorry that you feel that way. The only regrets I have are that I didn't make you and your mom my top priority as much as I should have. I know your mom felt the same. Old age gives you a unique perspective on what's important in life, and hindsight isn't always kind. Jamie, if I had it to do over again, I would spend more time taking you camping. I'd take your mom out on more dates. I would have been home for all of your track meets, your piano recitals, and your school open houses. A good father would have met your teachers and heard firsthand how impressed they were with you, not been told over the phone by your mom when I called from the campaign trail three days later. I regret all of those choices I made, and I'd give it all back for a chance to do it again."

"Oh…" That wasn't the response Jamie was expecting, and she was doing her best to sort through the emotions his words evoked.

"Please talk to me, sweetheart. Is this about that ranger who was assigned to help you, Fleming, or something? I was told he was the very best."

"She," Jamie answered.

"She?"

"Ranger Rowan Fleming is a woman, and yes, this is about her. I think I'm in love with her."

Her father cleared his throat. "Okay, well, are you—is this a relationship you plan to continue now that you'll be coming home or…"

"I don't know, Dad. I don't know what to do. She can't leave Alaska. Her mother isn't well and is a prominent member of her community, so moving to California isn't an option for Rowan."

"Okay, so you'll have a long-distance relationship. You're going to be a busy bee anyway, so balancing a brand-new relationship with someone who has just moved thousands of miles away from their home for you is not ideal. Long-distance might be for the best, anyway. Have you told the PWCA about the curlew yet?"

"No, you were my first call."

"Well, you'll want to call them right away so they can alert the media and set up interviews. Things will move fast, and you will want to devote all your focus to this for now. If you and Ranger Fleming are still an item in a couple of years, you can reevaluate things then."

Jamie watched the robin hop along the ground, searching for more worms to feed her babies. It stopped and looked at her, cocking its head almost like it was waiting to see what she would do.

"How did you know Mom was the one you wanted to spend the rest of your life with?" The leather creaked again, and Jamie suspected her dad was shifting uncomfortably in his chair.

"I felt like a whole person when we were together and broken when we weren't. Even though she's gone, I still feel that way. There were sleepless nights alone in a hotel room after long hours on the campaign trail when I should have been at home, with her, with both of you. That feeling of completeness was there from the beginning with your mother, and my life isn't the same without her. The grass isn't as green. The sky isn't as blue. The sun isn't as warm as it once was."

"Oh, Dad, I'm so sorry. I didn't know you were still struggling so much. I miss her, too."

"Does this ranger make you feel like that? Like I felt about your mom?"

"Yeah," Jamie said.

"I take it you're not coming home?" her dad asked.

"Would you be disappointed if I didn't?"

"That's not a fair question, sweetheart. Of course, I'll be disappointed. I miss you and can't wait to see you. Would I understand if you weren't ready to leave? Yes, I understand. You'll still need to honor your obligations to the PWCA. They funded your trip, and you owe them that."

"Absolutely. I can do most of that over the phone or on video calls. I know I'll need to go home and sort this all out. I just can't leave without knowing for sure what's happening here. We need to talk about so much, and she is still recovering from the attack. I don't want to push."

"What? What attack?"

Jamie had forgotten she hadn't even talked to him about everything that had happened. "It's a long story, but basically Rowan saved me from a mama bear and her cubs and was attacked. She'll be okay. The bear clawed her chest before I could get to the cabin to get a gun to scare it off. I got her to the cabin and called for help over the radio. A helicopter medevaced us out, and she's recovering in the hospital now."

"Jesus Christ, Jamie, are you okay?"

"I'm totally fine," Jamie reassured him. "I didn't get a scratch."

"I—please tell Rowan I owe her a debt of gratitude. You take care of her. It sounds like she's a good one."

Jamie smiled as her heart warmed with affection for him. "I will. I'll call tomorrow and fill you in on what's happened over the last few months. It's been a pretty wild ride."

"Sounds like it. I love you with all my heart, Jamie, and I couldn't be prouder of you."

She felt like a weight had been lifted from her shoulders. Not only because she'd had this conversation with her dad but also because she felt like she finally knew what she had to do. Now she just had to convince Rowan it was what she wanted.

CHAPTER THIRTY-TWO

Rowan released the tension she'd been holding when Jamie walked back into the room. There was a part of her that worried she'd gone home while Rowan was still sleeping and hadn't said good-bye. It was a ridiculous fear, Jamie wouldn't do that, but it had crossed Rowan's mind nonetheless.

"Hey."

"Hey," Jamie answered as she came around the bed and kissed Rowan on the lips. "How are you feeling, baby?"

The sound of someone clearing their throat startled them both. Rowan looked toward the door and saw her mother watching them with a curious look on her face.

"Mama, I'm sorry you got pulled down here. I know you hate to come to the city."

Her mom looked so confident and fit, it was hard to believe she was seventy-five and struggled with her health the way she did. You would never know it by looking at her, and she knew how important that was to her mom.

"I see you have a new friend. Is this the person who has kept you away for so long, Rowan?"

Jamie stepped back from the bed under Rowan's mother's scrutiny. "Mama, stop." Rowan reached out and took Jamie's hand, pulling her back to her position next to the bed. The pain from stretching made her groan, but she knew that if she didn't make things clear to them both, this could be an uncomfortable situation for them all.

"This is Dr. Jamie Martin. Jamie, this is my mother, Ahnah Fleming."

"I'm honored to meet you, Mrs. Fleming. You've raised an incredible person who has been invaluable to me over these last few months. I'm very thankful to you for sharing her with me. I know it was difficult for her to be away from you for so long."

Her mother nodded and walked to the opposite side of the bed as Jamie and kissed Rowan's cheek. "How are you doing? I talked to the doctor on my way in, and he said you had to have surgery but will be fine. Now that I can see you, I don't think you look so fine."

"Thanks, Mom." Rowan laughed and took her mother's hand with her right hand while still holding Jamie's with her left. It felt good to have them both with her. "Having you guys here is making me feel better already."

Her mother studied Jamie again. "What are your plans, young lady?"

"Mama," Rowan warned her. "Please don't be rude."

"I'm not being rude, sweetheart. I can see what this woman—"

"Jamie," Rowan corrected her.

"What this Jamie person means to you, and I don't want to see you hurt like you were before. We've only just put you back together."

"Mama, please." Rowan wasn't surprised by what her mother was saying. She had always been very protective of her, and when she'd moved back to Alaska from having her heart broken in two, her mother had been the one to piece her back together. That was when she started noticing little things here and there that concerned her about her mother's memory.

She was very thankful that this was one of her mother's more lucid moments but wished it was one where she was in a friendlier mood.

"Where's Steve?" Rowan asked. She had hired a private nurse for her mother soon after moving her into the senior care community. There was no way she could be with her every day with Rowan's schedule, and Steve gave Rowan peace of mind that her mom was being cared for.

"He's getting me water and a granola bar. I told him I wanted to come straight here to see you and wouldn't stop for lunch first." She looked at Jamie. "He's only bringing one granola bar, by the way. You'll have to get your own, Dr. Martin."

"Mama, seriously, stop." Rowan thought she would have to ask her mom to leave when Steve walked in with a cup of water and the promised granola bar.

"Here we go, Ahnah. I can tell from the tension in the room that I've arrived just in time." He handed her mom the food and drink and bent to kiss Rowan on the forehead. "How are you, child? You look a mess, but I can see from that sparkle in your eyes that this young lady is doing her part to make you feel better." Steve took Jamie's free hand that wasn't being held by Rowan and kissed it. "You must be the young woman who brought our Rowan home. We owe you a debt of gratitude, you beautiful thing. We've gotten used to having this one around and would notice if a bear had eaten her."

Jamie laughed as Rowan rolled her eyes. "I'm Jamie, and the pleasure is all mine. I'm just sorry I brought her back in this state. She was all shiny when I first got her."

The look of glee on Steve's face when he obviously realized that Jamie was going to play along with his silliness made Rowan thankful for the thousandth time that she'd hired him as her mother's nurse. Not only was he the most qualified, caring, patient person she'd interviewed for the position, but he also brought joy into her mom's life that had long been absent.

"Don't you worry, honey, a sweet little smile like yours will heal this old grump in no time."

"First, I'm not a grump," Rowan said, scowling at him. "Second, if I didn't know your heart belonged to Calvin, I'd be worried you were flirting with my girl." Rowan felt Jamie squeeze her hand and realized what she'd said. "I mean—"

"You have nothing to worry about. I have my sights set on someone already." Jamie winked at Rowan, and the gesture made her smile against her will.

"You guys are making me sick," Rowan's mom mumbled around a mouth full of granola bar. "When are they letting you out of here?"

Rowan groaned as she tried to sit up higher.

"Hey, let me help you," Jamie said. She gently guided Rowan to lean back and then used the bed controls to lift her body forward. Once Rowan was settled, she kissed her temple and sat on the edge of her bed.

"I'm not sure when they'll release me. Did they tell you?"

Jamie shook her head. "They said the doctor will be back later today but haven't told me any specifics about when you'll be able to go home."

"You're coming to stay with the boys and me until you're better. You can't stay in that house all by yourself," her mom said.

"Absolutely," Steve said. "Cal and I would be happy to look after you for as long as you need."

"I—that won't be necessary," Jamie said. "I'll be going home with her, if that's okay with Rowan, of course."

Rowan knew shock was written all over her face. "Steve, would you mind taking my mom to the cafeteria for some lunch?"

"I just had a bar. I'm fine," her mom argued. Rowan glared at her mom until she threw up her hands. "Fine, I want pancakes."

Steve chuckled and led her mom out the door. She could hear her loudly complaining to him about the cool temperature of the hospital as the sound of their footsteps faded down the hall. Rowan loved her mother more than anything. This ornery version of her became more common as her disease progressed, but Rowan knew it wasn't her fault.

"I'm sorry about my mom," she said once they were alone.

"Don't be. I was young, but I remember how much my Grandma Opal changed when her dementia progressed and how difficult it was for my mom. It's not their fault."

"She's always been feisty, but it has gotten worse as time goes on."

Rowan did her best to scoot over to give Jamie room to lean back against her on the bed. She wanted nothing more than to hold her. Jamie hesitated but finally gingerly leaned back, trying to remain more on the edge of the bed and only barely touching Rowan's shoulder so she wouldn't accidentally hurt her.

"How are you really feeling?" Jamie asked.

"Okay. Confused. What did you mean about going home with me and taking care of me? You can't put your life on hold just because this stupid bear thing happened." Trying to convince Jamie to leave went against everything her heart wanted. Rowan knew watching her walk out of her life would be the most challenging thing she'd ever done, but it was what had to happen.

"It's not only about you being injured, Rowan." Jamie slid off the side of the bed and pulled a chair over to face each other. "Well, not in the way you think, at least."

"You don't owe me anything, Jamie. Don't make a life-altering decision like this out of guilt. I've decided to try the long-distance thing."

"Really?"

Rowan nodded and kissed Jamie's lips. "Really. It won't be the best, but we'll figure it out. We have to, right? I don't think I can let you just walk out of my life without at least trying to make things work."

Jamie was silent for so long Rowan worried she'd made a mistake, and she'd changed her mind about wanting to try, even though she was leaving. Rowan would understand. It was probably the right thing to do, but it would hurt. "Unless you don't still want to make that work."

"That's not what I—" Jamie stood and paced at the foot of Rowan's bed. "I want this to work more than anything, and this isn't only because of what happened yesterday. I've been fighting these feelings for a while now but wasn't ready to admit to myself just how much you meant to me until I thought I was going to lose you. Rowan, I don't want to be without you. My career, the curlew, my position at the PWCA, it's important to me, but none of it compares to the way I feel when I'm with you."

The beeps from the monitors increased as Rowan's heart pumped faster. "What are you saying?"

"I'm saying I love you. I know we've only known each other for a few months, and this is all so confusing right now, but I love you, Rowan Fleming. Being without you isn't an option, so I'm saying I agree with you. A long-distance relationship won't be enough." Jamie wiped tears from Rowan's cheeks before kissing her lips. "Who knows what the logistics of all of this is going to look like, but if it's okay with you, I want to stay. I want to be here to help you recover and to see where things lead after that. I've kind of gotten used to having you around at this point."

This was everything Rowan had ever wanted, but part of her was still struggling to believe Jamie had thought everything through. "What did the PWCA and your dad say about the curlew?"

Jamie sat on the edge of the bed again and cradled Rowan's hand in hers. "I haven't spoken to the PWCA yet. We're a few days early, so they don't expect my call until Monday. I spoke to my dad, though." Jamie's smile was unexpected, but she hoped it was a sign that the conversation with her dad had gone well.

"Did you send him any of the videos?" Rowan asked.

"Hmm? Oh, it's all still at the cabin."

A jolt of panic raced through Rowan. "Why is it still in the cabin?"

Jamie gave Rowan a quizzical look. "We were medevaced out by helicopter, honey. I didn't exactly have time to collect our things before we left. I called Greg when we arrived at the hospital, and he's having someone pack everything up and bring it to your house. Someone is going to fly your plane from Ugruk to your place, too."

"Did he say who's flying my plane?"

"Someone named Garland or something?"

Rowan groaned. "Ugh, Garlyn? He better not leave one scratch on her. That guy thinks he's a cowboy."

Soft hands cupped Rowan's jaw as Jamie looked at her with pure adoration in her eyes. "I love you, Rowan Fleming. I don't care what it costs me. If I tried to walk away, I'd be leaving a huge part of my heart with you. I refuse to regret not at least trying to see if we can make this work. I need to know you feel the same."

All the reasons Rowan had convinced herself were valid for why they couldn't be together seemed to fall away. She wanted Jamie more than anything, and she wouldn't miss this chance at happiness because she was too stubborn to at least try.

"I love you, too. Let's make a life together."

EPILOGUE

Three years later

Jamie waved away the overwhelming applause of the standing-room-only crowd gathered inside the lecture auditorium at the University of Alaska Fairbanks. The book she'd written about their life-changing journey to find the northern curlew had made it to several best seller lists and there was buzz that the documentary was a contender come award season—even if most viewers seemed more interested in the real-life romance happening behind the camera than her many ornithological findings.

Oh well. Whatever got people hooked.

"Yes, one last question." She pointed to a woman in the front row.

"Dr. Martin, Cassidy Peters with *Wild Alaska* magazine, thank you for taking my question. In both the book and the documentary, you mention how profoundly this experience changed you as a person. I know your life has changed both professionally and personally. Could you elaborate on which change came as the biggest surprise?"

Jamie looked down at her notes. She'd done so many of these at this point that she'd had an answer for almost every question that was asked. Cassidy Peters was the first to ask her this specific question, and it caught her off guard. She searched the room until she found Rowan standing in the back. Brown eyes settled on her and brought the world back into focus.

"There were many things that surprised me. For one, I never would have imagined how resilient I could be. I scaled a rock cliff with only a rope tied around my waist. I went toe-to-toe with a mama bear and her cubs. Have you ever tried eating almost nothing but rabbit and salmon for three months?" The crowd laughed. "Professionally, I discovered it was the work itself that I found fulfilling, not a title or a place on the board." Jamie looked back at Rowan and winked. "I think the thing that surprised me the most was that none of that mattered. The job, the discovery, none of that mattered as much as love. I know that sounds ridiculous. I would have rolled my eyes if someone had said that to me before starting this journey, but it's the truth. Nothing makes me feel as complete as I do when I'm home with Rowan. That was by far the most surprising and most life-altering discovery I made."

Jamie closed her notebook and tucked it under her arm. "Thank you all for sharing this journey with me. I hope you find the thing that fulfills you in your life. When you do, hold on to it with both hands and never let it go. It can be as rare as finding a bird everyone thought was extinct. Thank you."

The room filled with applause as they escorted Jamie through the auditorium and into one last room where she would have her photo taken for the press. A half hour later, she exited the building and found a very sexy ranger casually leaning against her truck. It reminded her of Jake Ryan leaning against his Porsche in the last scene of *Sixteen Candles*. She was hot, and she was all Jamie's.

"Hey, Dr. Martin," Rowan said as she held the door open for her.

"Hey yourself, Ranger Fleming." Jamie climbed into the truck and unbuttoned the first few buttons at the neckline of her dress. She couldn't wait to get home and into something more comfortable. Fancy dresses, high heels, and makeup had never really been her style. After the last few months she'd had, she was ready to escape to their little piece of heaven so she could once again feel like herself.

"Is everything ready for us to leave?" The year before, they'd purchased land in a remote area of Alaska. Rowan had spent every chance she had building a cabin for them out of trees she felled on their own land. She had cleared a small landing strip a half mile from the cabin so they could easily access it without the need to hike all their supplies in. The most recent addition was a large deck on the front of the cabin that looked out over the beautiful little lake they fished and swam in when the weather was warm. It was heaven, and it was theirs.

"Yep." Rowan pulled onto the main road that led them out of Fairbanks toward their home. "Grizzly can't wait to see you."

"I can't believe you named him Grizzly." They'd rescued a sled dog puppy the year before that had broken his leg while training and could no longer endure the rigors of running the number of miles required to perform during a race. Jamie had fallen in love with him while visiting a friend's sled dog yard. After much debate, Jamie agreed to allow Rowan to name him Grizzly after the beast that had convinced her to stay in Alaska. She wasn't sure of the name initially, since it was also the creature that nearly took Rowan away from her, but now that Grizzly had grown into a big, fuzzy adult, it seemed appropriate.

"He can't believe you didn't bring him something from the University of Montana. Their mascot is a grizzly, you know?"

"I do know that, and who said I didn't bring him something back from there?" Jamie reached out and pulled Rowan's hand into her lap. "I can't believe it's finally over. Well, mostly over. They'll ask me to do things here and there, but the major book and documentary tour is complete."

"I thought this was what you wanted?"

Jamie watched the familiar landscape pass as they turned down the road that would lead them to their home. "It is. It was. I'm glad I did it, but I'm also glad it's done. I don't want to see or speak to anyone other than you and Grizzly for the next two months."

"Are you excited to teach classes at the university at the end of summer?"

"I am. I desperately need this time away, but I'm sure I'll be ready to bore some students talking about birds by the end. The school emailed me and asked if I'd be willing to take a group of students out into the field next summer for a week. I don't think they set any details in stone, but they were asking to see if I might be interested."

"That sounds fun."

"It does. I told them it would need to be early or late in the summer because we'd be at the cabin otherwise, but I think they're going to make something work. I also received an interesting call from the Discovery Network."

"You're kidding. When did this happen?" Rowan pulled into their garage and grabbed Jamie's bags from the back of the truck.

"Yesterday, just before I got on the plane. They want to discuss a possible show based in Alaska about the birds here. I guess they want to capitalize on the buzz from the book and documentary."

"Wow, that's amazing, sweetheart. I'm so proud of you." A loud bark bellowed from inside the house, followed by the sound of dog feet clattering against the tile floor. "Get ready for a Grizzly greeting."

The furry beast burst through the door and into Jamie's arms, almost toppling her over backward. "Hey, baby boy!"

"You really shouldn't let him clobber you like that. He's going to send you ass over teakettle at some point."

Jamie cradled her dog's face and kissed the top of his head. "Don't listen to that mean old mama. She doesn't understand how excited we are to see each other."

Rowan set Jamie's bags down and started unpacking them to take out the things they needed to go with them to the cabin. "Oh, I understand perfectly. I want to give you the same greeting every time I see you. I'm just better behaved and have some self-control. Unlike someone else I know." She gave Grizzly the side-eye.

"You're barely better behaved, and the self-control thing is debatable." Jamie wrapped her arms around Rowan and leaned up to kiss her on the lips. "I missed you so much."

The kiss deepened as Rowan pulled her closer. When they finally parted, Jamie checked the time on Rowan's wristwatch. "Are you sure we can't squeeze in a quickie before we leave?"

After one last check of her watch, Rowan lifted Jamie and carried her toward their bedroom. "You were going to have to take these clothes off and shower before we left, anyway, right? I should probably help you with that, just to be safe."

Jamie wrapped her legs around Rowan's waist and threaded her fingers into her hair. She was so hungry for her Jamie was tempted to suggest they stop in the living room because the bedroom seemed too far away. Since it was probably the last time they'd be there for a couple of months, she deepened their kiss and held on tight. Rowan used one arm to help hold Jamie against her body and the other to open doors and make sure they didn't run into walls as they made their way to the bed.

"I missed you so much, baby. Two weeks apart is too much," Rowan said when they reached the bed. She gently placed her on the soft comforter and dropped to her knees to remove Jamie's shoes. "These are pretty."

"They're Louboutin. It's the one luxury item I've used my book money for."

Rowan removed the other shoe and carefully set them to the side. "You know you're free to use that money on whatever luxury items you would like, right? It's your money and doesn't need to go into our family budget." She pulled her own shirt off before placing soft kisses along the arch of Jamie's foot, over her ankle, and up her leg toward her center.

"I know. Ungh." Jamie gasped when Rowan lifted the hem of her dress and kissed along her inner thigh. "You feel so good, baby."

"Mmm." Rowan hummed her appreciation when she finally reached the black lacy panties Jamie had intentionally put on that morning, hoping this very thing would happen when they were finally alone. "These are new, too."

"Yes, they are, but these were a gift for you."

Rowan grazed her teeth along the fabric, which sent a flood of wetness to Jamie's pussy. "I would argue that what's behind them is my actual gift, but I certainly appreciate the effort to wrap it so beautifully for me."

"Please, Rowan, I need you to touch me." Jamie was getting desperate. She was hesitant to speed things up, but her need to be touched was consuming her.

Nimble fingers pushed the edge of the fabric aside as Rowan uncovered her now extremely wet center. "It looks like you missed me, too."

"I did, desperately, yes." Jamie reached down to touch her own clit, but Rowan pushed her hands away.

"No, no, no, this is for me. Give me a minute to enjoy it." Rowan ran her tongue from Jamie's entrance up to her clit and sucked the swollen nub into her mouth before releasing it. "A minute to taste you and to appreciate how fortunate I am to have you in my life."

Warm lips returned to Jamie's pussy as Rowan drove her further toward the edge. "I can't take much more, Rowan." Jamie's hands gripped the sheets, resisting the urge to push Rowan to go faster.

The bed shifted as Rowan crawled up next to her and directed her to roll over onto her front. She heard Rowan unzipping her dress. Once she removed it, it left her in only her matching black lace bra and panties—soaked panties at this point. Wordlessly, Rowan guided her onto her back and gently traced a fingernail across the fabric of her bra.

"This is pretty, too. Also, for me?"

"Yesss…" Jamie hissed as Rowan dragged her nail across her nipple. "It's all for you, my love. All of it. All of me."

Rowan nodded and helped Jamie pull her panties down her legs and off, tossing them to the floor. Jamie leaned forward to take one of Rowan's nipples into her mouth and sucked. Her breasts were small, firm, and perfectly Rowan. "Take off your pants," Jamie said as she reached down to assist Rowan with her belt. "I need to feel your body against mine."

"Mmm." Rowan's direct communication skills had irritated her at one time, but now they were just part of the entire package that was Rowan. Now that she'd taken the time to understand and get to know Rowan more, she didn't need many words to comprehend what she wanted. Rowan communicated with her body, her touch, and her actions. Jamie was all for it. Not that Rowan didn't talk to her. She was very open about anything Jamie asked her. She just wasn't one to waste extra words to get her point across. Rowan was efficient, and that was something Jamie had learned she liked in a partner.

Rowan removed her pants and underwear, leaving Jamie the only one still wearing something. She reached up to remove her bra, but Rowan stopped her. "I want to see you with it on when I fuck you. Is that okay?"

Jamie nodded and ran her fingers over her own breasts while Rowan watched. "Well, are you going to fuck me, then?" She knew the effect her words would have on Rowan, and the power to excite her was heady.

"Should I use my cock or my fingers?"

Jamie had fantasized about Rowan fucking her like this while they were apart. "Cock, please, hurry."

Rowan hopped off the bed and quickly found the dildo and the briefs that worked like a harness in her bag. "I packed it to take with us, so don't let me forget to pack it again once we're done."

"We need to buy extra toys that we just leave at the cabin, so we don't have to carry things back and forth."

"Yeah, that would be a hilarious surprise when a bear breaks into our cabin and carries off an enormous dildo. If I was hiking and came across a bear carrying a dildo in its mouth, I just might die."

Jamie laughed. "Get up here, dork. Less talk about bears with dildos and more satisfying your girlfriend."

The bed dipped as she settled herself between Jamie's legs. Rowan reached over to retrieve a condom from the drawer and slip it onto the cock now securely strapped to her. "I didn't know we should use condoms with a toy before I knew you. I guess you learn many things when you date a doctor."

"Well, I'm not that kind of doctor, but I'm happy to give you any other sex advice you need."

"Really?" Rowan collected some of the copious amount of wetness from Jamie's pussy on her finger before slipping it inside. "I'll keep that in mind."

Jamie's hips pushed up, trying to take her deeper. "More, baby." Rowan slipped a second finger in and moved them in a rolling motion to stroke Jamie from the inside. "Yes, Rowan. Like that. So good."

"Are you ready for me, sweetheart?"

"Yes, now, please."

Rowan used Jamie's wetness to lubricate the cock. Jamie flinched when she initially felt the stretch of the head as it slowly pushed inside. Not having sex over the last two weeks left Jamie tighter than usual and taking the blunt head of the cock was almost too much.

"Do you like that, Jamie? Do you like having me inside you?" Rowan was always so considerate and loving. Always. She knew exactly how to check in to make sure Jamie was okay with what she was doing to her, but masked by dirty talk that made it hot. Jamie knew she could stop things at any time while still maintaining an edge of dirtiness she loved.

"Yes, baby, I'm so full. Fuck. You feel amazing."

Strong hips pumped faster as Rowan worked her way into Jamie's pussy. The feeling was incredible. She understood it was a dildo. The appendage inside her wasn't Rowan, but it felt like it was. She felt like Rowan was inside her, a part of her. It was as close as she'd ever felt to anyone, and she never wanted that feeling to stop. She wanted Rowan for the rest of her life.

Rowan's fingers found her clit and joined in the rhythm her hips had set in motion. Jamie knew she couldn't hold out much longer. She was so close to her release, and it was the most fantastic feeling in the world. "Don't stop fucking me, Rowan. Don't stop."

"I'll never stop, baby." Rowan grabbed Jamie's hip with her free hand and used it to pull her body against her, fucking her so deep it was almost too much.

"I love you." Jamie's mind was racing. A million thoughts jumbled themselves around until she wasn't sure of anything other than Rowan. Her love for this beautiful, strong, amazing person who had flown into her life and captured her heart. Nothing else mattered.

"I love you, too. Completely. Absolutely." Sweat poured from Rowan as she worked her body against Jamie's at an almost frantic pace.

Without realizing what she was saying before it had escaped from her lips, Jamie cradled Rowan's face between her hands, looked directly in her eyes, and said the only thing that she knew was certain in the world. "Marry me, Rowan."

Rowan's movement immediately stopped. "What?"

"Don't stop. I'm so close."

"But?"

"Rowan Fleming, fuck me, and answer my question."

A smile lit up Rowan's face as she leaned down to kiss Jamie and resumed her thrusts. "Yes, yes, I'll marry you. A thousand times, yes."

Jamie's world tilted on its axis as she climaxed so intensely, she worried she'd lose consciousness. Rowan slowed but continued her thrusts for another few minutes as she slipped her fingers between the dildo and her clit. Jamie caressed her body and whispered how good she felt inside of her until Rowan pushed in one last time and roared as her own orgasm overtook her. They both lay panting as they struggled to catch their breath. After a minute, Rowan gently pulled the cock out of Jamie's pussy and fell onto the bed next to her. Jamie rolled toward her and snuggled into her side. Completely content and thoroughly satisfied.

"Did you really just propose to me?" Rowan asked.

"Yes." Jamie nuzzled the soft skin on the side of Rowan's neck. "Is that okay?"

"Yeah. It's more than okay. I had planned to propose while we were at the cabin, but that's okay. I have a ring for you in my bag. You may have stolen my thunder, but it's kind of hot that you proposed to me while we were having sex."

Jamie pulled Rowan's lips to hers and kissed her. She wanted Rowan to feel how much she loved her, know that she was the center of her universe and that what they had was forever.

When they parted, Jamie wiped a tear from her cheek. "I'm deliriously happy, my love."

Rowan cupped her cheek and placed a gentle kiss on her lips. "Me, too. Ridiculously happy."

A bark pierced through their touching moment and made them both laugh. "Grizzly says he's happy, too, but wants to get going."

"I think he may love being at the cabin more than we do," Jamie said.

"I'm not so sure about that. How about we agree that we all love it equally?"

Another bark came from the other room, and they begrudgingly sat up and made their way to the shower. "Need some help in the shower, Dr. Martin?"

"Always, Ranger Fleming."

About the Author

Angie Williams, winner of a third grade essay competition on fire safety, grew up in the dusty desert of West Texas. Always interested in writing, as a child she would lose interest before the end, killing the characters off in a tragic accident so she could move on to the next story. Thankfully as an adult she decided it was time to write things where everyone survives.

Angie lives in Northern California with her beautiful wife and son, and a menagerie of dogs, cats, snakes, and tarantulas. She's a proud geek and lover of all things she was teased about in school.

Books Available From Bold Strokes Books

The Artist by Sheri Lewis Wohl. Detective Casey Wilson and reclusive artist Tula Crane are drawn together in a web of passion, intrigue, and art that might just hold the key to stopping a killer. (978-1-63679-150-0)

Cherry on Top by Georgia Beers. A chance meeting leaves Cherry and Ellis longing for a different life, but when Ellis's search for truth crashes into Cherry's insta-filter world, do they have any hope at all of a happily ever after? (978-1-63679-158-6)

Love and Other Rare Birds by Angie Williams. Ornithologist Dr. Jamie Martin and park ranger Rowan Fleming are searching the Alaskan wilderness for a bird thought to be extinct, and they're about to discover opposites really do attract. (978-1-63679-108-1)

Parallel Paradise by Mayapee Chowdhury. When their love affair is put to the test by the homophobia of their family, community, and culture, Bindi and Rimli will need to fight for a chance at love. (978-1-63679-203-3)

Perfectly Matched by Toni Logan. A beautiful Cupid named Hannah, a runaway arrow, and just seventy-two hours to fix a mishap that could be the best mistake she has ever made. (978-1-63679-120-3)

Slow Burn by Missouri Vaun. A wounded wildland firefighter from California and a struggling artist find solace and love in a small southern town. (978-1-63679-098-5)

The Inconvenient Heiress by Jane Walsh. An unlikely heiress and a spinster evade the Marriage Mart only to discover true love together. (978-1-63679-173-9)

Closed-Door Policy by Erin Zak. Going back to college is never easy, but Caroline Stevens is prepared to work hard and change her life for the better. What she's not prepared for is Dr. Atlanta Morris, her gorgeous new professor. (978-1-63679-181-4)

Homeworld by Gun Brooke. Headed by Captain Holly Crowe, the spaceship Velocity's crew journeys toward their alien ancestors' homeworld, and what they find is completely unexpected—and they're not safe. (978-1-63679-177-7)

Outland by Kristin Keppler & Allisa Bahney. Danielle Clark and Katelyn Turner can't seem to stay away from one another even as the war for the wastelands tests their loyalty to each other and to their people. (978-1-63679-154-8)

Royal Exposé by Jenny Frame. When they're grouped together for a class assignment, Poppy's enthusiasm for life and love may just save Casey's soul, but will she ever forgive Casey for using her to expose royal secrets? (978-1-63679-165-4)

Secret Sanctuary by Nance Sparks. US Deputy Marshal Alex Trenton specializes in protecting those awaiting trial, but when danger threatens the woman she's falling for, Alex is in for the fight of her life. (978-1-63679-148-7)

Stranded Hearts by Kris Bryant, Amanda Radley & Emily Smith. In these novellas from award-winning authors, fate intervenes on behalf of love when characters are unexpectedly stuck together. With too much time and an irresistible attraction, anything could happen. (978-1-63679-182-1)

The Last Lavender Sister by Melissa Brayden. Aster Lavender sells her gourmet doughnuts and keeps a low profile; she never plans on the town's temporary veterinarian swooping in and making her feel like anything but a wallflower. (978-1-63679-130-2)

The Probability of Love by Dena Blake. As Blair and Rachel keep ending up in the same place despite the odds, can a one-night stand turn into forever? Or will the bet Blair never intended to make ruin their happily ever after? (978-1-63679-188-3)

Worth a Fortune by Sam Ledel. After placing a want ad for a personal secretary, a New York heiress is surprised when the woman who got away is the one interested in the position. (978-1-63679-175-3)